A DRAGON'S DARE

D1096964

A DRAGON'S DARE

CHRONICLES OF AN URBAN DRUID™ BOOK 10

AUBURN TEMPEST

MICHAEL ANDERLE

DISRUPTIVE IMAGINATION

LMBPN Publishing
PMB 196, 2540 South Maryland Pkwy
Las Vegas, NV 89109

Version 1.00, September 2021
eBook ISBN: 978-1-68500-434-7
Print ISBN: 978-1-68500-435-4

THE A DRAGON'S DARE TEAM

Thanks to our JIT Team:

Rachel Beckford
Dave Hicks
Larry Omans
Deb Mader
Diane L. Smith
Dorothy Lloyd
John Ashmore
James Caplan
Debi Sateren
Paul Westman
Micky Cocker
Kelly O'Donnell

Editor
SkyHunter Editing Team

CHAPTER ONE

"It is a truth universally acknowledged, that a single man in possession of a good fortune, must be in want of a crazy Canadian crush."

Sloan chuckles and looks over the edge of the textbook he's reading. "That's how it goes, is it?"

I hold up my copy of *Pride and Prejudice* and tap the front cover. "You can't argue with the wisdom of ages. Jane Austen saw you coming a mile away, hotness."

He closes his book on antidotes of rare venoms and poisons and sets it on the table by the living room window. "I think living with my crazy Canadian crush is better described by, 'It was a bright cold day in April, and the clocks were striking thirteen.'"

I laugh. "That's a good one, for sure. What about, 'O, my luve's like a red, red rose.'"

"Oh, tonight yer a poet too, are ye. Yes, I like that one, though yer much more than a pretty flower. I think life within yer inner circle is more like, 'It was the best of times, it was the worst of times, it was the age of wisdom, it was the age of foolishness.'"

I burst out laughing. "Oh, that's good too."

"I've got one," Emmet says, coming into the kitchen and grabbing the handle of the fridge. "As far back as I can remember, I always wanted to be a gangster."

Sloan frowns. "I don't know that one. What book is it from?"

Emmet's mouth drops open. "That's Ray Liotta's opening line in *Goodfellas*."

"Och, that's why. I've never seen it."

"Seriously? What were you doing with your life all these years, Irish? You've got some serious learnin' up to do, my man."

I laugh, but he's not wrong. Sloan didn't grow up with pop culture and American movies as we did. There are so many things I want to share with him.

"Maybe for my birthday, we'll host a movie marathon pajama weekend. We can invite everyone, and they can crash here and hang out."

"It's yer birthday, *a ghra*. We will, of course, do whatever ye want. However, I think yer aiming low."

"You do? Why?"

"Because with wayfarers and immortals at your disposal, the world is quite literally at yer fingertips. Maybe we go on an African safari or learn to surf in Australia or have a party on a yacht upon turquoise waters. We could spend a few days touring the Caribbean with all yer family and friends."

"Hells, yes, now you're sucking diesel." Emmet stops hauling food and cans of soda out of the fridge and straightens. "I've always wanted to hoist the mainsail and jib my jab and swab the poop deck. That's an awesome plan."

"That sounds super fun," I say, chuckling at Emmet bouncing around the kitchen like he just ate five boxes of Mike and Ike's. "Let's save the Caribbean boat cruise for one of the boys. It seems Emmet, for one, would love it."

Emmet stops dancing and stares at me, looking aghast. "You're passing up our chance at a private Caribbean yacht party? Who are you and what have you done with my sista?"

"It will be awesome—I have no doubt—but if I get to choose

my perfect birthday, I kinda like the idea of Sloan and I spending a weekend without chaos. Maybe we can rent an Airbnb and get out of the city. We could enjoy some wine and local culture. That could be fun too, couldn't it?"

"It sounds heavenly, *a ghra*. I'll make it happen."

"What about a party?" Emmet asks. "Drinks at Shenanigans? Nothing for your brothers?"

I laugh at his indignation. "You can do that on *your* birthday. Besides, since when have you guys needed a reason to drink at Shenanigans? Like... since never."

Emmet rolls his eyes and goes back to grabbing up a stash of drinks and snacks from the fridge.

"Ignore his pouting," I say to Sloan. "His birthday is in July, and he can pick the Caribbean yacht party then."

"Are ye sure yer not interested in a blowout?"

"No. We have a blowout every year."

"Because blowouts are awesome," Emmet chuffs.

I laugh. "No doubt, my beloved brothers will try something— they always do. If we're not around, they won't be able to target me."

"Target you?" Emmet says, scowling. "You make it sound like an offensive attack."

"It *is*."

Sloan's gaze is ping-ponging between Emmet and me as we hash out the same argument we've had a hundred times. "What's this about?"

I roll my eyes. "They duffed my sixteenth birthday, and every year since, they've tried to surprise me with a massive surprise party."

"Have they ever succeeded?"

"No. I know all their tricks. For my twenty-first, I pretended to be surprised so the madness would end."

"Buuut...we saw through the act." Emmet digs out the serving tray and starts packing it with his haul. "We know all her tricks too."

"True. They've sworn they won't quit until they get a real win."

Sloan arches a brow and chuckles. "It seems if ye try every year, it'll never be much of a surprise."

"Right? That's what I've told them a hundred times, but they're a tenacious bunch."

Emmet chuckles. "It's grown to be a family challenge. We'll get her. One year, we'll get her good."

"Yeah, yeah, you keep talking, bro." I grin at Sloan. "I'll be on my toes for the next couple of weeks. There's no telling what they'll try to pull. So, yeah, if we sneak away and have an intimate celebration by ourselves, I'm good with that."

Sloan looks over at my brother. "Maybe one year ye should do nothing, and *that* will be the surprise."

I laugh. "That would be a massive surprise."

"Harhar." Emmet finishes with his stockpile to take downstairs. "You two are so entertaining."

Oh, right. "Speaking of entertaining, Dora's hosting a screening of *Rocky Horror* next month at Queens on Queen. She asked me to spread the word to the fam jam and let her know if we want to go and how many tickets we'll need."

Emmet grins. "Hells yeah, we do. That will be awesome. I'll break out my fishnets and garters."

Sloan's expression sours. "I'm not wearing stockings at a drag club."

Emmet's gaze narrows. "So, would you wear fishnets to places other than a drag club?"

I laugh at Sloan's look of indignation.

"No."

I wave that away. "That's fine. You can be Riff Raff or Brad. All your manly bits can remain covered."

Emmet bites into a pepperoni stick and waves it at us like a wand. "Not every man can pull off being Frank N. Furter, Irish. Don't feel bad."

"I don't. Not in the slightest."

Hilarious. Sloan has come a long way in the quest to pull the stick out of his ass, but he still has a long way to go. "I'll post the deets in the family chatroom and see who's interested in coming."

Emmet nods. "It'll be a blast."

I pull out my phone and add the info. "The last time we went to a showing, it was at the Regent Theatre, and I was Magenta. If you're set on being Brad, I'll be Janet."

"Oh! Invite Dionysus," Emmet says, busting a gut. "Can you imagine him at something like that?"

I love this idea more by the minute. "I bet Nikon will dress up."

A couple of notifications *ping* back at me right away. "Calum says he and Kevin are in for sure. Dillan too. He'll want a plus-one."

"Since when does D have a plus-one?" Emmet asks.

"No idea. Maybe the girl he hooked up with at Dionysus's house-warming? He said she was amazing. Or maybe he's planning ahead." Another notification *pings* in. "Nikon's calling Frank N. Furter."

Emmet scoffs. "He can call it all he wants, but that changes nothing. I can out Frank his Furter any day of the week."

I type that in and laugh at the *ping* of the next notification. "He says, challenge accepted, puny mortal."

The phone rings in my hand, and I jump and then laugh at myself.

"It's Liam, one sec." I answer the call and put him on speaker. "Hey bestie, you're on speaker. What's up? Is this about *Rocky Horror*? Shouldn't you be working?"

"I am. Any chance Sloan can *poof* you into the back hall? Something weird is brewing. I don't have a shield to tingle, but if I did, I bet it would be flaring right now with something *other*."

Sloan is already on his feet and jogging to the powder room by the front door, and Emmet is shoving his haul back into the fridge.

"We're on our way. Give us two minutes."

I stand and head toward the back hall to grab my shoes. Bending over the railing, I fill in the basement bunch. "Liam says something weird is happening at the pub, and he thinks it falls in our wheelhouse. He asked us to pop over and see if it's empowered. All aboard who's coming aboard."

Calum jogs up the stairs in his lounge pants and rounds the staircase to continue upstairs. "One sec. Let me get pants on."

As I grab my purse, Dillan, Tad, and Ciara barrel up the basement steps.

"I'm in," Dillan shouts.

"Yeah, sounds fun," Tad says.

I'm comin' too, Red. Bruin returns to me.

A minute later, the whole gang has gathered at the back door, and we're ready to roll.

Sloan *poofs* us into the downtown core, and we take form in the private hallway that divides Shenanigans from Shannon's and Liam's apartment above the pub. It's a tight fit for seven of us, but Dillan opens the door, and we pour out into the back hall of the restaurant.

A drunk guy coming out of the Lads eyes us up, confusion plain in his gaze.

I laugh. "Like clowns coming out of a Volkswagen, amirite?"

Without waiting for his opinion on that, we continue to the front. The blissful aromas of pub fare and beer hit us at the same time the upbeat Celtic rhythm pulls us into the crowd. I prairie dog my head over the crowd as I sashay through the mass of familiar bodies.

I meet the gaze of a couple of cops Da works with and wave. "*Slainte mhath.*"

The toast for good health comes back to me from all directions.

A whistle has me turning back to find Emmet pointing toward the booth wall. He's spotted a group clearing out for the night and moves to snag it.

I head to the bar to get the first round and find out what we're dealing with.

"Hey, Fi," Kady says as I step around the bar. "I didn't know you were coming in tonight."

"Me either." I hug her at the servers' station and carry on. "It was a last-minute decision."

"Just you?"

I grab a tray, set seven glasses on it, and start pulling the first pitcher of Guinness. "No. It's the usual suspects minus Kevin. He's busy at the gallery getting ready for some big event this weekend."

"Where are you camping out?"

"Emmet grabbed us a spot at six."

"Cool. I'll swing by and say hi once things settle down a bit later."

Liam places three beers and a bloody Caesar on her tray and waits for her to dissolve into the crush of bodies before turning his back to the bar so only I can see his face. "At the four top by the stage, do you see the swashbuckler nursing a cider?"

I find the wannabe pirate in question and chuckle. He's not so much a pirate as a slight guy with pale skin and flaxen-blond hair wearing a tri-corner hat. "Yeah, I see him."

"At first, I thought he was simply an odd duck, but hey, we get all kinds of kinds, so I didn't think much more of it. Then he ordered a flagon of apple mead and paid for it with this. Riley brought it over to see if it's accepted currency and I figured this has you written all over it."

He hands me a thick, copper coin and I chuckle. "Yeah, I suppose that pegs him as other. This is fae currency. I saw it when Dillan and I were behind the faery glass finding Moira."

"He seems like he had a night, don't you think?"

I take another look at the cider-sipping pirate and agree. His shoulders are rounded, his Friday night at the pub outfit a torn white tunic swathed to his hip and hanging open at the front. Ripped at the shoulder and splattered with the dirt and blood from his split lip, it's obvious he's been roughed up.

"Agreed. Any idea who was playing pirate punching bag with him?"

"As weird as it sounds, I think the two women standing at the high top under the speaker have something to do with it. They came in on his heels and locked their sights on him the moment they walked in the door."

I check out the women in question and yeah, something is off. They blend a lot better with the crowd than the guy, but there's something about them that triggers my need to stay alert.

Bartenders are a lot like cops in the way that over the years they become observant of body language and visual cues. That's compounded in a pub like Shenanigans, which off-duty cops heavily attend.

"Agreed. Something weird is going on. I'll check it out. Who did you say is serving that table? Riley?"

"Yeah."

I set the second pitcher onto my tray and strike off. "I'll keep you posted."

I drop off the two pitchers and the glasses at our table and keep the tray in hand. "So, we're wondering about the blond Jack Sparrow by the stage and how the two women watching him from the high top by the speaker were involved in his recent beating."

Dillan, Tad, and Sloan are on the side of the booth with a direct line of sight and can see without turning around. They take the first look.

"The man is a bit of a dandy," Sloan says, starting to pour, "but what makes Liam think he's empowered?"

"First off, point to you for using the word dandy, Mackenzie. It proves you're secure in your manhood. Back to the point of your question, he paid for his flagon of apple mead with this."

I set the copper coin on the table, and Dillan picks it up. "I recognize this. Fi and I didn't have any coin to open the town gate while in the Fae Realm. As we bartered with the trylle sentry, this was the money citizens used for their passage."

"And at the pub," I say.

"Yeah, there too."

Emmet takes it next. He and Ciara lean close to examine it. "So, we have a visitor from Faeryland?"

Ciara passes the coin to Tad to have a look. "Regardless of him bein' a visitor to our realm, what the hell is he doing using fae currency here? Surely he knows better."

"Maybe Shenanigans is getting a reputation as an otherworld hot spot," Dillan says. "There are druids, shifters, immortals, elves, and gods here fairly regularly. Maybe the news is spreading."

"I hope not," I say. "I don't want to bring that kind of attention to Shannon and Liam."

"True dat," Dillan says.

"All right, I'll go see what I can find out from Pirate Pete. Watch my six."

"It's one of life's simple pleasures, *a ghra*."

I laugh. "Cheeky and insouciant. I like it."

I make my way through the crowd and find Riley punching in

an order. "Hey, Liam's worried that the guy drinking cider by the stage is in some kind of trouble. Did he say anything to you?"

"Not much that makes sense. He talks like he's stuck in a cosplay role or comes from World of Warcraft."

"I think it's safe to say he's from out of town."

"Yeah, like from Ironforge."

I chuckle. "Do you mind if I check in with him and see if he needs anything? If he's in trouble, maybe I can direct him to one of my brothers."

"Knock yourself out."

Heading over, I assess his situation and position myself between him and the two women keeping a close eye on him. "Hey, is your cider all right?" I ask, pointing to his nearly full glass. "If you don't like it, I can get you something else."

He looks up at me, and wowzers, it'll be hard to pass off those eyes as human. Startlingly bright, he has one eye that is the most beautiful turquoise of a tropical sea, and the other is as green as a glittering emerald.

Sadly, marring the ocular beauty is a purple sheen ringing his eye socket, promising one heck of a shiner tomorrow. "Fash not. The mead is sufficient. It shall do."

"All right. What about some company? I can tell you're not from around here, and I'm a local. Maybe I can help you get sorted."

He meets my gaze, and while I have his attention, I release the glamor on my fae vision. Allowing him to see my 'other' serves two purposes. I'm letting him know I'm other too, and I can assess the status of him and the two women stalking him.

As I expect, his aura and intentions radiate in lovely champagne and blue swirls. The women aren't exactly evil, but they certainly are shady.

They aren't passionate though, so I doubt they're personally invested. The third-party muscle around here usually implies vampire mercenaries.

I know first-hand that roughing up an innocent is exactly the sort of thing the vampires do.

Once I finish with my evaluation, I replace the glamor over my eyes and resume my normal city girl persona. "The beauty of Shenanigans is that you're among friends here. If you need anything, let me know. I'm here for you."

His gaze sharpens, and he dips his chin. "Your kindness is well-received."

I tap my eye. "That's quite a bump you got. Would you like to come into the back and get some ice?"

His gaze skitters to the two women behind me and back. "Your offer is kind, but I must decline. My state of affairs prevents me from accepting at this time."

Right, but I'm not sure what to do to change his state of affairs in a room full of human patrons.

"Of course. If you change your mind, join us at our table." I gesture across the room and wave so that Dillan and Emmet wave back. "I'm Fiona, by the way—Fiona Mac Cumhaill."

At the sound of my name, the gold flecks in his eyes flash and sparkle, unlike anything I've ever seen in the human world. "Merry meet, Lady Fiona."

"Merry meet. And your name is?"

———

When I retreat to our booth, I remain standing and decline Sloan's offer to swap spots. If I want to sit, I can grab a chair and put it at the end of the booth. I'm good. He pours me a pint of Guinness and hands it to me. I sip from the edge of the glass and try not to stare across the room at our mystery pirate.

"So, what's his story?" Emmet asks.

I shrug and take another drink. "I'm not sure. I screened him with my fae vision, and he's a decent guy, but we're no closer to knowing what his situation is or why he has two very hostile women watching him."

"Do you know his name?"

"No. I asked him, but he didn't answer."

"Weird."

"Agreed."

Sloan tilts his head back and forth as if considering that. "Not so weird if he's of one of the fae races who believe a person's name holds power over them. In which case, he might not know you or trust you well enough to tell you."

Tad sets his empty glass down and swallows. "If someone knocked him around enough, he might be cautious about what he says and to whom."

I feel the current of subtext in Tad's words and my heart aches for him. It was no secret that he and his father had issues but having Riordan give himself to Mingin and try to kill him last week is still a festering wound.

"He's headed to the jacks," Ciara says. "Maybe Sloan or Tad should join him and portal him off if he needs an out."

"That's a great idea." I don't turn to look, but I step away from the end of the booth so Sloan can slide out. "Are the women following him?"

Emmet glances up over the edge of his glass. "Yep. Right on his ass."

"Okay, see what our wayfarers can find out. You're up, boys."

"This is a one-wayfarer job," Tad says. "I'll stay and finish my pint if ye don't mind."

Sloan straightens. "Where shall I take him if he agrees to go with me?"

"The safehouse at the Batcave?" I check to see if anyone has any better ideas, but it seems unanimous.

He nods. "All right. I'll be back."

"I'll come too." Emmet slides out. "Not as backup. I've gotta piss like ninety."

"Classy." I claim Sloan's seat and laugh. "You picked a truly cultured prince, Ciara."

My brother's newly betrothed brunette grins. "Emmet is as honest a man as ever there was and good-hearted about it too."

I raise my glass. "True story."

The five of us sit and share a pint for a few minutes until both Sloan and Emmet come back looking annoyed.

"Why do I get the feeling I won't like what you have to say?"

Emmet slides in next to Ciara and frowns. "Because you won't. It's a no-go on helping the guy out. He said to express his gratitude for your concern, but he truly cannot accept."

As they're relaying that info to me, the fae pirate exits the back hall and passes us on the way to the door…followed closely by his two women stalkers.

"Something is going on." I follow them with my gaze. "My skin is tingling with the energy of bad juju and my instincts are firing."

Sloan nods. "I don't disagree, luv, but there's nothing we can do if the man doesn't want our help."

I swallow another sip of beer and set down my glass. "Not entirely true."

Closing my eyes, I focus on blocking out the music and noise of the Friday night crowd and connect with my bear. *Bruin, there is a fae male with a tricorne hat leaving the bar with two women on his tail. Follow them and see if you can figure out what the hell is going on.*

On it.

"We'll see what Bruin turns up. If it's a domestic dispute and we have no business meddling, fine, but my gut says it's not. My instincts say we need to pay attention because something is about to happen."

Sloan frowns. "Oh, good. It's been a whole five days since we've had the world blow up in our faces."

I chuckle and hand him his glass. "Cheer up. Like you told your father. Your new life here is never boring."

CHAPTER TWO

"Calum and Kevin are buzzing around really feckin' early," Bruin grumbles, stretching his massive paw across my bedroom floor. "What's all the commotion about downstairs at the ass crack?"

It's not exactly the crack of dawn—or the ass crack, as he put it. It's going on eight-thirty, and in little people's land, that's nearly noon.

I roll to the edge of the bed and push back the curtains to see my grumbly fur mountain completely. "Saturday fun day with the uncles. Calum and Kev thought we could give Aiden and Kinu a break from chasing the monkeys."

Bruin chuffs, rubbing his paw over his black snout. "Children should be made to sleep in. Tie them down and gag them. That's what I would do."

"Then I guess it's good you're not in charge."

"I thought kids slept in until noon."

"I don't suppose that will happen for a few years yet. Sleeping the day away is more of a teenager thing."

"Or an ancient bear thing." He huffs but then grins and lets out a throaty chuckle. "Though it is funny as hell when the wee buggers crawl through the animal door to get in here."

"I got a video of that the other day. Hilarious." I roll out of bed and head into the bathroom to pee. "How did it go after you left the pub last night? Do we know anything more about who our fae pirate and those two women are or what's going on?"

"A bit. I know the male is an elf and fresh from behind the faery glass if I had to guess. I also know he doesn't much like those women, and they took something from him that he wants back."

"What kind of something?" I flush the toilet and run the water warm to wash my hands and wet a facecloth to wake myself up.

"I don't know, but it's important to him."

I dry my hands and rehang the towel. "Thus, the reason he wouldn't ditch them and accept the help from us."

"He likely couldn't risk it. Whatever it is they've taken from him, he's willing to endure a great deal to ensure he gets it back."

I grab my yoga pants from last night and pull them on and grab a clean t-shirt from my drawer. "Where did they end up? Do we have a location to go on?"

"That was weird. They escorted him to the harbor and took a ferry over to one of the three main islands."

"Which one?"

"The one farthest west."

"All right. What happened then?"

"They met up with two other guards outside a lighthouse. Everyone went inside. The door closed. That was the end of that."

I pull my two pendant necklaces off the corner of my dresser mirror and hang them around my neck. One is my Dionysus pendant, and the other is my Team Trouble security pendant.

"Why take a beaten-to-shit elf to a lighthouse on Hanlan's Point? Who are these people?"

He chuffs. "I don't interpret the intel. I only report what I see."

"Did you check out the lighthouse?"

"Yeah. I waited until all was quiet. I think what they took from him isn't a what. It's a who. When I went inside, there were two elves—the male we met and a female with her wrists bound."

"Seriously? Okay, well, that pieces a few things together. Pirate Pete wouldn't want to upset his captors if they have his sister or his girlfriend as leverage. Anything else to report?"

"No. That's all."

I bend over him and kiss his head. "Amazing job, buddy. Thanks."

"My pleasure. Are you going to the lighthouse to check it out?"

"I'll call this one into Garnet and see if he or Anyx can check it out right away. I've got a quick breakfast with the kids downstairs, then Sloan's *poofing* Dart and me to the stones to train with Dora. I've pushed off the training a couple of times already and have to give it my full attention or Dora will be pissed."

"All right. I'll nap in my den until yer ready to go. Make sure to wake me and take me."

"Promise."

He vanishes and caresses my cheek as he passes by and heads downstairs.

The sugary bliss of warm maple syrup seduces me as I descend the stairs. By the time I reach the kitchen, my stomach is growling, and my appetite is rising at an alarming rate. "Yummers. What's everyone eating?"

"A French-Canadian delight," Kevin says. "Grilled cheese and syrup."

I chuckle, heading over to the table to kiss Jackson and Meg good morning. "I know you *think* those two foods go together, Kev, but I'm not sold."

"Sweet and savory, Fi. You don't get an opinion unless you give it a try."

Jackson holds up a forkful for me to try and I make a face. "Pass. I think I'll stick with the tried and true grilled cheese and ketchup."

"Blasphemy," Kevin says. "Tell her, kids. Tell her my cheesy delight is amazing."

Jackson gives me a look that is all Aiden and holds his fork up higher. "You gotsta try new things, Auntie Fi. It's part of growin' up."

That is for sure Kinu's way of bribing him to eat vegetables, but I suppose I should lead by example.

Bending over, I accept the bite and assess the flavors blending in my mouth. Cheesy syrup. Weird.

"Well?" Calum asks, wiping Meg's hands and face. "I was a skeptic at first too, but after spending as much time at Kevin's parents' place as I did growing up, I learned to appreciate it."

I swallow and wave away Jackson's offer of a second bite. "No thanks, buddy. You eat it. I think I'll stick with the old faithful."

Kevin waves the spatula in the air and shakes his head. "I'm not sure we can still be friends. In my house growing up, syrup topped everything."

I snort and grab a glass from the drying rack. "Aren't both your parents battling with adult-onset diabetes now?"

"Well, yeah." He flips over the next sandwich. "Are you blaming the syrup?"

"Does a bear poop in the woods?"

Jackson asks, looking horrified. "Does Bruin poop in our grove?"

I grab the blueberry blast juice and pour myself a glass. "No, buddy. I'm sure he doesn't. It's a silly saying."

"Like, what goes around comes around," Calum says.

"Or, when life gives you lemons, make lemonade," Kevin adds.

"Or, I licked it, so it's mine," Emmet says, coming down the stairs to join us.

I laugh. "Why would you encourage that?"

Emmet snorts and heads straight for the pot of French Roast sitting on the warmer. "It was the genius strategy that got me through teenage hunger in a house filled with boys. It cut the competition."

"Says the turkey vulture."

Emmet sticks his tongue out at Calum and smiles at Ciara. She walked in on this conversation at the mid-point and looks both confused and slightly disgusted. "I didn't barf on stuff, babe. I only licked it. What can I say? In a household of six kids, you gotta get your elbows up."

"Well, that I agree with," I say.

I see the cogs in Jackson's head spinning. There's no way this isn't going to become a thing with him. "You don't have to lick things, monkey. Uncle Emmet is cray-cray, and you know how to share nicely with your sisters. You can't call dibs on more than your share."

"Says you." Emmet pours coffee into two travel mugs.

Kevin slides a grilled cheese onto a plate for me, and I accept it with a smile. "Perfection, thanks."

"What about the newly betrothed?" he asks. "You can't live on love alone. Do you guys want one?"

Emmet shakes his head, topping their coffees with almond milk. "No thanks. We're hitting the streets early and exploring. It's 'get to know your new home' tour number three. We'll grab brekkie on the run a little later at one of the diners."

I hand him the juice to put back into the fridge and point at the ketchup on the door shelf. "What's on the agenda for tour number three?"

"We're going down to Harbourfront for the morning by ourselves and meeting up with the fam jam at the ferry at one o'clock for a couple of hours on Centre Island."

I pause from eating and smile at the kids. "You're going to Centre Island today? Fun. Uncle's fun day is awesome."

"Are yous and Uncle Sloan coming, Auntie Fi?"

I think about my day and mentally shuffle things around. I'm meeting Dora for dragon training in the morning and planned to visit Suede to ask her about the elf this afternoon.

I want to ask if she's heard anything about a kidnapping in their community, but maybe I'll call her and take advantage of a trip to Centre Island.

From Centre Island, I'll cross the footbridge, walk around to Hanlan's Point, and check out that lighthouse. No need to call Garnet when I'll already be there.

"Yeah, buddy. I think that would be amazeballs. I'll call Uncle Sloan and see if he can come too."

"Yay!" Meggie claps.

"Yay!" we all say back.

"Good morrow, mighty dragon mistress," I say, bowing to Dora in a flourish of hands and arms. "One sweet blue boy and his much less impressive bonded human counterpart reporting for dragon boot camp."

Dora straightens to what must be six-foot-six with the heels of her boots. She's killing it in pink and gray camo with fuchsia hair. "You joke now, but you might not think it's funny when we're finished. I've been known to be a taskmaster."

"You've been known to be a lot of things."

She nods. "Very true."

I kiss Sloan goodbye and send him packing. "Thanks for the ride, my love. I'll call you when we're ready for a pick-up."

"That's fine. I'll be at STOA on my computer."

"Happy relic hunting. I hope you find something über cool and super powerful today."

He chuckles. "You say that every day."

"It's true every day. *Go n-eirí an t-ádh leat.*"

He grins and smiles at Dora. "Good luck to you too. Work her hard, Dora. No mercy."

When he *poofs* out, I laugh and face my instructor. "He's right. Be whoever and whatever you think you need to be to get Dart and I synced up to be a dynamic dragon duo."

"That's a good attitude, cookie. Let me finish what I started here before I lose my place. Then I'm all yours."

I leave Dora to her spellbook and take Dart to explore the stones. "These are like the ones in Ireland," I tell him. "That's what Dora is working on. She's going to create a standing portal from our stones to the ones at Drombeg in County Cork. That way, if you ever need to get back there or the Queen of Wyrms needs to get here, there's a quick and easy passage for you."

Dart tilts his head as I explain, but in the end, he thumps his tail on the grass. I think that means he understands and likes that idea.

He's grown a lot over the past months. He's gone from a little guy that could climb into the palm of my hand to the size of a large dog to the size of a large elephant. That's his adolescent size. His super-sized form is as long as a city bus and twice as tall.

With massive wings.

And blows fire.

So cute.

I press my hand against the frill behind his cheek and work on our connection. When Gran does this, she can communicate with him flawlessly.

In no way do I pretend to possess the magic mojo of the amazing and accomplished Lara Cumhaill, but I'm hoping it'll come with time. "Do you miss being at the lair with your mother and your siblings, baby boy?"

Images flash into my mind like impressions of emotion: him playing with Scarlet, her digging them an escape tunnel to leave the lair without permission, and her sad face when he was readying to leave.

"I'm sorry you're sad. If it's too hard and you miss your Ireland home too much, you don't have to stay here. I don't want you to be sad and lonely. I can visit you in Ireland more often. Whatever you need, we can make it work."

His mind shifts to having fun with Bruin, Manx, Doc, and Daisy, and being out in the grove with me, and saving me from Xavier last week, and going to the Beltane celebration.

"So, you're not totally sad and lonely. That's a relief. I understand. You're happy with your life here but also miss your little sister."

By the grunt he lets out, I think I got that right.

"Well, she'll always be your sister, and maybe when Dora gets the portal linked, we can visit her."

That seems to cheer him up.

Something crackles behind me and the air charges with a magical pulse of energy. The hair on my arms and the nape of my neck stand on end.

Breathing in, I get a cloying whiff of something that smells a lot like old baby powder. It's grossly sweet but tainted and musty at the same time.

Then it dissipates and drains away.

"What was that?" I ask, heading back to Dora.

"A trial run powering up. I think this side of the portal is almost ready. If Nikon can transport me to the corresponding stones later, I'll work to bring Drombeg online as well."

"Noice. You rock, girlfriend." I pat Dart and urge him to come with me to join Dora. "So, where do we start with our training?"

"First, I want to establish how firmly developed your bond is. You mentioned that Dart feels your emotion and knows to come to you when you're in trouble."

"That's right. Patty said he would get agitated when he felt my pain or struggles."

"What about you? Can you sense his emotions when you're separated?"

"No. Is that bad? Should I feel him like he feels me? Am I falling short already?"

Dora rolls her eyes and smiles. "Take a breath. Rome wasn't built in a day, and dragons don't meld with their counterparts overnight."

"All right. So, what do we do?"

"Relax your mind and see if you can follow the bond the two of you share. Envision it as a physical tether between the two of you, a rope or a cable or a braided tangle of vines."

I lay on the grass next to my dragon, to do as Dora says. Shamans can see things on other planes. Once I figure out where this manifestation of our bond lies within me, I can focus on strengthening it.

Closing my eyes, I shift through my mind and body, searching for the tie that binds.

I have no trouble finding my happy place where Brendan's spark resides and where I retreat and regroup when life is at its worst.

I feel Bruin where he's resting peacefully after a late night out following kidnappers and captives.

I don't feel anything that resembles a dragon bond.

After trying for what feels like ages, I sigh and open my eyes. "I've got nothing."

She tents her fingers together and frowns. "Nothing? You're sure?"

"Yeah. Why do you sound so surprised?"

"Because you've been able to retreat inwardly since the beginning, and that was long before you knew how or why you could. The bond is there on Dartamont's side. I'm not sure why you aren't able to find it."

Me either.

It's been almost two months since I learned about my Celtic shaman abilities. Why can't I do this?

I sigh, and Dora drops to the grass to sit next to us. "Maybe if we start from the *very* beginning, understanding the big picture might help. A bit of history—or perhaps it's closer to mythology—might give you better insight into who and what Dartamont is."

I look at my blue boy and frown. I think I have a strong grasp on who and what my boy is. There's no sense arguing though because you don't know what you don't know, you know?

"It is written that millennia ago—before humans evolved from survival to living and became enlightened enough to form tribes and then communities—there was a great war between the gods and giants."

I chuckle. "Giants versus gods? Doesn't seem like it would be much of a war? Aren't giants a little dim-witted to be taking on a pantheon of gods? Or maybe that's why they *did* take on the gods, because they didn't realize how FUBAR things would get."

"No. I'm not talking about the giants in the modern sense of large, simple-minded creatures, but giants in their original form, which were much like the ancient gods themselves."

"Oh, okay. Gods versus giants. What was the war about?"

"The giants were arrogant, omniscient beings who cared nothing for the earth and its inhabitants. They believed humans and animals were inconsequential and therefore irrelevant. The abundance of nature's resources was all the giants craved. They consumed without consideration and caused chaos."

"Nice guys."

"The gods were also arrogant, but they saw the flaws in the giants' ways. They recognized nature's bounty as finite and respected the evolution of man and beast. They committed to establishing balance."

"So, a war between chaos and balance."

"That's right. It wasn't a battle like the wars humans have where hundreds of thousands of men and women clash and die over a few years or even decades. There were only maybe a hundred gods against a hundred giants, but the battles raged on and off for centuries."

"What does this have to do with dragon training?"

She holds up a finger and winks. "Everything, for if there were no wars between the gods and the giants, there would be no dragons."

"How so?"

"As I mentioned, gods and giants were balance and chaos. They were essentially the omniscient version of yin and yang."

"All right."

"So when the blood spilled by foes mixed and fell to the earth, there were instances when that powerful fluid found sources of fae prana, and the magic triumvirate was complete. The power of their essences took hold, and just as life evolved from the primordial ooze, dragons were born. Wyrms, Westerns, and wyverns were the founding species, but later, through evolution, drakes, basilisks, and serpents grew into existence as well."

"That's how the basilisk sperm was able to fertilize the queen's eggs? Because they're genetically linked?"

"That's right. And a lucky thing too because as far as I know, the Dragon Queen of Wyrms was the sole survivor of all dragons. I believed them extinct entirely."

I glance up at my blue boy and tug on one of the spikes on his neck. "Thankfully not."

"Thankfully not," Dora agrees. "It should also explain to you why dragons are not and will never be your pet or your child. They're powerful beings with equal parts chaos and balance. Dartamont will be taught right from wrong and, for the most part, he will likely make an earnest effort at choosing wisely, but you cannot change what he is by nature."

"What is that?"

"He is a dragon—a great and mythical beast that needs to be respected."

"I do respect him."

"No, Fi, you don't. You *love* him and believe training him will be like training a dog or your nieces and nephew. It won't. There's a reason why dragons live in seclusion. They aren't naturally wired to live by rules."

I think about that, and yeah, she has a point to some extent, but I don't think she's completely right.

"Do you think I made a mistake by bringing him here? Is this going to blow up in my face?"

She shrugs. "It likely will to some degree, yes."

"So, we shouldn't try?"

"No. What I'm saying is that as a young dragon, Dartamont yearns to be with you and will do his best to conform to your world, but as he ages and grows stronger, his needs won't be met by these stones and sleeping in your backyard. He will stray. There will be exposure and people will notice when he swoops down into a dog park and eats all the dogs."

I sigh. "You're harshing my mellow here, Dora."

She nods. "You asked for hard truths, so here it is. Me helping you is equally about training you as it is training him. You need to stop looking at this like inviting your nephew over for a sleepover. Dragons in a city is a bad idea."

"Wow. Don't hold back."

"There's no sense shooting rainbows and sunshine up your ass."

I look at Dart and rub the ache in my chest. "Okay. Consider me enlightened. I'll expand my thinking and really start preparing for our future."

"Good."

"How much time do you think I have before my life doesn't fit him and we're in trouble?"

She shrugs. "A year? Maybe two?"

That's a huge blow. I was thinking maybe Sloan and I could retire to Ireland in a decade or two, but a year? I'll miss the day-to-day of the kids growing up and have to forfeit everything I love.

I swallow. "Wow. Consider my day ruined."

"Don't look at it that way. We live in a world of magic and marvel. You have time to think of something. I just need you to be thinking."

I draw a deep breath and exhale. "That's fair. I'll brainstorm with Sloan. He's the smartest person I know. Between the three of us, I'm sure we'll think of something."

"Good girl. I truly hope we do."

CHAPTER THREE

As bummed as I was when Dora burst my dragon bubble, after almost two hours of working with Dart on communication and connection, I can breathe again. We're a great team. It'll work out.

Everything happens as it's supposed to.

Dart and I were a lock from the first moment he poked his little head out of his egg, and our gazes met. That's not a mistake intended to make either of us suffer. There's an answer out there, and it will be great.

The important part is that Dora gave me a shake.

Dart isn't my baby boy. He's a mythical creature with equal parts balance and chaos, and I have to acknowledge both sides of him and love him for who he is and not who I want him to be.

Much like I had to get used to Killer Clawbearer's desire to shred his enemies and Birga's thirst for blood.

Human morals and ethics don't apply to life in the empowered world.

"Yer quiet, *a ghra*," Sloan says as we take form in the shade of our backyard grove.

"Dora gave me a lot to think about. She said she would

be tough on me, but I assumed that referred more to the physical training than crushing my illusions."

He arches a dark brow. "That sounds ominous."

A giant, scratchy tongue slaps up against the side of my neck, and I chuckle, helpless against Dart's goofy grin. I scrub my knuckles across his snout and he grunts.

The image he projects to me is one I'm getting very accustomed to. "Hungry again? You're not a dragon. You're a bottomless pit."

Sloan scoffs. "Yer boy is always hungry. The two of us need to find him something that fills him up."

"He's been here a week and has eaten a deer and a calf and some rabbits. What we need is the dragon equivalent to pasta. How do you carb-load a dragon?"

Sloan laughs. "Yer lookin' at me like I have an answer to that."

"You have an answer to most things. You're my druid guru and guide in life and love."

He grins. "And yer full of it."

Dart shuffles off in the direction of his nest, and I take a moment to claim a hug. "Tell me having Dart here isn't a colossal mistake. You don't even have to believe it. I just need to hear you say the words and I'll believe it enough for the both of us."

Sloan hugs me and lifts me off my feet. "Dart is a welcome addition to our home and our family. Not every plus-one we add will be an easy transition. It doesn't make them any less a part of our little family. Yer Fiona-feckin' Cumhaill. Ye'll figure it out."

I draw a deep breath and let his reassurance strengthen my conviction. "Hells yeah, I will. No man left behind—that includes dragons."

Calum and the kids come out of our house at the same time Kevin comes out onto the back deck with Kinu next door. He holds up a backpack and an insulated cooler. "We're all set. Mommy even packed us lunch, didn't she, kids?"

"Yay, Mommy!" Dillan prompts them.

"Yay, Mommy!" they repeat.

Sloan chuckles, kissing my temple and setting me back on my feet. "They really are so easily amused."

I laugh. "Who, the kids or Calum, Kev, and Dillan?"

"Lady's choice."

The Toronto harbor is a five-minute drive from our house straight down Parliament Street and east a couple of blocks. We park in a public lot a block north of the ferry terminal and walk down Bay Street with the new two-seater jogger stroller I bought for them with Brendan's money.

As a family, we agreed that Brendan would appreciate his life insurance money going toward the lives of the next generation of Clan Cumhaill.

When we were growing up, things were tight. We had what we needed but never any extras. For us, it was hand-me-downs and making do our entire lives.

There was no money for extracurricular sports or clubs or video games or anything like that. Once Aiden started working, then Brendan, they paid for Calum, Dillan, and Emmet to play community hockey, but by then, they were so far behind in skills any dreams of the NHL were shot.

It's one of the reasons we were all so eager to work and make our own money. I bought my first mascara and blush with the money I saved working the hostess stand at Shenanigans.

Not the next-gen Cumhaills. No sir.

Meg and Jackson are riding in a luxury stroller with reclining seats, adjustable suspension, and rear lights and reflectors for night walks.

Emmet calls it the chariot.

"Uncle Emmet!" Jackson calls, waving to Em and Ciara waiting under the awning of the ticket kiosks.

"Hey, monkeys! Are you guys ready to run away and join the circus?"

Jackson knows Emmet well enough not to fall for that. "No. We's going to the rides on the island."

"Rides?" Emmet shakes his head. "No. I think they took all the rides away. Now kids have to work on the island, cleaning up sticks and raking leaves."

Jackson looks at Calum. "Is dat true?"

"Not even a little bit. Uncle Emmet is teasing you."

Jackson narrows his gaze and nods. "Thought so."

"Ponies," Meg says.

I nod. "Yep. There are ponies, and goats, and alpacas, and ducks. It'll be so fun."

"Ciara and I grabbed the tickets." Emmet flashes us the receipt. "We're ready to roll."

Calum turns the chariot toward the stroller entrance, and we're on our way. "Let the good times roll."

The ferry ride to Centre Island takes ten minutes. Then we spend the next hour riding the antique carousel, taking the mini train around the amusement park, and corralling two crazy kids having the time of their lives.

Since the birth of the twins less than two weeks ago, Kinu and Aiden have had their hands full. There haven't been any all-day events to get the bigger two kids out of the house.

"Ducks!"

I follow Meggie's extended finger to the waddling group of quackers on the bank of the duck pond. "Have we got any loonies left for bird food, Kev?"

He checks the pocket of the chariot where we opened the roll and pulls out a bunch. "Yep. Lots. Looks like it's a lucky day for the ducks."

"Lucky ducks." Jackson giggles. "That's a silly saying."

"Yes, it is, buddy." I chuckle. "Your Cumhaill sense of humor is coming right along."

Emmet takes the money and heads off to the concession stand to buy us each a bag of food for the birds. When he returns, he's laughing and points us farther down the pond. "Let's go that way. A tourist family is feeding Canadian geese over there, and they're running out of food."

"Good call." Dillan picks up Jackson and swings him around in circles as we walk.

"What's wrong with the geese?" Ciara asks.

"Regular geese, nothing," I say, "but Canadian geese are vicious. They'll hiss and bite you for no reason—especially ones conditioned to think humans should feed them."

Calum nods. "Once you've been on the receiving end of a few of them, you learn to be wary. They used to be really bad at the zoo too."

"They don't look menacing."

Emmet laughs. "Yeah, when tourists come, all they see are cute little geese. Canadians see evil velociraptors ready to strike."

Ciara looks skeptical. She catches Sloan's attention and lifts her chin. "Are they pullin' my leg?"

"I don't think so. They warned me off them a few months ago."

"Oh, wait." Emmet points. "Watch. Tourist family ran out of food."

We all turn to watch as a family of four finishes feeding a group of geese. The dad shows them his empty hands, but they don't have the good sense to clear out.

"What?" Dillan says. "They think they can hang out with them?"

"See. They aren't turning into monsters," Ciara says.

"Uh-huh," Kev says. "Give it a minute."

The geese realize the gravy train has stopped and start their offensive. They waddle closer, grunting and intimidating the dazzled feeders. When the people don't meet the goosey demands, they start going for the lowest-hanging fruit.

"Are they targeting the wee ones?" Ciara asks.

"Sure are."

The geese advance, hissing and snapping. Mom tourist grabs up the toddler and retreats. Dad tourist takes the hand of the older one and swipes his foot through the air, shouting at the angry birds.

That doesn't go over well at all.

It's too late for a graceful retreat.

The attempt to intimidate the birds has made them mad. They swarm forward. The kids screech as the parents rush to the closest picnic table and climb the bench to stand on the tabletop.

That's enough to hold off the siege, but they're trapped if they want to stay out of reach from snapping beaks.

"Should we help them?" Ciara asks. "We can talk the geese down."

Calum shakes his head, laughing. "And ruin this amazing life lesson? No, they're safe enough now as long as the swans stay in the water. The geese will lose interest soon enough and go back for a swim."

"Birdies biting." Meg frowns.

"Just those birdies, Meggers," Kevin says. "We'll find you some nice duckies to feed."

"Duckies don't bite?" Jackson asks, obviously rethinking the whole bird feeding endeavor.

"No, buddy," I say. "Ducks are super nice. When they nibble food, it tickles."

The nine of us continue down the duck pond further and find a hungry bunch of ducks to feed. They quack and waggle their tails and peck and poke their beaks into our palms, chomping up the pellets of food. Jackson is brave enough to feed them by hand, but Meg prefers to throw hers onto the ground.

When my pellets are gone, I brush my hands together and look around. "Sloan and I are venturing off for an island walk. We'll be back in a bit."

Dillan frowns. "Seriously? At a children's park? That's just wrong."

It takes a moment—"No, dumbass. We're going over to Hanlan's Point to check things out."

"Noice," Dillan says.

Emmet snorts. "I didn't peg Irish for a nude beach kinda guy."

Calum barks a laugh. "It's too cold for that. Wait for summer."

Dillan chuckles. "Oh, yeah. Great point. Don't hang out with your wang out during shrinkage weather."

Sloan frowns. "Yer all a bunch of eejits. Bruin tracked the guards of the battered elf to the Gibraltar Lighthouse at Hanlan's Point. Fi wants to check it out. How ye got from that to me displayin' my johnson is beyond me."

"Oh, well, that's much less interesting." Emmet gestures toward the road leading back to the pier. "Have at it. Buh-bye."

I wink to the kids. "Secret druid business. We'll catch up with you guys later, okeedoodle?"

Jackson makes an earnest attempt to wink at me and grins. "Okeedoodle."

Sloan and I part from the Cumhaill outing and meander our way around the big red barn that houses the animals for the petting zoo. Once we get back to the ferry dock, we hang a right and follow the lakefront road toward Hanlan's Point.

"The Gibraltar Point lighthouse, on the Hanlan side of Centre Island, was built in 1808 to protect ships coming into Toronto harbor from washing ashore during storms," I say, reading Sloan the history from the Hanlan's Point website. "Due to shifting landmasses, it now stands inland."

"I don't suppose a lighthouse set in from the water is of much use as a lighthouse," Sloan says.

"I suppose not. It says here that its first lighthouse keeper, JP Radelmüller, was murdered and dismembered by two soldiers from Fort York."

"That's grisly."

"Yeah. They recovered his jawbone years later but never found the rest of his body."

"Why would soldiers kill the lighthouse keeper?"

I scroll through the article and read on. "Authorities believe he had a home distillery and was brewing beer. They suspect he was actively known as a bootlegger to the soldiers. One night, two men, John Blueman and John Henry, got too drunk. It's believed Radelmüller cut them off and they didn't take it well."

"Dismembering the man fer not sellin' them his beer is more than not takin' it well."

"Agreed. Oh, but listen to this… It says the ghost of poor old John Paul Radelmüller returns every summer and people can hear his howls from one end of the island to the other."

Sloan arches a brow at me and frowns. "Yer makin' that last bit up."

"No, I'm not. That's what it says." I hold up my phone so he can see the island webpage.

He grunts and grimaces off toward the water, his easy demeanor suddenly stiff.

"What's that face about?"

"This is my normal face."

I laugh. "No, it's not. That is not your usual surly scowl. That's a new surly scowl. What did I say to flip your switch?"

"Nothing. Yer being ridiculous."

"Your pants are on fire, Mackenzie."

We walk along in relative silence, but I keep my gaze on him. He's terrible at staring contests and can't withstand the pressure.

By the tensing of his brow and the pursing of his lips, he's either having an aneurysm or is about to crack.

About. To. Crack…

"All right, fine," he says, his breath escaping in an annoyed exhale. "I'm not a fan of ghosts."

I burst out laughing. "You? You, the man of logic and reason is afraid of ghosts? That's hilarious."

"Why? Poltergeists and vengeful spirits are nothin' to laugh at. When an enemy is attackin', I prefer the kind that will fall from a weapon's strike or the impact of a spell. Ghosts are deadly business."

"Wait. What?" I strike my hand out and stop him in his tracks. "Ghosts are real?"

He scowls down at me. "Of course they are. Why would I be leery of them if they weren't real?"

"Point to you. Okay, now I'm a little afraid. Why is this the first I'm hearing of this?"

"I don't know? I suppose there are still a great many preternatural creatures you aren't aware of. Ye've been livin' the life fer less than a year."

"True, but what a time we've had, eh?"

He looks down at me, and his trepidation about the ghost drains away, replaced by a crooked smile. "Och, I suppose it's been all right."

I laugh. "Yeah, good call. Let's not oversell it. I'd give it all right. Mediocre at best."

"Mediocre?" He grabs my wrist and *poofs* us off the road and behind a cluster of trees in the background. Pressing me up against the rough bark of an old oak, he cradles my jaw in his palms, claims my mouth, and proceeds to kiss me like he's missed me.

When he pulls back a moment later, we're both breathless and I'm thankful for the tree at my back.

"I think we can do better than mediocre," he says, pegging me with a heated gaze.

I swallow, my mind spinning and my heart pounding at the base of my throat. "Yeah, way better."

As much as I'm tempted to abandon the lighthouse idea and have him *poof* us home to have the house to ourselves, I can't seem to get the image of the beaten elf out of my mind.

"Ugh…why do I have this compulsion to help people even when they don't want my help?"

"Because yer Fiona-bleeding-heart-Cumhaill."

I laugh, grab his hand, and tug him back toward the road. "I'm not a bleeding heart. I had a boyfriend in high school who told me that when they gave out the girl genes, I was nowhere in sight."

Sloan's head whips around, and he's sweet enough to look appalled on my behalf. "He did not."

I hold up three fingers in the Girl Guides salute. "He totes did, and there were similar opinions from other guys too. I'm not girly enough for most guys."

"Obviously ye dated fools before me. I love the fact that yer not like other girls. Ye can kick my ass if yer fired up. Ye don't need constant stroking and reassurance. Ye speak yer mind and are frank about it. Yer my perfect girl."

I chuckle. "You have odd standards for perfection."

"No, I don't."

"Since it skews in my favor, we'll agree to disagree. Come on. The lighthouse is up here. We need to be quiet if we don't want to tip off the mysterious women kidnappers that we're coming."

"Have ye given any thought to what yer goin' to say to these possibly vampire, hired thugs?"

"No, but I'll think of something. I always do."

CHAPTER FOUR

B ruin. *You up for a quick spin to see if the guards from last night are still hanging around the lighthouse?*

I'm always up for a chance to throw down.

True story.

Sloan and I wait in the wings until he breezes back. *All clear. No sign of anyone.*

"Where did they go?"

I can't tell ye.

"I take it Bruin says there's no one here?"

"That's the report, yes." With no reason for stealth, I tromp out of the brush and reclaim the footpath leading to the lighthouse.

"Well, poop. Now I'm disappointed."

Sloan glances over at me. "Ye were hoping we'd have a run-in with the mysterious elf captors?"

"I was hoping for something." I try the door. It's locked, so I press my palm against the latch plate and let myself in. *"Open Sesame."*

Sloan laughs. "Ye realize that's not the real spell, don't ye?"

"Intention is everything." I turn the rusty old knob and push the door open. "It's never failed me yet."

The hinges creak in protest as I force the swing of the red, wooden door. "It wouldn't kill them to spray a bit of WD-40 on that."

"I think this place has seen better days."

"I think it's seen better centuries."

There's not much to the interior. It's a claustrophobic, twenty-foot hexagon with a threadbare twin mattress against the wall and stairs up the middle of the structure leading to the lamp room above.

"The article says this is the oldest existing lighthouse on the Great Lakes and one of Toronto's oldest buildings."

"It shows." Sloan sweeps his foot through the remnants of teenager trespassing. He toes the empty beer cans and chip and Dorito bags. "Looks like someone had a good time here. Do ye think it was yer elf kidnappers?"

I frown down at the leftover debris and shake my head. Then I pick up one of the cans and sniff it.

"What are ye doin'? Put that down. Ye don't know where it's been."

I snort. "Sure I do. Right here. Some kid hung out with his buddies. They polished off a six and smoked up. It wasn't our thugs, though. These are old. No scent or drips of beer. If I didn't know better, I'd question that there even was anyone here last night."

"So now yer a forensic expert?"

I sort through the discarded food wrappers and look around. "I may have gleaned a few things after cleaning up after my brothers a time or two."

The two of us search the main body of the lighthouse. It doesn't take long. There's no sign of anything we can use in my search to help out an elf in trouble.

Sloan takes the first step and starts to climb. "Who knew having older brothers would be such an education fer a little sister."

Once I've exhausted the idea of finding anything useful on the floor, I start up the stairs after him. "Oh, I was educated on a lot of things that maybe I shouldn't have been. Da was gone a lot. He had to pick up extra shifts and off-duty gigs to keep things going. It left a lot of opportunity for questionable behavior."

He doesn't question me on that, which is likely a good thing.

"Not that we did anything too bad. Just ill-thought-out shenanigans mostly."

He still doesn't say anything...which is weird.

"Hotness? You all right?" I hustle up the last few steps and burst into the lamp room. It's a circular space with a large glass cage in the center for the lamp and windows all the way around.

Sloan is standing a couple of feet from the top step, stiff as a board and focused on the far side of the room.

"What's wrong? What do you see?"

"Ye don't see him?"

"Him who? The ghost? No. Do *you* see him?"

Sloan holds his hand out for me, and the moment our fingers mesh, his bone ring expands my vision beyond the visible realm —and there he is.

The ghost is staring at us with the same amazed confusion as I'm sure we have on our faces. He's a rather short man in his fifties, wearing worn and torn clothes that have seen better days.

Thankfully, even though he was murdered and dismembered, he looks whole. Still, he'll never be mistaken for normal because he's a faded sepia color and a bit see-through.

Looking at him is like staring at an image in an old photo. Or getting your saloon picture taken at an amusement park.

Only this isn't amusing.

Hokie doodle—I'm staring at a ghost.

The air isn't cold like they always say in movies. In fact, with the entire room around us being glass, it's quite warm and stuffy.

"Hello, John Paul," I say, hoping he isn't one of those poltergeists or vengeful spirits Sloan was worried about. "How's things in the lighthouse these days?"

Sloan scowls at me. "Are ye daft?"

"What? I've never made first contact with a ghost before. At least I said something. You're standing there with your mouth hanging open, looking like a freeze ray shot you."

I give my attention back to the man standing next to the lamp controls. "Forgive me. I'm a first-time ghost whisperer, and I'm not sure of the protocols."

Ghost John Paul says nothing.

I chuckle at the sound of that in my head.

Sloan pegs me with a glare. "Did I miss the part where somethin' funny happened?"

"My bad. I was just thinking he's Ghost John Paul...it reminded me of Pope John Paul and struck my funny bone. Not the same, I know, but it made me chuckle."

"Maybe ye can leave yer funny bone out of things fer now and focus on the crisis at hand?"

"Sure, I can try." I straighten, press my shoulders back, and smile at the faded brown man. "You can leave your post now if that's what's holding you here. Other lighthouses do what this one used to. You're free to pass over or move on or whatever it is you need to do."

He opens his mouth, and it seems like he's going to say something, but it doesn't come.

"Maybe it's been so long since he spoke, he doesn't remember how. Or maybe this is a jawbone thing...do you think? Do we need to track that down to make him whole so he can talk?"

Sloan frowns. "It's more likely he's been trapped in this state for so long, he's lost himself and his humanity. When was he killed?"

I take out my phone and look that up. "German-born John Paul Radelmüller, murdered in 1815, remains the lead character in Toronto's most enduring ghost story."

"Were the men who killed him caught and put to justice? Maybe he's looking fer closure."

I scroll further down the page. "It says, authorities arrested the two men, and they were charged and faced a jury, but it ultimately acquitted John Henry and John Blueman of the crime."

"Och, well, I'm sorry to hear that, sham. Is that yer trouble? Do ye seek justice before ye pass over?"

John Paul's mouth continues to work, but no sound comes out. It's freaky and gives me the willies.

There's no sense staying here. If he won't say anything and we don't know what he wants or how to fix him, there's not much we can do.

Shifting, I point at the stairs in case he doesn't understand me. "Okay, well, we gotta go. Don't worry, I promise, I'll talk to some people and find out what to do to help you. We'll be back."

When I turn to leave, he lifts his arm, and the door downstairs slams shut and locks.

A gust of cold air hits and a shiver runs down my spine. "Okay, creepy just got unnerving. Him not wanting us to leave isn't good, is it?"

Sloan stiffens. "I don't think so, no."

"Like it or not, we can't stand in a lighthouse all day and night."

"What do ye suggest we do? The man is amicable enough at the moment. If ye mention leavin' again, it might set him off."

I don't like the sound of that.

The frozen still and mute ghost is triggering alarm bells left and right. I have no interest in an angry and vengeful version of Ghost John Paul Radelmüller.

"Do you have unfinished business?" I ask. "Or maybe an object tethering you to the lighthouse?"

Sloan frowns. "Where'd ye get that?"

"*Supernatural*. When all else fails, sometimes I ask myself what would Sam and Dean Winchester do?"

"Are they the brothers with the classic car?"

"Baby, yeah. '67 Chevy Impala."

He shakes his head. "All right, I'll play yer game. What would yer Winchester brothers do?"

"They'd find the grave of the dead guy, dig it up, then salt and burn the bones. If the body is already burned, the spirit is possessing an object. Once you know what object, then you salt and burn that."

He turns on me. "Absolutely not. Desecration of the man's grave is not the answer. That's likely to get the two of us haunted until the end of days."

I shrug. "Fine. We'll ask around and see who knows about ghosts. Considering he doesn't want us to leave, I'm thinking *poofing* is our best bet."

"Och, I don't think he'll like that either."

"Damned if you do. Damned if you don't."

He sighs and shakes his head. "Must ye say such things? I'd rather not be damned at all...and certainly not while we're lookin' at a man that's been dead fer more than two centuries."

Sloan's voice, usually deep and smooth, is getting pitchy and thin. It's pretty funny, actually. Sloan's easy to rile with nonsense and impropriety but he's usually rock-solid on the empowered stuff.

Seeing him afraid of ghosts is fun for me, but I suppose there's no sense tormenting him.

"You're really not good with ghosts, are you?"

"No."

"John Paul? I don't want you to go all *Candyman* on us. We're going to figure this out and help you, I promise. We'll make this right. Just hang in there." I squeeze Sloan's hand and nod.

Thankfully, he reads my mind and a moment later we're back behind the red barn on the other side of Centre Island.

"Well, crappers. That did not go as planned."

"No. It didn't."

CHAPTER FIVE

By the time we get Meg and Jackson home and unwind after a day of fun, the Cumhaill fam jam is bagged. Emmet and Ciara head upstairs for a nap before dinner. Calum retreats to the basement to check on Tad, and Kevin jumps in his truck to pick up some beer before the store closes.

"What a weird day." I flop down on the couch. "A dragon, a ghost, and a coerced elf...it sounds like the beginning of a bad joke."

Sloan strides straight into the kitchen and turns on the faucet to wash his hands. Then, he fills the kettle and sets it on its base to start the boil. "Life is stranger than fiction, they say."

In *my* life, that's even more strange.

"I can't believe ghosts are real. I honestly didn't know that."

"Ye don't know what ye don't know, *a ghra*. Until ye do and then ye do."

I giggle and pull my über-soft lap blankie over my legs. "That was profound, Mackenzie. Truly transcendent thinking."

He grins, puttering around, putting away the clean dishes. "It's been a long day. I'm not at my peak."

"Me either." It bugs me that I haven't been particularly

productive. "Is it strange the shock of being face-to-face with a ghost is wearing off?"

"I don't know. Ye seem to have a higher tolerance than most for the odd and unusual."

"Right? Who knew crazy things like that would become commonplace in druid life?"

"I think commonplace might be overstating." He pulls out the molasses cookies. "I've been living an active druid life for decades and have only encountered a ghost twice before today."

"Twice? Do tell? Is that why they freak you out so badly? Did you have a bad experience? Were you haunted? Or probed?"

"No. I think yer mixin' ghosts with aliens on that last one." The kettle boils and clicks off, and Sloan pours it into our mugs to steep. "No, both ghostly encounters were while I was touring an ancient building of some historic significance admiring the history and architecture. Once was in Paris and once was in Rome."

"I see how ghosts might have dominion over haunting old buildings in those places. What did you do?"

"I did what any sane person would do. I pretended I didn't see them and raced fer the door."

"Hilarious, but not helpful. Now I've got an elf in trouble, a ghost who needs releasing, and Dora says Dart needs a lot more than what I've allotted for. It's been one helluva day."

"Let's look at one problem at a time." Sloan bobs the tea bags in and out of the water with the little string. "What can you do about the elf?"

"I want to call Suede and talk to her. I'd also like to talk to Xavier and see if his people are involved. I'm almost positive the women intimidating the elf last night were vampires."

"Both good thoughts." He adds a splash of milk. "What about the ghost? Who do ye know that deals with entities like that?"

"I have no idea. Maybe I could call Garnet and see if he knows someone. Do you think Dionysus would know anything about ghosts?

He grabs the handles of the two mugs and the container of Gran's homemade molasses cookies and joins me on the couch. "I honestly couldn't hazard a guess to what Dionysus knows. The man is an enigma."

I chuckle and blow across the top of my tea. "He's fun. I heart him big."

"I know ye do, and with good reason. He's saved yer life more than once, so fer that, he shall always be welcome in our home. On the flip side of things, ye have to admit he's a bit of a disaster."

I laugh and sip my tea. "I know. Is it odd that makes me love him even more? It doesn't matter that he's an ancient Greek god or that he's had millennia to figure his shit out. He's a work in progress like the rest of us."

Sloan settles in on the couch beside me and passes me a cookie. "So, where do ye want to start?"

I swallow my tea and take a bite. The cookie is sweet and strong and dusted with sugar on top. The blend of molasses and ginger makes me groan out loud. "I could seriously get addicted to these."

Sloan grins. "Most of my favorite childhood memories revolve around Lara and her cooking. In that one way, my childhood was truly blessed."

I take another bite and savor the flavor. "Let's sit here, not think about all the things hanging over our heads, and eat cookies until they're gone."

"All right, but ye'll make yerself sick."

"Soooo worth it."

Sloan is right, as usual. I eat *waaay* too many cookies and feel gross afterward. Still, I forge on. I seem driven to volunteer myself for things that are none of my business.

I say it's my helping spirit.

Dillan says it's FOMA. It's similar to FOMO—fear of missing out—but it's a fear of missing action.

I can't say he's completely off-base, but I don't think he's nailed it either. If the world played nice and everything was calm, I would happily sit home and make myself sick on Gran's baking.

Everyone isn't playing nice, and things aren't calm.

After scrolling through my contact list, I tap Suede's name and connect the call.

"Hey, there," she says on the second ring. "I was just thinking about you."

"Yeah? Dare I ask in what context?"

"A while back you mentioned your birthday was around the due date of the twins and hoped they'd be born on your day. The twins are ten days old, so I figured it has to be soon."

"Just under two weeks. They came earlier than expected and ended that plan. You've got plenty of time to prepare if you want to call and sing."

She laughs. "You joke, but I might do that."

"I look forward to it. Elves are good singers, right? Legolas was a bard of tales."

She laughs harder. "Yes, elves generally can carry a tune, but Legolas was a fictional character."

"Same diff."

"Nope. Not even a little." I hear someone in the background, and she mutes for a second before coming back online. "Sorry, I'm being beckoned. Was there a reason for this call or did you just want to hear my smooth elven voice?"

"Actually, there was a reason." I fill her in on what happened last night at Shenanigans and about the guards maybe being vampires and ask if she knows anything.

"One blue eye and one green eye?"

"Yeah, like really beautiful, brilliant coloration too."

"It sounds like Trym Willowleaf. He's the son of one of the wealthiest elven families in Canada. Good guy. Smart. Friendly."

"Canada? After speaking to him, I would've sworn he was from the fae realm."

"Well, if it is Trym, I can see why. First off, his family is very traditional and speaks formally. Secondly, he lives almost exclusively behind the fairy glass and sources items to ship here to his father. They're dealers in fae product here in this realm."

"Black market kind of stuff?"

"Oh, no. It's legitimate. It's simply cross-realm import-export."

"From what Bruin saw, we think someone's blackmailing him to do something with the threat of harm to his girlfriend or wife? A woman was being held prisoner. Is there any way to find out for sure?"

"I think the more important question would be why would someone seize him and force him to comply."

"Okay, I'm listening."

"The import warehouse in the fashion district has state of the art, high-tech security. Trym designed it. My guess is if they're coercing Trym, it has something to do with gaining access."

"Why? What kind of fae tchotchke would someone want so badly?"

"The Willowleaf family don't import fae knickknacks, Fi. They are fae weapons dealers. You want an enchanted spear; you go to them. You need a fire mace; they have them. Staffs, wands, armor, knives, shields...they have it all."

Well, crappers.

"So, if someone were readying for a turn of the tides when the world's darkness tries to take hold and cull the goodness, that would be exactly the place to rob to stock up on artillery for the Culling."

"Wow, your mind goes straight to the worst-case scenario, doesn't it?"

I run my fingers through my hair and sigh. "It didn't use to, but now...yeah. If someone hired vampires to track down and force Trym to give them access to the warehouse, they would need to take something important to him to leverage."

"Like the fiancée he adores."

"Yeah, and if he's anything like the men in my life, he'll take a beating to keep her safe."

"Well, yeah."

"All right. Let's assume that bad guys want a cache of fae weapons, and they're forcing Trym to comply with their agenda. We'll have to stop the robbery and get his fiancée back."

"The Willowtrees have strict protocols in place to keep bad people from acquiring their cache of weapons. If people are trying to steal them to avoid the restrictions, it's because they have bad things planned."

"That's my thought too." I meet Sloan's gaze across the room and roll my eyes. "As much as I hate that scenario, it's possible, and therefore we should check it out. Where is the warehouse?"

"Offhand, I don't know. I'll have to do some digging and get back to you."

"Okay. If you don't mind, can you do it quickly? The guy, Trym, if it is indeed Trym Willowtree, got pretty battered up last night. Once they get what they want, I don't suppose they'll keep him alive long after."

"Wow, you are dark today."

"Sorry, it's been a day."

"Okay, I'll get on it and text you."

"Thanks." I end the call and sigh.

"I take it, we've got trouble," Sloan says.

"Just another day in the world of good versus bad."

49

"Take a left here." I point at a narrow side street passing between buildings. "There's a Green P behind here."

"A Green P?"

"Yeah." I point at the big green P on the parking lot entrance sign. "It's called a Green P lot."

Sloan doesn't comment. He finds an empty spot, pulls in, and I hop out to run to the payment kiosk. Once I have the paid slip, I jog back and hand it to him.

"Put this on the dash. I only paid for an hour, so try to focus and not get swept away by your inner urge to karaoke."

"I'll do my best." He places our parking receipt on the dashboard of my SUV and locks things up. "Do you think it wise to crash the private night out of the vampire companions?"

"Sure. Laurel invited me to drop in and say hi, and I need to talk to Xavier."

"What makes you think the king of the Toronto seethe will be in attendance? An all-night karaoke bar in Chinatown doesn't seem to be the kind of place a man like Xavier would attend."

"He's here. When I spoke to Karuna about what it means to be Xavier's companion, she told me he's very protective of her and the others. My instincts say he'll be here in the background somewhere."

"Do ye think ye can walk right up to him and ask him about whether or not he hired out the muscle involved in kidnapping and torturing a pirate elf?"

I shrug. "That's my plan."

Sloan chuckles. "Of course, it is."

I squeeze his arm and offer him what I hope is a reassuring gaze. "It'll be fine. He feels guilty for trying to kill me last week and hey, if I can leverage that to keep fae weapons from falling into the hands of bad guys, I'm willing to risk annoying a vampire."

Sloan and I step inside the front doors of the Dragon City Mall and find the Echo KTV Karaoke bar. The front entrance is glitzy and glammed up in gold and black. I'm about to ask the girl at the cash register where I'd find Xavier's party when I spot two men I recognize.

I wave as I pass the desk and smile. "I'm good."

"You can't go back there," the girl calls out. "It's a private party."

"I know. Thanks."

By the time we close the distance, Xavier's men have pushed off the door and are frowning at me. "What the bloody hell are you doing here?" the mouthy Brit vamp snaps at me.

"No need to get your panties in a wad, Oli," I say. "I was invited to come over and say hi to the girls. I also hoped to have a moment with Xavier."

"Like fuck. Piss off."

Sloan stiffens. "Mind yer language. I'd appreciate ye not speakin' to Fiona like that. No need to be rude."

"Showing up here uninvited is rude. Calling me names is rude."

I wave that away. "I asked you your name when we ate lasagna together. You didn't want to share. Oliver is a perfectly lovely British name. It's better than hey you or yo vampire man. Now *that* would be rude."

He moves faster than my eyes can track and pins me against the opposite wall. I'm ready for it and release Bruin with a mere thought.

My battle bear materializes beside me.

Bruin roars his annoyance at them mistreating me, and both the vampires seem taken back.

"He'll rip you to shreds and end you before you blink. It will be senseless and stupid because Laurel invited me, and Xavier will be pissed you let your personal bias affect newfound respect between him and me."

"Lady Druid." Xavier opens the door and takes in the standoff. "What a pleasant surprise. Laurel mentioned you might drop by."

I give Oli a shit-eating grin.

"It seems you forgot to set out the welcome mat. I was expressing to Peaky Blinders here that if he doesn't let me go and back off, it will force me to defend myself and that won't end well for him."

"There's no need for defensive action. Oscar will let you go now and issue a heartfelt apology." The tone of Xavier's voice is calm and smooth, but there is an unmistakable warning threaded beneath the surface.

With a look that promises retaliation, the furious vamp releases his hold on my shoulders and takes a step back. "My apologies. You caught me off-guard."

By walking the sixty feet from the front door in plain view? Yeah no, I don't think so.

"I understand completely. Not everyone takes to my charms. I'm a bit of an acquired taste, but I'm told I do grow on people."

"Much like an invasive vine," Xavier says.

I chuckle. "Ooo, can I be poison ivy... although poison ivy isn't a vine, like other ivy. Why do they call it ivy, do you think?"

Xavier lets that mental freefall go unanswered.

Gesturing at the door to the private room behind him, guard number two opens our way. "Perhaps you should collect your bear before you terrorize some unwitting staff member."

"Oh, good idea." I nod at Bruin and tap my chest. "Thanks, buddy. Sorry you didn't get to kill anyone."

"Maybe next time," he says.

I chuckle. "Yeah, maybe."

CHAPTER SIX

Xavier ushers us into a private room where more than thirty people are drinking, eating, and having fun. The party room has long, black leather couches with black lacquer and gold tables and strobe lights gently swirling dots of colored light over Xavier's family of vampires and human feeder companions.

A day in the life of vampire blood donors.

It's not nearly as gross and creepy as I thought.

Xavier picks up two flutes of champagne from the bar and gives Sloan and me each one. "I am pleased to get a chance to meet with you and express how sorry I am about what happened. I still owe you a dinner, but with everything that happened, business matters have demanded my full attention."

I shrug off his concern. "I'm fine. Between the flowers and the gift cards and the chef for a night—he was fantastic, by the way—and everything else you've sent my way, you've more than expressed your regret."

He tilts his head to the side and frowns at the puncture marks on my throat. The fact that he had the strength to pierce my body armor is either a testament to how out of his mind he was or how powerful he is as a creature of "other."

I'm afraid to know which.

"The incident was one hundy percent an accident. No part of me thinks you meant for it to happen. I don't blame you. Honestly, since it worked out in the end and we ended Galina, I'm fine to put it behind us."

Xavier lifts my knuckles to his lips in an old-fashioned gesture. "That is incredibly generous of you, Fiona. I don't know if I would be so forgiving if positions were reversed."

"I guess it's good our positions aren't reversed."

Xavier sweeps his hand toward the leather couches. "Please sit. Help yourself to food or anything you like."

There's a shuffle of a few people to make room for us, and my high school friend Laurel comes over.

I've never met the man she's with, but I recognize him from the day I visited Xavier's bloodline in the bunker. I assume he's her vampire companion Benjamin.

Xavier steps to the other side of the table and takes his seat next to his companion, Karuna. "All right, let's start with introductions. Sloan, you met Laurel, and this is Karuna, and neither of you has met Benjamin. Am I right?"

"No. It's a pleasure." Sloan extends his hand to Benjamin.

"Nice to meet you," I say.

"Likewise." Benjamin is an ordinary-looking thirty-something guy with sandy blond hair and brown eyes. He's the type of person who could walk through a crowd, and no one would take notice. They certainly wouldn't think he's a vampire walking among us.

Laurel grins, her ponytail waving behind her as she leans in to hug me. "It's so exciting to see you again and to know we can be friends."

I sense more than see Benjamin's concern.

"What, does that bother you?" I ask.

"My apologies," he says. I think if he had blood flowing, he would be blushing right now. "Laurel is free to do as she wishes with her spare time, and I know how excited she is to reconnect with you. My concern stems from people seeing her in old circles. There was a reason why people killed her father. Spending time with you might put her in danger."

From the look in his eyes and the tone in his voice, I get no sense that he's territorial or controlling. He truly cares about Laurel's safety and worries I might put her in harm's way.

"I won't pretend that being around me is safe. Even if her father didn't have enemies, people around me tend to get drawn into dangerous and dramatic situations. I acknowledge and respect your worry."

Laurel rolls her eyes. "Don't do that. Don't let him think he's right about this. I'm looking forward to getting caught up on what's happened with our friends since I've been living my second life."

"There's no reason we can't do that and still keep you safe. I can come to you, or we can talk on the phone, or if you have a safe house like Karuna, I can meet you there. We don't have to go shopping or be seen in public if it keeps you safe."

Laurel looks frustrated but not upset. "Fine. As long as you're not ditching me."

"Me? Never gonna happen, chickie."

Xavier raises his glass. "To new beginnings."

We all drink to that.

The champagne is crisp and chilled, and I like it very much. I take another sip and figure Xavier must like nice things like Garnet does.

Men from days gone by often do.

"Since we're toasting to new beginnings, I want you to know how much I appreciate you taking the time to educate me on my prejudices against your people."

Xavier's brow arches and his mouth curls in a slight smile.

The look is odd and out of place on him. A stern-looking Korean man, he's not one for smirks.

"Did I say something funny?"

He takes another sip and swallows. "Not funny, but it did strike me as humorous that while I was well behaved and polite in all things, you thought me a murderous monster. Conversely, when I lost control, attacked you, and nearly killed you, you now appreciate my species and give me thoughtful consideration."

Sloan chuckles as he sips from his flute. I know what he'll say before the words fall from his lips. "I tell her almost daily she's ridiculous. Honestly, her odd way of thinking is one of the things I love about her most. She's never boring."

With everyone chuckling at my expense, I reach for the appetizer platter on the coffee table ahead of me and decide to bring up the vampire guards who kidnapped that elf. "Speaking of never being boring, last night something happened. I wonder if I can ask you about it without offending you."

I pop the Thai chicken bite into my mouth.

Amazeballs.

I reach for another in case my choice of conversation gets me kicked out. Damn. Can I get this whole platter to go, please?

"You were saying, Lady Druid?"

"Oh, right." I take another sip of champagne, hoping it will help me find the right words. In my family, I'm known to say exactly the wrong thing at the wrong time, and I've never had a filter between my mind and my mouth, but I've been working on it.

Xavier isn't the kind of man I want angry at me—especially after we just started being friendly.

Well, *friendly* might be an exaggeration, but he hasn't tried to kill me in the past week, so that's an improvement.

"Your warning is appreciated. I will try not to take your question as an offense. Please proceed."

"Last night, my friend at Shenanigans grew concerned about a pub patron who looked scared and quite beaten up. From what we gathered, he got scuffed up and tried to ditch his attackers and get to a public place. We thought he might need help, but both Sloan and I encouraged him to come with us, and he declined."

"And what does that have to do with me? Why do you think I would be offended?"

"Because the women guarding him seemed to be vampire muscle hired for some nefarious purpose."

Xavier's mouth turns up again. "So, if something nefarious is happening and vampires are involved, then I must be behind it?"

"No, I'm not saying that. I simply wondered if you might know something about it. Have you heard anything, say on the vampire hotline or at the water cooler?"

"Vampire hotline?" He looks to Benjamin. "Did anything come across the hotline about an elf abduction?"

"Nothing about an elf abduction." Benjamin bites back a smile. "There was something about a bunch of us going to the Eaton Centre tomorrow to check out the spring sales event and grab a smoothie."

Everyone gets a chuckle out of that at my expense.

Even Sloan.

"Et tu, Brute?"

He shrugs. "What? That was funny."

I roll my eyes. "Okay, yeah, sorry. I just thought you might know."

Xavier sobers and shakes his head. "There's no vampire hive-mind, Fiona. We are not Borg."

I grin. "You know about the Borg?"

"I'm a vampire, not a neophyte."

Karuna laughs. "The companions keep things lively and current. We try to keep them hip on pop culture to help them blend into the passing centuries."

"My point is," Xavier says, casting Karuna a genuinely warm

gaze, "there are many seethes and many agendas in the vampire community. Being the king doesn't mean I know all and see all. Usually, things get brought to my attention after the fact, and I am more an enforcer of consequence."

I snag a mini eggroll and dip it in the plum sauce. "Got it. Sorry."

"It's fine. There is much to learn on both sides of this fence, isn't there?"

I nod. "What about ghosts? I have more than one problem swirling around me at the moment. Do you know anything about ancient murder victims who haven't passed over?"

The vampires stiffen, and Xavier grows serious. "No. Vampires do *not* like ghosts."

The way he says that brings my hackles up. "Why?"

"They are a different type of undead, and we steer clear of one another. My advice would be to do the same. Ghosts do not fall under your usual pet projects, Lady Druid. They are dangerous."

There is not one ounce of drama in Xavier's words.

I try not to take offense to him implying my crime-fighting is me playing at pet projects—after all, I asked him for the same courtesy only moments ago.

The point is, he truly doesn't like ghosts and doesn't want me anywhere near Ghost John Paul.

"Thanks for the warning. I'll give it more thought before I do anything about him."

My phone buzzes at my hip and I check the incoming text. "Excellent. Suede sent me the address of the Willowtree weapons warehouse. Maybe we can solve one of these mysteries tonight."

Xavier lifts his chin. "Willowtree? That's who you believe the elf in trouble is?"

"It's only a working theory, but yes."

"In that case, perhaps I should accompany you. The Willowtree family is powerful. If vampires are involved in nefarious behavior as you suspect, I should ensure there is no backlash to our community."

"You coming along would be great, but I don't want to tear you away from your party."

Laurel cracks up. "Xavier always finds a valid reason to leave before his turn at the mic. Rumor has it he has the velvet voice of a thirties crooner."

Xavier's lip curls in disdain. "I assure you that's an exaggeration. No one needs to hear me caterwauling. Escorting Fiona into a possibly dangerous situation involving vampires is much more important."

I shrug. "Well, whatever your reasoning, we're happy to have you join the fun."

Suede mentioned that the Willowtree warehouse was in the fashion district, which isn't that far from Chinatown. At eight o'clock at night, it takes us less than ten minutes to get from the karaoke bar to a vacant parking lot down the street from the address on my phone.

"I think this is close enough." I unbuckle my seatbelt and lean forward to see out the front windshield between the two front seats. "If there are bad guys inside, there's no sense tipping them off to our arrival by driving up to the front door."

"If there are bad guys inside," Xavier says, "what exactly is your plan to proceed?"

I grin at the king of vampires and shrug. "I'm more of a go with the flow, live by the seat-of-my-pants kind of girl. My plans generally go FUBAR anyway, so I find it's better to take things as they come."

Xavier frowns and looks out the front windshield of my truck. "You plan to force entry into a high-security, privately owned warehouse filled with powerful fae weapons without knowing who is inside or even if this is, in any way, tied to the elf you wish to help?"

I wince. "It sounds terrible when you put it that way, but yeah, that's the general gist."

Sloan makes one of his Irish throat noises that I interpret as him implying I'm as ridiculous in front of other people as I am in front of him.

Hey, a girl's gotta be real, amirite?

The three of us bail out of my truck and stick to the shadows as we cross the front lawns of three other warehouses until we are where we want to be.

"We're not going in completely blind," I say. "I asked Dillan to meet us here with his cloak. He's surveying the land and will pick up anything hinky we might need to know about."

Xavier frowns. "Has anyone bothered to contact Graymor Willowtree to ask if maybe his son is in trouble and check the security on the warehouse?"

I shake my head. "No. If it was Trym we met last night, sounding the alarm would put him in more danger. I think it's a 'better to ask forgiveness than permission' kinda moment."

Xavier doesn't look convinced. "Is it my imagination or do you have a lot of those kinda moments? For an enforcer of the guild laws, you run loose and free with the laws yourself."

I frown at the vampire. "You didn't have to come. If a little B&E for a good cause is against your code, you're free to wait in the truck. Strange, though, I didn't picture you as a guy afraid to stir up trouble."

Xavier tugs the sleeves of his dress shirt below the cuffs of his tailored suit jacket. "Oh, I'm not afraid. I'm simply pointing out your standard mode of operation is messy and haphazard. Criminal endeavors take a certain amount of thoughtful planning and finesse."

"Life is about the journey, not the destination."

Sloan chuffs. "Maybe that's been your problem all along, *a ghra*. When dealing with lethal opponents, it's definitely about the destination."

I wave that away. "You know what I mean."

He's about to say something else when I cut them off by pointing across the parking lot.

Dillan is making his way toward us, nearly invisible under the cover of darkness. "Hey," he says as he joins us. "I checked the building perimeter and climbed onto the roof. The place is reinforced like Fort Knox, but a few minutes ago, a dozen people went inside. The alarms and security are off now."

"Excellent. Did you see the elf from last night or a woman prisoner?"

"Both. The girl looked relatively unharmed, but the pirate elf isn't looking so good. I think the beatings and bruises we saw at the pub were a warm-up act. It looks like the main event took its toll."

I sigh. "We need to get in there fast and stop this."

Sloan scowls at me. "Did ye miss the part where he said there are a dozen people in there? This is a weapons warehouse, Fi. Which means they'll be armed more heavily than us and they outnumber us three to one."

"I hear what you're saying. I still think we need to move. Trym's been through enough, and we can't allow people inside there to get away with those weapons."

Dillan pulls out his phone and starts moving his thumb across the screen. "It never hurts to call in backup, baby girl. I'm sure Nikon can have the gang here in a snap. Better safe than dead." He looks over at Xavier standing beside me. "No offense."

Xavier gives him a cool once-over. "None taken. Being dead has worked out rather well for me."

Not for the first time, I wonder who Xavier was before he became a vampire.

"Hey, there they are." I wave over Nikon, Emmet, Calum, and Dionysus. "Thanks for coming."

"Wouldn't miss it," Dionysus says.

"Shit. You're dressed up. Did I screw your plans? Crap, this is Kevin's gallery night, isn't it?"

Calum shrugs. "Don't worry. Once we get you sorted out, Saturday night can resume in full swing. What are we looking at?"

I fill them in on what I learned at the lighthouse this afternoon and from talking to Suede and Xavier.

Emmet frowns at the warehouse. "You think the kidnappers are inside getting stocked up on fae weapons to kick our asses at a later date?"

"I'm not sure what the motive is, but yeah. Dillan says we're looking at a dozen hostiles as well as our elf friend from the bar last night and his girlfriend."

Calum faces us and puts his fist forward into the center of our huddle. "It's musketeer time. Let's spread out and getter done."

We all reach forward and do the same—except Xavier, but I give him a pass.

After a friendly round of knuckle bumps, we're good to go.

Dillan points and fills us in on the logistics. "There's a door on the front and side and loading bays at the back. I say Fi and Sloan take the front door. Nikon and Calum take the side, and I'll take the back with Emmet and Dionysus."

"You missed someone," Dionysus says, pointing toward Xavier.

Dillan shakes his head. "The king of Toronto vampires can decide for himself what he wants to do."

Xavier dips his chin. "I appreciate you realizing that."

Dillan pulls out his phone. "I have the farthest to go to get into position. Give me a sec, and I'll text when I'm ready."

I nod. "Sounds good. Safe home, everyone. Keep it right and tight."

"Ready and steady," Calum says.

"Wired and fired," Emmet says.

"Rough and buff," Dillan says.

"Hammered and stammered," Dionysus says.

I laugh and get ready to rock. The seven of us fan out and close in on the warehouse as Dillan suggested. When Sloan and I get into position at the front entrance, I check the surroundings while he opens the front door.

"Be safe, *a ghra*. If I have to choose between you or an elven stranger or weapons getting on the street, I choose you every time."

I reach up onto my tiptoes and kiss his cheek. "I heart you too, hotness. How about a soak in the hot spring tonight when we get home? It's been a long day."

"That sounds lovely. It's a date."

My cell phone buzzes in my pocket, and I pull it out to glance at the screen. "Okay, we're on. Dillan is ready to move."

We open the door and hurry inside.

The moment we step into the public front, all hell breaks loose, and we're on the run.

The shouts of men, the clang of metal on metal, and the sizzle of magic-powered weapons discharging in the back permeate the air.

As I weave through the maze of offices at the front of the business, Dillan shouts for Emmet to get down.

A split second later, Emmet shouts that he's hit.

The corridor leading to the back passes in a blur, my blood rushing through my veins and thundering in my ears. "Bruin! Find Emmet and help him."

I barely feel the change in pressure as my bear releases from my chest and rushes forward.

The door to the back warehouse is open, but racks of black wooden crates screen my vision.

I don't slow down to assess my entry.

Calling Birga onto my palm, we round the last crate and rocket straight into the warehouse war.

CHAPTER SEVEN

"Surprise!"

I put my brakes on—which is hard with adrenaline fueling my muscles—and stumble to a stop. The warehouse is a massive empty space. No weapon stores. No hostile robbers with kidnapping victims. Instead... it's my family and friends...and Dart and Manx...

"What the fuckety-fuck?"

"Happy birthday, baby girl." Da raises a glass, standing in front of the refreshments table.

I shake my head trying to figure out what is happening. My brothers have their phones up, recording me as it sinks in. "Seriously? You set me up? It's all a hoax?"

"You said we'd never get you," Emmet says, "but *tah-dah*... we got you good, sista."

"Damn straight we did," Dillan says, the two of them smacking palms.

I turn and look at Sloan, who dares to look amused. "You knew about this the whole time?"

"Och, of course. Someone had to ride it out with ye to make sure ye didn't spear an innocent bystander."

"Been there, done that." Nikon grins and holds up his drink. "I can't advise it."

My poor hamster is so disoriented. "So there never was a Trym Willowtree? And he was never in danger? The whole thing was bogus?"

Suede moves in from behind the grinning wall of my family. "Hey, girlfriend." A handsome elf follows her. "Meet my friend, Trym."

The elf from last night is the only one here who has the courtesy to look abashed. "Merry meet, Fiona. Apologies for the deception. Suede assured me you would be up for the lark and would take it in good humor."

I run my fingers through my hair and draw a deep breath. "Yeah, of course. It'll take a minute for my adrenaline to settle."

Suede laughs. "You should've seen your face."

"Oh, I can help you with that." Dillan steps forward, activating the screen of his phone to play back the video.

Yep. He caught me barreling around the last row of crates hell-bent on getting to my brother and stopping whatever attack he was taking.

I release my call on Birga and draw a deep breath. "You intend on showing that to everyone you come across, don't you?"

"Hells yeah. This shit is gold."

I think about the bruises on Trym last night and how intricate the deception was. "Was Liam in on it?"

"Guilty as charged, Fi," my bestie says, winking at me from the crowd.

"What about Bruin tailing the kidnappers to the lighthouse at Hanlan's Point?"

I find my bear among the crowd, and he lets out a deep throaty chuckle. "Och, no. I spent the night in the forest with my girls and fed ye my lines this morning."

"And the impromptu trip to take the kids to Centre Island was a ploy to get me to search the lighthouse?"

Emmet grins. "Yeah, that and also a great place to take the kids to tire them out on Saturday fun day with the uncles."

"And the ghost?"

Sloan grunts beside me and shakes his head. "Och, no. That was all yer magnet fer mayhem. That angry apparition scared the bejeezus out of me."

"What about those two vampire women who roughed up Trym? I scanned them with my fae sight and tracked all kinds of shady and violent."

"Sorry, cookie." Dora waves. "I may have cast a little spell on the girls to fool you. You know what they say, 'to keep the story interesting, you got to raise the stakes.' You had to believe Trym was in real danger."

I turn to Xavier next. "You were in on this too?"

He shrugs. "Not so much me, as Laurel and Karuna. When I mentioned to them that I'd been approached to participate, Laurel got so excited I couldn't say no."

"Trojans! Trojans!"

I follow the call of my high school field hockey chant and wave at the arrival of Laurel, Karuna, and Benjamin through the side door.

I run my fingers through my hair and try to grasp the scope of this prank. "Man, you guys really got me. I've been freaking out all day about the poor guy who got beaten up by vampires and forced to give up magical weapons to save his true love. How the hell did you come up with that?"

Emmet pegs me with a look. "What, you don't think we could come up with something so diabolically detailed and dastardly?"

I laugh. "I *know* you couldn't. So, 'fess up. Whose idea was this?"

Dillan scoffs. "Rude. We could've totally come up with this idea. We've got cunning nailed down."

I laugh harder. "Yeah, right. So, who was it?"

The boys turn and look at Ciara.

Emmet's new betrothed is standing stiff and biting her bottom lip. "The boys promised ye'd take it in good humor. Are ye pissed at me?"

I bark a laugh and shake my head. "No, I'm not pissed. I'm inspired. Damn. I never saw it coming. Sloan and I even had a conversation last night about the boys always trying to surprise me. I told him I was on my toes and *still* I had no idea what was happening."

Her smile is pure relief, and I realize once again how hard she's trying to fit into our family.

"Ciara, you never got the chance to meet Brendan, but he would've thought this was epic. Congratulations, you've earned your first Cumhaill Oh Henry! award. It was a prank well-planned and well-executed. You win the night."

Emmet's grin is so filled with pride and love as he wraps his arms around his bride, my heart aches for him.

All I've ever wanted is for my brothers to be happy.

Good for them.

I glance around the room and find Myra and Garnet standing with Zxata by the food. Patty's with Dart and the other companions over by the couches. Andromeda and Maxwell are over by the bar. Aiden, Liam, and Shannon are next to the bouncy castle. Gran and Granda are looking a little alarmed at the pool of Jell-O. Tad and the other heirs are grinning at the penis piñatas.

Wow, the gang's all here.

I eye the decorations and giggle. "Dionysus, did you help plan this party?"

He waggles his brows underneath his brown curls. "I was in charge of ambiance. What do you think?"

I laugh and study the surroundings. "You nailed it, buddy. Everything is perfect. Best birthday party evah! The only problem is there isn't any music playing. Emmet, would you please get us started?"

Da lets out an f-bomb and points at my brother from across

the crowd. "Don't ye dare play that asinine hillbilly song. Pick something nice for your sister's party."

Emmet seems put out by Da's demand. He scrolls through his phone and grins as the Latin beat of Shakira fills the air.

The guests who don't realize this is a tribute to Brendan might be a little confused, but it's a perfect choice to start an evening of family fun.

I nod, opening my arms. "Let Fi's twenty-fourth surprise birthday bash commence."

"Are you having fun?" I ask Gran and Granda a little while later. "I'm trying not to drink too much too fast and to remain responsible and respectable in front of my grandparents. It's difficult in this crowd."

"Och, tons of craic." Gran leans in for a hug. "We're so pleased to share yer birthday celebration with ye, luv, but Granda and I are going to leave shortly."

"So early? There's still plenty of night left."

"Aye, there is," Granda says. "But yer Gran and I offered to watch over the wee twins for an hour or two so Kinu can have a bit of fun with the family."

"Aw, that's a great idea. Thank you." I hug them both and kiss each of them on the cheek. "If I don't see you before you go back, thanks for coming. Also, Sloan and I were talking about coming your way in the next few weeks."

"Or sooner," Nikon says. "Dora is almost finished with the preparations for the Drombeg circle. After a bit more testing, it'll be time to put the stones into action and see if the dragon portal works."

"That is exciting," Gran says. "Ye certainly have mixed things up, my dear."

"Fer druids and the fae community alike," Granda adds. "Ye make us prouder every day, *mo chroi*."

After another round of hugs, Nikon snaps Gran and Granda back to the house, and I head over to say hello to Myra, Zxata, and Dora.

"Are you guys having fun?"

Myra looks at me and laughs. "More fun than we probably should have. Dionysus came over and asked Garnet to join him in a match of man-on-man Jell-O wrestling. I'm not going to lie. I spat my drink out my nose."

I can tell by Dora's and Zxata's expressions it was as funny as I imagine. I look around the warehouse to see if I can find our mighty lion alpha. "Where did he go?"

"Not surprisingly, immediately after Dionysus asked him, something incredibly important came up at work, and he had to go."

"Oh no. I'm sorry Dionysus scared him off."

Myra waves it off. "Don't be. The look on his face was entertaining enough for me to giggle for the next decade."

Dora points up at the camera attached to the steel beams above her head. "Part of the full Dionysus ambiance package set up by the Greek god of partying is that there will be still shots and videos available after the event."

Myra nods. "We're hoping it caught that moment on tape so I can relive it over and over again."

I cover my mouth with my hand. "Oh, poor Garnet. I would've warned you away from Dionysus but I can't. I adore him so much."

Dora smiles. "You do tend to gather the misfits and unwanteds in life."

I know she includes herself in that category, and I shake my head. "I love the misfits and unwanteds in life. They're the people who make each day interesting and fill my heart."

I've never gotten into Dora's choice to leave her male persona behind and bury Merlin in the past. I'm not sure if it's any of my business.

Who am I kidding?

It's *none* of my business.

Still, I wonder. Was it simply how she identifies her true self or is it also an attempt to reinvent herself? I know she did a lot of things she wasn't proud of and wanted to leave in the past.

Was becoming Pan Dora a way to start again?

Maybe one day I'll have the guts to ask her.

"Dartamont is having fun." Dora gestures toward my dragon shooting fire at a row of raised targets in the rafters. "Who is that with him and Calum?"

I glance to the far end of the warehouse and find Calum with his bow nocked and ready to fire at a target no closer than two hundred feet in the distance.

"That's Eros, a god friend of Dionysus's. Are they having an archery competition?"

Zxata laughs. "That's ambitious."

I meet his gaze and shrug. "I've been meaning to look it up. Who is Eros? I know the name. He's a Greek god too, right?"

The three of them look at me like I'm clueless.

"Yes, duck," Myra says. "Eros is the Greek name for the man you might know better as Cupid."

Well, crappers, that makes *sooo* much sense.

I palm my forehead. "Of course, he'd be close friends with Dionysus. One's the God of Fertility and Ecstasy. The other is the God of Love and Passion. Their dominions practically overlap."

"It also explains how he's such a marksman with his bow and arrow." Dora points at the show of skills. The four of us watch the friendly competition for a few more shots. Then it's back to the party.

"Never a dull moment." I smile at my family and friends.

"Now, if you'll excuse me, I see Emmet in the inflatable castle. Gotta bounce."

Laughing at my joke, I run off to join the fun.

"Time to battle!" I shout, much later in the night. I call Birga to my hand and point at the people still standing. "Dillan, Ciara, Dionysus, Calum, and Tad on that side of the mat. Me, Sloan, Emmet, Kevin, and Eros on this side. Choose your weapons."

Sloan jogs over and scowls at me. "What are ye talkin' about, Fi? Everyone's banjaxed. Now is not the time to draw weapons."

"Do you say that because you're afraid to fight a girl? C'mon, hotness. Admit it. You're scairt."

He shakes his head. "No. I say that because ye cried inconsolably for two days when ye skewered Nikon. Ye may be blitzed, but somewhere in there, ye don't want to go through that again."

The warehouse is spinning, and his voice sounds smooth and sultry in my ears. "I like the way you talk, Mackenzie. It makes me tingly."

He grins. "That's lovely of ye to say, *a ghra*. Maybe that's a sign we should call it a night."

"No way, Jose. The birthday girl is the last man standing. Now, who wants to Jell-O wrestle me?"

"I do!" Dionysus, Eros, and Nikon say at once.

"It's a Greek trifecta. Hellenistic and hedonistic. I accept the challenge."

"No, she doesn't." Sloan grabs the hem of my shirt and pulls it back down my ribs. "Clothes stay on, Fi. Yer not stripping down and Jell-O wrestling with yer friends. It will make things terribly awkward fer ye tomorrow."

"How about penis piñata?" Emmet points at the papier-mâché man parts hanging from the rafters. "There are ten pinatas and about that many people left. We just need ten sticks."

Dionysus snaps his fingers, and Em's got *Star Wars* lightsabers in his hand.

"I'm a Jedi!" I shout, reaching for a blue one.

Emmet hands the weapons out, and we jump around getting the feel of them. "Okay, no super strength. No powers. It's natural muscle and aim only. You gotta whack your johnson without any help."

We all bust up laughing, and it's even funnier that Emmet has to recap his words to figure out why we're all cracking up.

"Okay, yeah, so, whack your johnson, and the first one to free the candy wins."

"Candy?" Dionysus asks, genuine surprise flashing across his face. "You're supposed to put candy in them?"

I giggle. "Yeah. What did you put in there?"

"Not candy." He grins at me. "I thought you bought the piñatas and went with a theme. There's really good stuff in these. Way better than candy."

Hilarious.

Now I'm dying to see what he's done. "You're right, dude. Candy's overdone. I'm sure what you thought up is much more interesting."

"Useful too. And before any of you begin to panic… batteries *are* included."

"Oh, lord," Sloan says. "Now I'm afraid to play and get rained down upon by dildos and sex paraphernalia."

I grin. "Then gird yer loins because we're doin' this and endin' the night with two shares of goodies."

"Did I forget to mention," Emmet says. "Only the winner gets to keep the rewards."

"Oh, game on." I swing my blue lightsaber. "I'm taking home the toys."

"Dream on." Ciara does some fancy saber work of her own and positions under a pinata opposite me. "It's on, Cumhaill."

"Don't underestimate the elf," Suede says.

"You're all going down." Dora joins us and calls a saber from Emmet's hand across the space. "I've got a foot and a hundred pounds on you girls. You're going home empty-handed."

Dionysus flashes himself into a black and white referee's costume and lifts his whistle. "Ready positions. And... Whack!"

CHAPTER EIGHT

I wake with a jolt, and even before I open my eyes, I have an overwhelming sense of, "Oh, shit. Where am I and what did I do?" It's a terrifying sensation, especially with the brain-swirl of still being half-drunk and knowing the lack of boundaries my friends and family tend to have.

Prying one eye open a crack, I scan my surroundings...inflatable panda...bumper cars...rock wall...

I'm in Dionysus's penthouse apartment.

And yep. I'm in his bed.

I look down at myself and have no idea why I'm wearing a Wonder Woman costume, but I'm thankful I'm dressed. Someone shifts behind me and groans.

I tense and glance over my shoulder.

Oh, thank the goddess—it's Sloan.

We're in the wrong bed, but it's the right guy.

Yay, me!

Dionysus shuffles in wearing only a kilt and bunny slippers. I'm about to ask about that when I get distracted. He's carrying a tray with a couple of mugs, and the moment I smell the coffee and morning after brew, I sit up and hold out my hands. "Bless you. How did you know?"

"Gran gave me the recipe when I was there building the tree-house. I figured now would be the perfect time to try it out. Kevin said it smells like festering assholes while it's brewing, and he's not wrong."

"No, he's not, but it works so well at fixing the morning after the night before we overlook that."

I blow across the lip of the mug and sip the magical concoction. Once the tiny sip goes down without too much revolt, I take a few bigger swallows. "What happened? How'd we end up here in your bed?"

"You don't remember?"

"Bits...but nothing after the piñata whacking and nothing about me being Wonder Woman and crashing in your sheets."

"Well, nothing bad or inappropriate happened if that's a concern."

Thank you, baby Groot.

"I didn't think so, but it's nice to hear."

He looks down at me, and I'm struck once again by the sincere sweetness that seeps through his brash and sassy bravado if you take the time to watch for it.

"Fi, you drew your line in the sand, and I would never allow drunken great ideas to go against your sober wishes. You told me once I'm safe with you and to trust you to be my friend. The same goes for you with me."

"Thanks, dude." I hold up my fist to bump. "I'll hug you for that later when the remedy has kicked in, and I can move without worrying I'll barf on you."

"I appreciate that." Sloan groans and Dionysus leans around me to get a better look. "That man has an amazing ass."

I glance back and chuckle, pulling the black satin sheet to cover Sloan's glorious nakedness. "I may have noticed that once or twice myself."

Taking another sip, I check myself inwardly and find I'm

feeling better already. "Okay, tell me what happened after the piñata contest."

"Once the piñatas were thoroughly pulverized, you, Suede, Dora, and Ciara overruled Emmet's edict and split the winnings. After that, the night progressed with an admirable amount of drinking and revelry. The bouncy castle was a crowd-pleaser as was the margarita slip and slide."

"And the costume?" I glance down at myself. It isn't a Hallowe'en kind of costume where the bodice and armor are printed with the designs of Wonder Woman. This is a burgundy leather bodice with the gold eagle embellishment over my breasts and a blue leather skirt. I lift my fingers to my forehead and probe the metal tiara. "What's this about?"

"You wanted to try out my VR room and said to make you Wonder Woman. It was your night, so I outfitted you. Then, when you had enough and crashed, I put you in here so you could sleep it off."

"Thanks. That's sweet. At what part of the night did Sloan get naked?"

He chuckles. "That was during strip Halo. That boy is no good at video games. The rule was that every time you died, you had to take a layer off. He was bad. So bad, in fact, when your brothers and Kevin were shooting him for the fun of it, he was too drunk to realize that friendly fire was taking him out ."

I chuckle. "That sounds about right."

When he stands to leave, I set my mug down and stand to hug him. "Thanks for my party. It was the most fun I've had in ages. You're a great friend, and I lurve you big."

He pulls back and kisses my cheek. "You're welcome, Fi. And to be honest. This friend thing is new to me. I've never had a female friend before. Only lovers and women sizing me up to become lovers. Thank you for not wanting me sexually and not trying to seduce me. It makes me feel special."

I chuckle. "You're welcome."

"You're alive," Dora says at the druid stone circle late that night.

It's after eleven, and the sky is black and moonless, leaving us in almost complete darkness to work in the skies unseen. Sloan *poofed* Dart and me over to meet with our mistress of dragon training, and I'm excited to see where the night takes us.

"I'll leave ye to it, then." Sloan winks at me and lifts his hand to give Dora a polite wave. "Nikon asked me to stop over and help him move some furniture in his house. Then I'll make my way back."

"Sounds good. Thanks, hotness."

When it's only the three of us, Dora looks me over. "How was your day? Are you up for this?"

"Yeah, I'm good. It was a bit rough this morning, but between Gran's remedy and Ciara's sober pill, we managed. It was a solid recovery, PJ day."

"I bet." She steps over to Dart and bows her head. "Hello, Dartamont. Are you ready to work on your fated bond, young master?"

Dart nods, and Dora holds up her finger.

"Try to project your thoughts like we practiced yesterday morning."

Yesterday morning? Man, it feels like ages ago.

Dart looks at me and stares.

I meet his gaze and strain against the silence of the night to hear him communicating with me.

I get nothing.

After an honest effort, he blows a huff of steam out of his nostrils, grunts, and slams his tail against the ground.

"It's fine," Dora says. "Come lay down, and we'll try something else." Dora points at the grass, and he lays down. Then, she smiles at me and points at the spot beside him. "You too, cookie."

I do as I'm told and have a feeling I know where this is going.

"You need to find and acknowledge the bond the two of you share. Dartamont will continue to get frustrated if he can't communicate with you. He's all-in and bonded. You need to meet him halfway for this to work."

"I am all-in, and I want it to work."

"I believe you, but there's something else. A part of you isn't making the connection we need for the two of you to become truly bonded. You need to figure out what that is and why it's preventing you from accepting the entirety of the bond."

I draw a deep breath and lay down next to my blue boy. "Okay. Let's do this."

"Close your eyes, and focus on the energy of Dartamont's presence. Dragons are mythical beasts with immeasurable amounts of arcane power within. Open your senses and learn the feel of his power signature."

I do as Dora says and draw a few deep, calming breaths. Of course, I can feel Dart beside me and feel his presence, but Dora wants more than that.

She wants me to feel his *magical* presence.

With my eyes closed, I sift through the impulses my sense receptors are processing. I hear his heavy breaths sawing in and out. I feel the warmth of his breath as he exhales. Twisting my neck from side to side, I release the tension within my muscles and focus.

There is something.

I follow the impulse tickling my consciousness. Retreating into myself deeper, I follow the subtle brushing of my instincts.

I'm on the right track.

I learned a couple of months ago that part of being a Celtic shaman means that I can access different planes of existence than most. It's like a meditative state, but it's more…it goes deeper than that.

Once again, I have no trouble finding my happy place where Brendan's spark resides and where I retreat and regroup. I envision that place within me as my metaphysical heart. It's where my love for my brother is rooted. We're bound by blood and by choice, by pulling together in times of heartache and growing together in times of celebration.

I bypass Brendan and my happy place and find Bruin's presence at the core of my chest. I envision this place as my metaphysical solar plexus. My bond with Bruin lends me strength and power. His presence has become familiar and necessary—a comfort.

So, what does my bond with Dart represent and why haven't I been able to find it yet?

I remember what Dora told me to look for yesterday. She said to envision my bond with Dart as a physical tether between the two of us. She said it might manifest as a rope or a cable or a braided tangle of vines...

But neither of the other two bonds I've formed manifested like that for me.

Instead, I think those bonds are more chakra-based. Brendan is my heart and fills me with compassion, healing, love, and mindfulness. Bruin is my solar plexus and brings me confidence, power, and transformation.

So where does Dart fall within that scope?

The impact of what Dora was saying hits me.

Dart is more than a hatchling baby reptile that loves me because I was there when he cracked through his egg. Dragons are living history and mythology. They are divine and born of The Source.

As fierce and powerful as he is, he's also sweet and happy and protective of those he loves.

He's a being of magic and power, and—if his mother is any indicator—one day he will embody wisdom and enlightenment.

If my bonds are chakra-based, I need to stop searching in the core of my body and search my mind. Dart represents my connection with cosmic energy.

He's my crown.

Just like that, it becomes clear where the block was. I was looking at it all the wrong way. Once I realize our connection stems from my crown, the bond appears.

I envisioned the tether joining me to a beast as fierce as a dragon would be thick and strong. I figured it would be steel or one of those thick chains that hold ship anchors, but it's not.

I lift my finger and tap the glimmering blue and silver band of undulating light. It's beautiful and graceful, and I'm humbled to look at it.

It's part of me...*he* is part of me.

The release of my mind is like opening a window and getting that first faceful of fresh air. I breathe it in and welcome the flow of incoming energy.

Dart? Can you hear me?

He shuffles closer, his large snout hovering over my chest. *You did it. Can you hear me?* Dart's voice isn't at all as I imagined. He doesn't sound like a boy or even an adolescent. He has the strong, deep timbre of a man.

Have I been projecting my perceptions on him all along? Dora told me he wasn't my baby boy.

Fiona? Please answer. Can you hear me?

Oh, yes, buddy, I can. I had to figure it out in my way. I'm sorry it took me so long.

That is our past. Now that our bond is complete, we can focus on the future. You are mine, and I am yours. It will begin.

He speaks those words with a great deal of authority and expectation. *What will begin?*

The union.

Who knew my dragon boy was so cryptic. *What does that mean?*

That has yet to become clear. The union differs for all pairing bonds. In the centuries past, the binding connection between dragon and rider has manifested in countless ways.

Did the dragon queen teach you about that?

No.

Patty?

No. It simply is.

How do you know about it if it wasn't something you were taught?

It simply is.

"I take it you've made the connection?" Dora says. "Have you formed your link?"

I open my eyes, and she's standing over us. "Yeah, he told me our union will begin but can't tell me what that means or how he knows. All he says is, 'It simply is.'"

The words seem to strike a chord with her, and I'm not sure why. Dora plays things close to the vest. I understand that in her life as Merlin, there were things she did that she regrets. She was a bit of a drunk and a jerk, but I also sense some deep wounds.

Why would a person considered one of the greatest and most powerful druids of all time walk away from his or her life and bury that part of themselves?

"Dora? Are you okay?"

"Yes, of course, girlfriend. Why wouldn't I be?" It's a rhetorical question because she straightens and holds out her hand to help me up.

"When Dartamont speaks of things beyond his knowledge and can't explain where the knowledge comes from, it's because dragons pass their history and wisdom down through their genes. He was born knowing everything and yet nothing."

"That's cool and not confusing at all."

She chuckles. "It will become clearer as the union takes hold. He's right about that. Now that you've completed the link and welcomed the connection, things will change between the two of you."

"Change how? We don't need to change. We're good the way we are."

She chuckles, her voice deep and graveled. "Oh, honey, you have no idea what you're in for."

"No, that's what I'm asking. What am I in for?"

Dora strides over to the altar stone and grabs a wide strip of black leather with handles on it.

"What's that?"

"It's a dragon spike saddle. You may have noticed while riding a dragon there isn't much to hold onto."

"I did notice that. Dillan and I wrapped ourselves around the spikes on his back when he super-sized, but it was restrictive because we had to link our arms and legs around to keep from flying off. Then, when the centaur guards attacked, we couldn't defend ourselves."

She stops in front of Dart and smiles. "Transform into battle-size for me, please, Dartamont."

Dart does as he's asked and super-sizes.

Dora grabs his elbow spike and swings up onto his shoulder like one of those trick cowboys that mounts a horse from the side as it runs by. Then she walks over the arch of his ribs as if she's done it a thousand times.

When she gets to the first large spike along his spine, she presses the black leather against the spike and speaks a few words in tongues.

The leather wraps around the spike like a bandage around a finger. Then she waves at me. "Come. See if this is in the right spot for you."

I didn't watch her carefully enough to see how she got up on his elbow the way she did, so I go the route I have in the past.

Dart lowers his head, and I climb up behind the frill plates at the back of his neck and hike uphill to his back. "See if what's a good fit?"

Dora moves out of the way and signals for me to move in ahead of her. "Stand here, widen your feet and brace them at the ridges of his two shoulder scales, then grab hold of the handles on the saddle."

"Oh, I get it." I frown at the handles. "Why are there three?"

There are two small handles spread out toward the sides and one long one facing me in the center.

"The side ones are for two-handed flight, and the center grip is for when you need to draw your weapon and fight. Becoming comfortable releasing your grip and maneuvering during battle will take training and time. Now that your bond is complete, you'll have plenty of that."

The way she says that... "What do you mean?"

She offers me a sad smile. "You are bound to a mythical immortal, and his power and energy are now part of you. The union has begun."

My mind stalls out on that. "Hubba—wha? Are you saying that once this union thing takes hold, I'll be immortal?"

She shakes her head. "Not immortal in the sense that Nikon or Dionysus is. Violence and magic and a million things can still kill you...but you won't age and die for a very long time."

"Like how long? Decades? Centuries? Millennia?"

She shrugs. "I can't say. I'm fourteen hundred and eighty, and I still look forty-five."

Two things hit me at once...

First, Merlin must've had a dragon bond back in the day. Maybe that's part of the reason Dora turned away from her powers and heritage.

Second, I might never go gray.

CHAPTER NINE

I sleep restlessly and wake to the warmth of Sloan's hand rubbing my shoulder and coaxing me out of pained turmoil. "Shh...*a ghra*. It's one of yer nightmares, luv. All is well."

I blink awake and draw a steadying breath. My chest is tight as I swipe my cheeks dry. "All is *not* well. What will I do without you and my brothers and my friends?"

I told Sloan about the revelation of my dragon bond extending my life when we got home last night, and while explaining it out loud, I remembered what Nikon said about life as an immortal. About the pain of losing loved ones and life becoming monotonous and lonely.

I don't want that.

I always admired Brendan's drunken thirst for life and pictured myself as much the same person. I relish gathering life experiences—good more than bad—and think there is a natural expiry date to our existence.

Not that I want Gran or Granda or even Da to pass, but I accept that the generations before you won't always be with you. That doesn't include Emmet, Calum, Dillan, and Aiden...and not Kev and Kinu, Meg, Jackson, and the twins...and not Sloan.

"I can't outlive all of you. It'll break me."

He hugs me tighter and brushes my hair out of the way to rub a hand down my back. "Ye said it's longevity, not immortality, right?"

"Yeah, that's what Dora said."

"While that's a wonderful gift and would probably mean everlasting life fer most people, ye tend to suffer brutal injury more than most. Odds are ye'll be killed long before yer family dies."

"Yeah? You think so?"

There's barely a glimmer of light in our King Henry fortress of solitude, but I don't miss him rolling his eyes. "I do. You'll likely die some horrible, bloody death and leave us all to mourn ye."

I let out a deep breath and nod. "Thanks, hotness. That makes me feel loads better."

"Of course it does. Now, let me cuddle ye and keep yer nightmares at bay so we can both get a few more hours of rest."

I roll over, give him my back, and snuggle in. Yeah, he's right. Odds are, I'll die long before them. Just because I *could* live for centuries doesn't mean I *will*.

That does make me feel better.

Just like that, Sloan Mackenzie rights my world once again.

Monday mornings are usually unwelcome in my life, but when Sloan *poofs* our household to the Acropolis for a day of productivity, I'm excited to get started. The last couple of days have kinda kicked my ass. I'm looking forward to doing the ass-kicking today.

"First stop, eighth floor," Calum says, in a spot-on impression of a TTC subway announcer. "Badass Bootcamp for the betrothed. Getting hot, sweaty, and tired, but without the orgasms."

Emmet snorts. "Says you. Enter at your own risk."

I cringe. "TMI, dude. We work out on those mats."

Ciara laughs. "Don't worry. If anything happens, we'll be sure to sanitize appropriately."

"Very much appreciated," I say.

"Yeah," Calum says. "Make it pass the blacklight."

We drop Kevin off next on the ninth floor. He's working solo on a collaborative art piece at SASS, the Studio of Art, Sculpture, and Sexiness, while Nikon is off helping Dora work on the Ireland end of our standing portal. Kev and Nikon have been enjoying their resurrection of the lost art of Greek fresco painting.

Calum and I get *poofed* to ten and left outside the Team Trouble Batcave. We're committing the day to work on the light-house ghost issue.

Sloan, of course, wants nothing to do with it and leaves us to our quest.

He *poofs* down to lucky number seven to STOA, Shrine of Toronto's Objects and Antiquities. He has an estate representative coming at ten to discuss the terms of entrusting him with a few pieces his client believes should *not* be bequeathed to his heirs.

Well, they won't find anyone more responsible and dedicated to securing and preserving the power of ancient and enchanted objects.

Calum unlocks the entrance security with his pendant, satisfies the scanner, and opens the door to enter our headquarters. Garnet and Andromeda are chatting at the long conference table in the main room and stop talking as we enter.

"Hey, guys," Andy says. "What are you two up to this morning?"

Calum breaks into an eighties breakdance arm wave and starts singing, "If JP haunts the lighthouse room. Who you gonna call?"

"Ghostbusters!" I raise my fist.

"If he won't pass on and is full of gloom. Who you gonna call?"

"Ghostbusters!"

Garnet gives us a total deadpan stink eye, but Andromeda appreciates our efforts.

A moment later, Dionysus appears next to us. "Did I hear you say we're ghostbusting today?"

"Why, yes you did, and yes, we are. Wanna come out and play with us?"

"Absolutely. A man can only spend so much time alone in a VR room before it gets pathetic. I am a god of fantastic. Pathetic doesn't suit me."

"No, it doesn't," Calum says. "Welcome aboard the ghost-busting troop. We came to learn about ghosts and what we need to do. Does anyone here know anything?"

Andy shrugs. "I think you're supposed to dig up the grave, salt the bones, and burn them."

I laugh. "Are you a *Supernatural* fan by any chance?"

She grins. "Uh-huh. Fifteen seasons and those boys were amazing in every damn one."

"Are you team Dean or Sam? I'm a Sam girl, myself. I go for those tall, broody, smart types."

"Yes, you do. I'd take them both in a hot minute. A girl's got to have choices."

Calum chuckles. "*Supernatural* fandom aside, do we know how to release the ghost of a murdered lighthouse keeper that's been stuck for two centuries?"

That's a no all around.

"Thankfully, ghosts are quite rare," Garnet says. "Getting rid of them depends on why they're stuck here in the first place. Are they bound to an object or another person? Did they die a horrible, unjust death and seek vengeance? Do they have unfinished business and need closure? Are they super powerful and evil?"

I make a face. "I don't like the sound of that. Strike the last one from the list."

"Good call," Andromeda says. "I like the closure one. Then you can be like the *Ghost Whisperer* and transition him to the light. I'm sending positive vibes that your lighthouse man needs you to find his lucky coin or something benign."

"I appreciate that. Let's hope your prana power extends to soothing ghosts."

"Let's hope."

After an hour of searching on the Internet and talking to Myra about any good books on ghostly releases, we're no closer to figuring out what kind of ghost John Paul Radelmüller is or what to do about it. We assume he's either a traumatized spirit that died so suddenly and violently he doesn't fully comprehend he should've passed, or he needs his body reassembled. Or he has unfinished business and needs to say something to his wife and daughter, who are both long dead.

So, locate, salt, and burn it is.

Dionysus snaps us home to get supplies. Then he takes the three of us to the Gibraltar Lighthouse at Hanlan's Point to start our ghostly adventure using the Winchester approach.

With iron pokers in hand and a duffle filled with three different boxes of table salt—Morton, Sifto, and Windsor—we fan out in the scrub around the outside of the lighthouse.

"From what I read, authorities believed JP wouldn't have entertained Blueman and Henry inside the cramped staircase of the lighthouse but in his keeper's cottage constructed alongside it. The article said there was a cozy cabin here until about 1950."

"That's only seventy years ago." Calum searches the ground. "Surely there will be signs of a foundation or ruins to show us where to start."

Dionysus shakes his head. "If two hotheaded drunken soldiers

—both Irish, I might add—got denied liquor and killed and dismembered the man who cut them off, they wouldn't have done that in the man's house with his wife and daughter present."

"No. They wouldn't."

"Dismembering a body is hard work and very messy," he says with a little too much conviction. "They would've dragged him away and done the deed somewhere close by but far enough away from the cottage that the man's family didn't know where. Otherwise, when the authorities investigated, they would've found the bloody scene."

"Good point," Calum says. "According to an account of the time, the soldiers were stationed at the military blockhouse on Gibraltar Point, which guarded entry to York's harbor. The small detachment garrisoned there often visited the lighthouse keeper for drinks. It says here they were just over a mile's walk along the sandbar from Radelmüller's beer keg."

"Which way is the military blockhouse?" I ask, scanning the scene.

Calum studies the screen on his phone and pulls up a map. "That way."

"Okay, so between here and there, they must've buried the body."

"Oh," Dionysus says, straightening. "Do we need one of those machines to x-ray the earth and show us where the bones are?"

I shake my head. "No. If the bones are anywhere around here and hidden within the earth somewhere, that is solidly druid domain. We'll be able to call them up to the surface."

I focus on what I need to happen and revisit Sloan's spell after our first big battle at the druid stones.

Springtails, earthworms, snails, and slugs,
Millipedes, mites, beetles, and bugs,
Decomposers feast and flourish,
Body in the soil to nourish,
Bones shall rise in heaving surrender,

Exhume John Paul for eternal splendor.

I nod at Calum, who raises his palms. *"Detect Magic."* The tingle of Calum's power rushes over me.

Dionysus and I follow him deeper into the scrub, north toward the city. What starts as a low vibration in the distance soon becomes a tangible thrum in my bones.

I know from my studies with Granda that energy surrounding both birth and death is concentrated power. From the sensation of what's happening in front of us, I think the violent passion of murder might increase that ten-fold.

"Do you feel that?" I hold up my palm.

Calum swallows and winces. "I do. It's leaving a bad taste in my mouth."

"No wonder John Paul can't rest. That's nasty."

The three of us continue forward until we get to the edge of a small bay. In the center of the small body of water, there's a piece of land no bigger than two hundred by three hundred feet.

"The bones are on that little island?" Calum asks.

"It likely wasn't an island two hundred years ago, but yeah, I think so." I turn to Dionysus and smile. "Would you mind being our ferryman over to that little mound of dirt?"

"My pleasure."

A moment later, we're standing on what's known as Hanlan's Island, and the taint of powerful anger and betrayal grips my throat, making it hard to swallow.

"Purge Malevolence," I say.

A gust of a crisp, May breeze blows in, and my spell swirls the air for a few moments. When it dissipates, it sweeps the poisoned energy away. I breathe deeply, thankful for the reprieve, and my nerves begin to settle.

"That's better."

"Much better." Calum runs a hand over his forearms and shakes himself.

Dionysus seems curious more than bothered. Trudging forward, he explores for a bit before bending and pointing at the ground. "I think you've unearthed your lighthouse keeper."

Calum and I follow and watch as a massive army of creepy crawling creatures squirm and scramble to the surface and surrender the bones of the dead. Old bones now spot the long, green grasses of spring.

I unzip the duffle and pull out the three baskets I grabbed from the storage room before we came. "Excellent. Everyone, start gathering."

Calum blinks. "You brought our childhood Easter baskets to collect the bones of a dismembered murder victim?"

"We were in a rush, and I couldn't think of anything better. Besides, when was the last time we went on an egg hunt?"

Calum laughs. "You couldn't think of anything better? What about Ziploc bags? A plastic shopping bag? A laundry basket? I can think of half a dozen things."

"Nah, baskets were cuter."

Dionysus picks the blue one and smiles. "I like the baskets, Fi. I've never been on an Ostara egg hunt."

———

It takes close to an hour to scour the burial site of John Paul Radelmüller, which if Dionysus had felt inclined to god power for us, would've taken us minutes. He didn't offer, so I didn't ask.

Not for a minute do I think the God of Wine and Ecstasy has simply decided to slum it with the mortals of Toronto and build a life here.

I'm not complaining. I love having him as part of our cohort of crazy, but something is going on with him.

It's like he's hiding from being a god and wants to pretend he's normal for a bit.

I understand the impulse and support it…

Except, it feels like whatever he's hiding from is hurting him.

I'm happy to give him time to sort through it and the love and support he needs while he does, but if he needs to buckle down and deal with something, he'll have to address it sooner or later.

"Is that everything?" Calum braces his back with his hand as he winces and straightens. "Who knew there were so many little bones in the human body?"

"Um…everyone." I smirk at him. "There are two hundred and six bones in the human body. That's common knowledge."

Dionysus frowns at the pile. "We only have two-hundred and five."

"Seriously?" I look from him to the pile we've amassed on the small tarp we spread out. "Do you know that or are you screwing with us?"

Dionysus grins. "As much as I'd love to be screwing with the two of you, we're archeological professionals. There are two hundred and five bones."

"Well, poop." I search the ground where we've been toiling all morning. "Where's the last one?"

"Got it. Mystery solved." Calum lifts his finger and smiles. "They found the jaw bone, right? It wouldn't be here if the police had it."

"Right you are, Sherlock," I say, once again content with our pile of the exhumed lighthouse keeper. "Do you think that bone was destroyed or locked in an evidence room somewhere?"

"Did they have evidence lockup in 1815?"

I shrug. "You're the cop. Don't you know?"

He laughs. "They must've left that part out of the training academy."

"But we need to destroy all the bones to release him, don't we?"

"According to the Winchesters." Calum dumps the last of his basket onto the pile, and the bones skitter and clatter down our lighthouse keeper mountain.

"Maybe cleansing the bad juju and destroying these will be enough either way," I say.

Dionysus grins and hands me his basket. "Maybe he's already feeling better because you dissipated the nasty murder energy."

"Do you think I should go check? Maybe we should try again to figure out if he has unfinished business."

Calum's brow comes down in a pinched scowl rivaling Sloan's. "Didn't you say he tried to lock you and Irish in the lighthouse and got testy about you leaving?"

"That was when bad juju was strangling his bones."

"You're talking out your ass. You don't know if anything changed. He could try harder this time to keep you as his precious."

I wince at the image of a hunched-over Gollum wanting to keep me as his own. "Yeah no. Me no likey."

"I'll go with you," Dionysus says. "If he gets possessive, I'll get you out of there."

I try to shed the creepy sensation of equating Ghost John Paul with a demented, google-eyed Sméagol, but my brother has ruined it for me. "Yeah, I don't think I can go alone now, thanks to Calum. You know how much I hate Gollum."

Calum chuckles. "Yeah, I do."

CHAPTER TEN

At my request, Dionysus brings Calum and me back to the center of the druid circle, and we look for a spot to set out the bones. Having been here in another era, I know the area beneath the altar stone is where the druids established their fire pit. That doesn't work now. Not with the massive stone pillars and plinth we use as the altar.

"Dionysus could probably move it temporarily, couldn't you?" Calum asks.

"Sure. Where do you want it?" he asks.

I point to the side. "Just out of the way while we do this would be great."

Dionysus snaps his fingers, and the stone altar appears ten feet to the right of its original position.

"Perfect. Thanks."

Standing over the newly cleared spot, I look down and assess what we're dealing with.

The ground isn't charred and littered with ash like it was when Fionn took me back to the original Drombeg to eat salmon with him, but we're making this replica ours, so we might as well honor what came before.

"We'll set the bones here and get them ready." I press my hands against the grass and clear it with my powers to leave only a circle of dirt. "Then, depending on how it goes with John Paul, we'll either burn them right away or help him with whatever he needs doing, then burn them."

Calum kneels on the edge of the circle and unzips the duffle bag. "Do I need to say any words of exorcism or anything when I burn them? I'm not great with Latin, but I'm decent at rhyming."

I chuckle. "I don't think so, but hey, this is my first ghost banishment. What do I know?"

"Diddly squat, like the rest of us."

"True story."

When we have the bones grouped, salted, and doused in lighter fluid, Dionysus and I leave Calum to guard the unlit pyre and return to the Gibraltar Point Lighthouse to see if John Paul Radelmüller is haunting today.

Stopping outside the red door, I scan the grey brick of the lighthouse and rally my courage. "Have you ever dealt with ghosts before, Dionysus?"

He lifts a shoulder. "Not the kind of ghost you described, no. Over the ages, I've encountered people in different phases of undead or those resistant to pass to the Elysian Plain, but none like this who simply stay locked in one place haunting their old life."

"It's horrible, don't you think?"

"I do." He frowns at the lighthouse. "If something locked me into a life of haunting a place, I would want a castle or a village or someplace to stretch my legs. This little lighthouse would be worse than prison."

"Maybe another reason John Paul was cranky and reluctant to let us leave."

"Or Calum's right, and he's an evil spook."

I hope not. "Once we know for sure, I'll feel better about

sending him off in a ball of flame. If he needs to show or tell us something to rest at ease, I'd like to offer him that chance."

"You're a good person, Jane."

"Thanks, Tarzan. It takes one to know one."

After a deep breath to strengthen me, I press my hand on the lock plate and get things started. *"Open Sesame."*

The lock releases, and I push the red portal open to step inside. "Should we have a safe word to signal a quick retreat?"

"Whatever you like." Dionysus cranes his neck to see the opening to the lamp room above. "What about rapscallion. I've always liked that word."

I chuckle. "I wonder why?"

He grins. "What are you implying, Red?"

I climb the first step and cast a glance over my shoulder. "Stay close, please."

He shifts, and before I make it to the third step, the warmth of his body presses against my back. I look back at him. "Maybe not that close."

"A woman who knows what she wants and how she wants it. I respect that."

I chuckle. "Behave. Let's get this over with and get some lunch. I'm hungry."

"Me too. Ghostbusting gives me an appetite."

The two of us make it to the top of the stairs and step onto the lamp room floor. I spin Sloan's bone ring on the knuckle of my thumb. At first, I don't think the ghost is here. Then the hair on the nape of my neck stands on end.

Scanning the six-foot-round room takes a fraction of a second. He's not there one moment...then he is.

"Hello, John Paul. Remember me?"

The man's gaze narrows and his jaw works to open and close his mouth. Like the first time, no words come out, but I get the sense he's trying to say something.

"We found your body. You can rest now. You can pass and maybe find Magdalene and Arabella."

The names of his wife and daughter seem to give him pause. He falls still, and his gaze narrows on me.

"You remember them? Magdalene and Arabella? If you believe in the afterlife, you can take comfort that they'll be there waiting for you to join them. That would be nice, right?"

Despite my intention to offer him comfort, the mention of his family seems to rile him more.

Dionysus slides his hand into mine, and he squeezes. *Anytime you're ready, Red. This guy could challenge Medusa for most creepy death stare.*

I squeeze his hand back to show him that I hear him and understand. "Is there anything we can do or find or help you with to ease your transition?"

He throws his hand up and the downstairs door slams and locks like it did the last time.

A rush of dark energy builds in the lighthouse, and his gaze hardens. I try to swallow and calm myself, but my throat is clogged, and my heart is hammering.

When he lifts both hands, the glass walls of the lightroom shake and rattle. From the seam of the window frames, blood seeps down like macabre shades being drawn over the windows.

Check, please.

"Rapscallion," I say, my voice coming out pitchy.

Dionysus and I reform at the druid altar, and I faery fire the pyre. "I'm done. The. End. That was way too Carrie at the prom for me."

The three of us watch the bones burn until Nikon and Dora snap in to join us.

"No marshmallows?" Nikon asks.

"Sorry. Not this time."

The Greek looks closer and frowns. "Is that a human you're burning?"

"It was at one point, yes. Now, we think it's what's tethering a seriously creepy and cranky ghost to the lighthouse on Hanlan's Point."

"Where the nude beach is?"

"Yeah, there but further inland."

Nikon grins at Calum and Dionysus. "I think we should investigate this ghost sighting more thoroughly."

I chuckle. "Simmer down, Greek. The beaches aren't open until July."

"Disappointing. All right, make a note to revisit the scene in a few months and ensure the ghost issue is taken care of."

"Agreed," Calum says. When he looks at me, he shrugs. "A good druid is a thorough druid."

"I'm sure that's true."

Dora barks a laugh and strikes off toward the stone columns encircling us.

"How did it go in Ireland?" I ask. "Did you get the Drombeg side of the portal linked up and connected?"

"I believe so. I won't know for sure until we test it."

"How do we do that?"

She places a hand against the first of the two entrance stones, and a crackle of magic snaps in the air. "It's a dragon portal, girl-friend. We test it by sending your dragon through the portal. Bring Dartamont back tonight after dark, and we'll see if we're in business. You better bring Irish too. He should join you on the test run in case it doesn't work, and you need to portal out before you hit the ground."

I blink, not liking the sound of that. "We're going to hit the ground?"

"Not if it works."

. . .

As much as I don't like Dart being the test subject for what Wallace called arcane magic, there's no getting around the logic. It's a dragon portal.

It takes a dragon to activate it.

Still, I'm leery about it. My brothers, the Greeks, and Kevin are more excited than leery. While I'm having a bit of a meltdown, they're the ones pulling up lawn chairs with a cooler of beer.

"How does the portal technology work, exactly?" Sloan asks Dora as we prepare for the first portal leap.

Dora points at the stone ring encircling us. "I spelled the stone circle to act as a power accumulator. It focuses the energy and the intent of the dragon and allows it to pass through to another set of rings spelled for the same purpose."

That sounds simple enough...for an extremely magical and dangerous mode of travel.

"The more powerful Dartamont gets, the more he will be able to do here."

I frown. "What do you mean?"

"I mean, we're going to work on getting Dart to and from Ireland, but once he's aged and become powerful enough to become an Elder Dragon, he'll be able to navigate not only distance but also time."

"Time? Like, he could go in here and come out of say, Stonehenge in the ancient past?"

Dora nods. "Because Stonehenge was an active portal at that time, yes."

Dillan cracks the tab on a Guinness and pours it into a frosty mug. "Is anyone else getting a serious *Stargate* vibe from this?"

Emmet nods. "Yeah. So, what if the Goa'uld have a dragon and want to come here? Are we opening ourselves up to more trouble?"

Dora looks over toward the peanut gallery and frowns. "While it's possible, it's also unlikely. Like I mentioned, travel has to do with the power *and* the intent of the dragon. For an Elder Dragon to travel from the past to here, he or she would have to know not only the location of this circle but the time it was active with portal magic."

Sloan nods. "So, a dragon in Arthurian time wouldn't know about our circle and us and so couldn't access this portal."

"That's right."

"That's cool." I'm thankful we haven't opened Toronto up for invasion. "What if we go back and meet dragons, and they want to follow us home?"

"It won't happen," Dora says. "First of all, Dart won't be powerful enough to breach time for another century, at least. Even when he is, if you went back, you certainly wouldn't broadcast where and when you're from, or you'd be opening the door for unwanted guests."

"Fair enough," Sloan says. "I take it from yer breadth of knowledge of all things dragon and yer longevity, ye had a dragon of yer own at one time, aye?"

The flash of despair that shadows her gaze is gone before the others notice. Sloan and I seem to be the only two that catch it. Dora turns her back on us, pointing toward the outer stones.

"Back in Arthurian time, there were a dozen such standing circles and the dragons used them freely as part of their daily lives. I was fortunate enough to be part of that culture, no matter how unworthy I was of the honor at the time."

"Hindsight." I feel bad for the conversation going sideways on her. "As far as your worthiness, I imagine if a dragon bonded with you, he or she saw the same strength and honor in you that we all see."

She doesn't turn to look at me. Instead, she claps her hands, strides off across the flat plain of the circle, and grabs one of the two spike saddles off the grass. "Come, Fi. We'll practice aerial maneuvers before the test. Grab your saddle and join me. Time to train your dragon."

Dora puts Dart and me through a series of aerial drills, and I am, as always, in awe of her. Sure, she's lived almost fifteen hundred years, but she's also amazingly skilled and powerful.

"Dartamont, take us higher, young man." When Dart starts pumping his leathery wings, climbing toward the night clouds, she shifts her hold to one hand and pegs me with a sober look. "Okay, girlfriend. We're going to simulate a freefall, and you will remount in flight."

"Hubba-wha? You want me to fall?"

"Yes, but only briefly. Your job is to right yourself so you're falling feet first, then I'll instruct Dart on how to approach and intercept. Time your reconnection to land on his back close enough to grab your saddle handle. I suggest *Feline Finesse* and *Diminish Descent*."

She raises her finger, and I feel the surge of her power building up.

"Wait! I'm not ready—"

The pulse of energy knocks me backward through the open air and the wind whistles in my ears. There are a terrifying few seconds while I topple ass over end and I'm not sure which way is up or down.

"Feline Finesse." As my magic takes hold, so too does gravity. I figure out very clearly which way is down and my mental pistons start firing once again.

Using my arms to alter my drag, I get my feet under me. *"Diminish Descent."*

That helps too.

I blink against the sting of wind and hair lashing at my eyes and make a mental note to keep a pair of swimming goggles in my pocket from now on.

Cranking my head around like an owl, I search for the approach of my dragon.

I feel him before I see him.

My racing heart suddenly slows, and I sense the strong and steady *thrump-pump, thrump-pump,* of my dragon.

Turning to my left, I catch sight of him as he breaks from the clouds and dips his head, soaring toward me.

Shit. What did Dora say to do next?

Dammit, I freaked out so much about the "freefall" part, I missed the landing instructions.

Land on my back, Dart says into my mind. *I shall try to time it so you can grab hold of your saddle.*

Right. *Good one, buddy.*

I gauge how far he is from me and take a quick look down at the rapidly approaching ground.

Crap on a cracker. We don't have enough space for a mulligan on this.

Looking down is likely a mistake, he says. *I am nervous enough without feeling your heart race.*

I make an immediate attempt at calming down. *Sorry. I have faith in you. We're a dynamic duo. You ease in, and I'll stick the landing, promise.*

I feel the connection between us, and it's more than his voice and his heartbeat. I feel his worry and fear too. He's determined but afraid.

We can do this, Dart. Keep coming.

He does. In a move more graceful than a creature of his size and strength should be able to commit, he closes the distance between us and slows as he swoops twenty feet underneath me.

I spot where my feet will land and realize too late that I won't be close enough to reach the handle of my spike saddle.

Fuckety-fuck. What now?

"Gust of Wind." My feet make contact a moment before my spell hits me with a gale force. I'm thrust almost ten feet toward Dart's head and hit the spike coming out of his spine. Hard.

The world goes wonky on me for a second...but when the stars stop spinning, I have a hold on the handle of the saddle.

I won't get any points for the artistry of presentation, but I think, in this case, the judges down below will be happy I'm no longer plummeting toward becoming a puddle of goo on the ground in front of them.

Great job, buddy. Our success was way more you than me.

The result is all that matters in this case.

True story.

When we land, I read the hostility of the incoming storm and hold my hands up to stop Sloan before he goes off. "It's fine. I'm fine. It probably looked a lot scarier from down here than it was."

Sloan glares at me. "Are ye sayin' ye enjoyed plummetin' toward yer death and that I'm overreactin'?"

"I didn't enjoy it, but Dora was right. Being thrown from Dart's back is a possibility, and it's better that I have an idea of what I'm in for now before griffins are swiping at me or witches on broomsticks are attacking."

He throws a heated glare at Dora, and though I feel like I should intervene, there's no need. Sloan would never lose his cool on a woman, and Dora can certainly take care of herself.

"Sorry for the drama, boys," she says. "Fi's right. She and Dartamont need to work together in moments of urgency, and simulating life-threatening situations is the best way to develop those muscles."

Sloan lets out a throaty chuff and flails his hands. "Ye didn't *simulate* a damn thing, Dora. Ye forced her into a life-threatening situation. Ye made her fall off a fledgling dragon, and it could've killed her."

Dora presses her lips together and frowns. "It might've looked like that from here, but I wouldn't have let anything happen to her. You know that."

"Of course he does." I peg Sloan with a look and extend it to my brothers, who are equally as annoyed but are thankfully restraining themselves from making a scene. "We all know Dora is capable in the world of dragons and magic as well as thoughtful about cause and effect. It's fine. I'm fine. Everything is fine."

Dionysus chuckles. "That's it, Jane. Say it loud. Say it proud. They might believe you."

Nikon's the next to chuckle. "Well, this is super fun, but weren't we invited to see you test the dragon portal? I for one am excited to flash to Ireland and see if you come out the other end."

I blink and focus my attention on him. "As opposed to what? To us *not* coming out the other end?"

He holds up his hands and backs away. "My bad. I didn't mean to imply anything."

I wave his apology away. "No. It's fine. I'm still a little keyed up from the falling off the dragon exercise."

"If it makes you feel any better, you plummeted with style."

Emmet laughs. "And you didn't pee your pants. I'm pretty sure I would be standing here in pee pants right now if we'd reversed the roles."

I grin at my goofball brother. "Thanks, Em. That does help."

It takes a few minutes for the hard feelings between Sloan and Dora to subside, but once they both extend their apologies for letting emotions affect their view on things, we get back to the reason for our gathering.

Testing the dragon portal.

"All right," Dora says, talking to Sloan, Dart, and me. "You'll need to come at the center of the rings with a good deal of speed, but the more important aspect is the angle of entry. Anything from forty-five degrees to one-thirty-five degrees to the ground should work. The closer you get to ninety degrees, the better."

My mouth falls open. "So you want us to take a perpendicular swan dive straight at the ground?"

"Technically, it'll be a dragon dive," Dillan says, cracking open another beer.

"Thanks for that, D."

"That's what I'm here for." He sits back in his folding chair and sips.

I roll my eyes and get back to the issue at hand. "So, we're nose down and coming in relatively quickly. When do we know if the portal's working?"

"The rings should glow on approach. Once you're in your dive and Dartamont's intention registers with the spellwork I've cast, the stones will light up in a golden orange ring for you."

"As long as that happens, we're good to pass through?" Sloan asks.

Dora nods. "Yes. They'll either engage or not. There won't be any guesswork. If they're glowing like a ring of fire, enjoy the ride. If they don't, your first choice should be to abort. If it's too late and Dart has too much downward momentum, you'll need to portal them higher so he can pull out of his dive."

"Can you do that, hotness?" I ask.

He nods. "It shouldn't be a problem. I've never tried to materialize in the air before, but I don't see how it'll be any different."

"It won't," Dora says. "You should feel my magic power things up."

"Wouldn't it be better if you're with us?" I ask. "Then your magic will be close and in full swing."

Dora looks apprehensive. "This is your moment, cookie. Yours and Dartamont's."

I chuckle. "Oh, it's so not. I'm totes happy to share the moment if it means you're with us. I would feel a thousand times better."

Dora frowns but gives in. "All right. If that's what you want. I'll take the third spike and go as an observer. I won't step in unless things go sideways."

"Good enough. I feel better already."

Dora nods and gestures at Nikon. "The moment we pass through the portal, snap to the Drombeg rings in Ireland and welcome us through. I'm assuming Fi, Sloan, and Dart might like to visit. I'd like to come home. I have plans tonight."

Nikon nods. "We've got this."

I snort. "Says the guy *not* portaling through the earth's core."

Nikon winks. "We all have a part to play, Red."

Dora claps her hands. "All right, team. Here we go."

There's a huge difference between learning things in theory and experiencing them in practice. Me falling from my dragon is one example of this, and diving practically face-first at the solid ground is another.

"Okay, buddy," I say as we bank with the wind and align ourselves with the stone circle below. "We can do this. The rings are going to glow if they're set up properly and burst into a ring of gold and orange to give us the go-ahead. Everybody ready?"

I get a half-hearted affirmative from Dart and Sloan and try not to let that bring my faith down.

Dart gives his wings a couple of muscled pumps, arcs up, sweeps his wings back, and we dive.

Straight.

Down.

CHAPTER ELEVEN

There's a moment of suspended awareness—like we exist on a plane neither here nor there. My heart trips in my chest, and for a second, I wonder if we might be lost in here forever.

It's over in a second...

a split second...

a picosecond...

As fast as that is, the fear is intense, and when we break through to the other side, relief washes over me.

Then confusion.

When we dove into the druid circle in Toronto, it was close to midnight, and the sky was dark. When we emerge on the other side, the sun is hot and at its zenith overhead. Something isn't right.

If it's midnight in Toronto, it's five in the morning in Ireland. I expected the gray sky of dawn with the promise of the sunrise.

Instead, the sun is a golden ball of fiery flame over a canopy of crimson and auburn leaves, its brilliance promising a glorious autumn day.

Sloan curses behind me, and I know he's piecing it together too. We're not in Kansas anymore.

We're not in Ireland either.

"Dora? Where are we?" Switching to grip the center handle on my saddle, I twist backward to meet her shocked expression.

"It can't be."

"Can't be what? Where...or when?"

All of those questions apply because it's obvious by the forested lands below and the flags waving at the castle in the distance that *when* is the most important question.

"Ye did it again, didn't ye?" Sloan says behind me.

My mouth falls open. "Rude. I did nothing. I'm a passenger on this crazy train like—"

Dart lets out a shrill screech and pitches right, forcing me to get a better grip or face the very real possibility of taking another header into the open air.

I survey the sky—

A spear soars through the air and narrowly misses the leathery flesh of Dart's wing.

"Incoming!" I search the ground. Rolling hills. Forested lands. An expanse of sea waters all along the coastline. I point when I find the catapult towers manned with spiked cabers. "There. At seven o'clock. Who are they? Why are they firing on us?"

"We have dragons coming in hard and fast on the right," Sloan says.

"Tough as Bark." I turn to Dora and call faery fire to my palm.

When a crackling purple ball of magic comes at us, I swing back and release the faery fire to intercept. The collision of magic makes a thunderous *crack* and the incoming dragons hiss and rear.

The rider on one of the startled dragons is nearly thrown and sneers at me.

I release the handle of my saddle and hold both hands in the air. *"Wind Wall."*

"Sleet Storm," Sloan says behind me.

The force of my windstorm and the icy shards of Sloan's sleet storm blows the beasts back to a respectable distance.

The dragon riders seem both surprised and insulted.

Sorry-not-sorry.

I check my gang for damages. "Are we good? Everyone okay?"

"We're good," Sloan says. "Dora? What the hell is going on?"

Dora shakes herself out of whatever shock she's in and releases the handle of her saddle. As if she's jogging up a street sidewalk and not a panicked dragon evading incoming forces, she climbs the arch of Dart's spine to join me at the first spike.

Gripping the left side handle, she stands as straight and sure as I've ever seen her. "Stop the assault, Fi. Drop your armor and veil me while I do the same."

I do as I'm instructed and release a subtle shielding to keep Dora from drawing attention. It's not so much a veil as a suggestion for people to look away and not take notice of her.

Pulling off her wig, Dora releases the electric purple mane into the air. It flutters and falls toward the ground like a wounded exotic bird. Then, she passes a hand up her body from her waist to the air above her head.

In the flash of a moment and a surge of magic, she transforms into the man I've only spent time with once before—in Camelot.

Gone are the glittering gold eyelashes, fuchsia lipstick, and bell-bottom pink camo khakis.

Instead, the man in front of us is unmistakably Emrys Merlin, the legendary magician of days of old.

He steps out from behind me and scowls at the lead dragon rider. "Pelleas of Lisvane, you drunken fool, cease your advance. You are liable to kill someone."

The rider who leads the dragon offense scowls, looking confused. "Then our intent is clear. What are you playing at, Merlin?"

"I play at nothing except bones and women. Now disengage your offense and return to your post. You have no foe here."

"I am an officer of the guard. A great many strangers are arriving for the tournament. It is our task to evaluate them and intercept possible hostiles who might use the celebration as a way to infiltrate."

Merlin opens his hands to his sides. "There were no hostilities until you attacked us without provocation."

"Why do you fly upon a blue dragon and not Empress Cazzienth?"

Merlin grunts and rolls his dark chestnut eyes. "I escort my niece to the castle through the autonomous sky. Dartamont is her dragon. You struck against him as if he poses some dire threat. Why? He is a hatchling, a good and honorable dragon."

Pelleas looks Dart over and frowns. "He is not an identified dragon of the court, and therefore we can give no quarter."

"Free dragons need not be feared merely for the sake of them not being under the court's control."

"Free dragons are dangerous. If we can't control them, we can't trust them."

The three dragons in their control each wear a wide leather band cinched around the ankle of their hind leg. I feel the magic binding them, and it's sharp and uncomfortable.

"You shackle them to obedience by keeping them on a magical leash?" I say. "That's horrific."

Pelleas, a scruffy brute of a man, sneers at me. "The matters of dragons and realm safety are beyond your understanding, little girl. Don't bother yourself trying to understand."

Seriously?

"Dragons are amazing, intelligent creatures of strength. Shackling them to obedience is what will make them dangerous."

"It seems your niece needs a leash herself, Merlin." The speaker is a tall man with dark red hair and a scruffy goatee. He possesses a striking resemblance to Ewan McGregor and would be attractive if he wasn't wearing a look that suggests there's a nasty smell under his nose. "Speaking of obedience, perhaps you could teach her some."

Merlin grumbles. "My niece is fine the way she is, and the argument about free dragons is best left to the tavern. Return to your duties, gentlemen. There is no cause for alarm here."

"That is for us to decide," Ewan says.

The narrowing of Merlin's gaze is subtle, but I'm close enough to feel the rise of his ire as his power builds. "You grow bold, Sigberht. Does the king know of your thirst for conflict? Is this the welcome the dragon guard offers visitors to the kingdom?"

He looks us up and down and frowns. "The king is a boy overwrought with the grief of a father lost. The dragon guard will run the land until he gains a foothold."

Merlin's fingers curl into fists at his sides. "Does the king share your views? No, strike that. I shall ask him myself when he arrives. I shall also mention your undeserving attack upon innocent citizens."

Pelleas frowns. "Had the female not fired upon us, there would be no cause for concern."

I cluck my tongue. "Had the female not defended herself, her dragon would've taken fire and possibly been injured for no reason except for men wanting to flex their muscles and piss a line in the sand."

The man scowls at me. "Who are you to speak to us in such a manner?"

"My niece, Lady Fiona," Merlin snaps. "Fiona is right. She had every right to defend her mount. You neither identified yourselves nor voiced any demands. You simply fired upon us unbidden."

"As is our right," he hisses.

"Then your system of law enforcement is severely lacking," I say. "Innocent until proven guilty is a thing...or at least it will be."

The redhead, Sigberht, grips the hilt of his sword at his hip.

"Your niece would be better suited to joining the females in the weaving shed and not meddling in matters of men and getting herself killed in the process."

My laughter bursts out of me and carries on the breeze. "You're just pissy because I put you in your place. I wasn't meddling, and if there were a throwdown between us, you three wouldn't be here harassing us. You'd be on the ground somewhere licking your wounded pride."

The men don't seem to appreciate my response.

Pelleas scowls. "You should consider teaching her manners, Emrys, or someone else might take it upon themselves to do it for you."

I chuckle. "Bring it, asswipe. My daddy taught me never to shy away from a fight."

"My point exactly. The ladies of Tintagel do not behave in such a manner."

"Then it's a good thing I'm neither a lady nor from Tintagel. Problem solved."

Merlin raises a hand and frowns. "Peace, all of you. My niece is a skilled druid and a fine dragon rider. It would be best not to assess her based on what you deem an appropriate character for a lady of the land. She is a strangling vine, not a shrinking violet."

Their gazes narrow on me.

"Then she's come to find herself a man of good standing at the tournament who can tame her impulses and make a lady of her yet."

I chuckle. "I'm not on the market for a husband. If I were, I guarantee my guy would know better than to try to tell me who I could be."

"Then it seems the men in your life thus far have done you the disservice of not teaching you your place."

Sloan tenses and is about to chime in, and I wave him off. "It's fine. Don't bother."

"Off with you, now." Merlin holds up his fists. They are snapping with gold sparks as the wind around us picks up. Dark clouds begin to form and blow across the sky. "Another word from any of you and I will strike you down from the heavens."

Sigberht considers the threat, then tilts his head and the three dragons drop back and peel away.

When they've soared back to the forest below where I saw the spear catapults, I turn to Sloan and Dora. "Rude much? The weaving shed? Seriously?"

Dora huffs. "They've never encountered a woman of your character and...willfulness, shall we say."

Sloan arches a brow. "Fi is an acquired taste."

I chuckle. "In my defense, they sucked balls as our welcoming committee."

Merlin grins. "That was three of the twelve Dragon Guards of Tintagel. They aren't a bad bunch, but there are certainly a few of them who believe their positions perched atop a dragon gives them the power to bolster themselves over the lowly citizens."

"It seems they like their women to recognize that," Sloan says.

"That's not cool," I say. "Bowing down doesn't work for me in any century. Maybe I should check out this tournament of champions they were talking about and throw my name in the hat."

Dora...or—I guess Merlin—frowns. "No. You should not. You can't take on all the fights all the time."

I grin. "Come to think of it, a few of my report cards said that. Didn't stop me in the fifth grade. I doubt it'll stop me now."

Dora rolls her eyes. "If you don't mind me assuming the helm, I'll take us somewhere safe, and we can try to figure out what happened and why we ended up here."

Glancing back at Sloan standing almost ten feet behind me on the next spike, I consider her request for the driver's seat. "Yeah, sure, no problem."

A reassuring squeeze to my wrist and a tingle of magic bolster my confidence. "Feel the movement of your dragon and anticipate. The two of you are bonded, and your union is taking hold. You're a graceful girl. You can get back to Sloan without issue."

I'm not so sure, but then again, I've felt the same way about every druid challenge I've faced so far.

Giving my mentor the benefit of the doubt, I release the thick leather handle on my saddle and give it a go. Mimicking Dora's movement of a few moments ago, I jog back to Sloan's extended hand.

It's a bit like walking on the deck of a cruise ship. Mostly steady but a dip and sway to level out as I go. When I get back there, I squeeze Sloan's hand and wink. "Ha! That was kinda fun."

Sloan looks pale for a black man. "Glad ye think so. It wasn't much fun fer me."

Once I've got a hold on the saddle handle and am settled at the second spike with Sloan, Dora steers Dart out over the open water and entices him to pick up speed. The wind whistles in my ears and I squint against the glare of the sun reflecting off the surface of the vast, blue sea.

Tintagel Castle sits atop the rocky cliffs of a jut of land fingering out into the sea. It's pretty much an island, except for a narrow land bridge that connects it to the small fishing town on the mainland side of things.

Assessing the area around the castle, I try to pick out where we're heading. Are we arcing around to the rocky plateau on the cliffs somewhere? There are some dragons near tents over there.

There's a courtyard in the center of the castle buildings. Maybe there—

"Hold on," Dora says.

No sooner have the words been spoken and Dart dives straight down at the water.

What? Why?

Sloan mutters something ungentlemanly behind me and shifts me from the side handle to stand in front of his chest. Caging me between his arms, he grips the side handles with both hands.

I follow his lead and do as Dora says, securing a firmer hold.

We hit the water with a great deal of velocity, but instead of the jarring impact I'm expecting, we slide beneath the surface like a high-caliber bullet shot into a pond. The next entertaining surprise is that the water doesn't close in on us.

Whatever Dora is doing, there's a bubble of oxygen within a shielded area streamlining us through the sea.

"Incredible," Sloan says behind me.

I glance back at him and smile. "I'm glad you finally get to join me on a time adventure, hotness. Castle life is going to blow your mind."

"I'd say I'm glad as well, but I think I'll weigh in after we see what we're in for."

"Always my pragmatist."

Dora must be communicating with Dart on a telepathic channel because my boy seems to know exactly where he's going.

Like a sleek river otter in the water, he navigates the rocky shoreline with more grace and deftness in his movement than a creature of his size and heft should possess.

We continue, deep beneath the surface of the sea, and then, quite suddenly, he turns into a dark opening and takes us through a passage under the land.

Up and over jagged rocks, first veering right through a wall of seaweed, then pitching left to squeeze through a fork in the land.

We breach the surface and soar into the air as Dart stretches out his wings and uses his forward momentum to thrust us clear of the seawater.

As the spray of our launch falls away, he pumps his great, blue wings and lifts us higher.

A shiver races up my spine.

The air of the underground cavern is cool and damp and surprisingly fresh for the size of the space.

Dora throws her hands out toward a plateau up and to our right, and light streams from her palms to guide our way. When the magic hits the stone above a wide, flat platform, the illumination absorbs directly into the stone of the cliff, and the plateau glows in magical light.

Dart course-corrects and rises to take us three hundred feet above the sea pool where we emerged. He pumps his wings to climb toward the plateau, then reverse thrusts to hover and touch down like a pro.

When the ride comes to a complete stop, Dora slides off without a backward glance. Sloan and I follow her lead...no, his lead...oh, this is confusing.

Dart releases his super-size and shrinks down to the size of my blue boy. Not that he's small in any way. His adolescent size is now as big if not bigger than a full-grown African elephant.

I round the elbow spike on his front leg and reach to scrub my knuckles over his center horn. "Great flying, buddy. You are awesomeness dragonified."

I smell dragons here, he says into my mind. *Old and powerful dragons.*

That concerns me.

"Hey, Dora...oh," I step closer and drop my voice. "Are you Dora here or Merlin? I'm confused about how to address you."

He shrugs, and it's still super odd to see him not in his fabulous drag form. "It's customary in my world to use the name and pronoun of the person you see in front of you. Like this, you should call me Merlin...or, I suppose, Uncle."

I chuckle. "Right, because I'm your niece."

"Until I figure out when we are exactly and why we're here, I think that's best. I'm not the most popular man in history, but the people who matter respect me and will respect that you belong to me while we're here."

Sloan frowns. "Why *do* ye think we're here? Ye said the destination is the dragon's intent. Do ye think Dart brought us here?"

"No, I—" He holds up his finger to pause the conversation, and his gaze locks on the massive dragon exiting a cave opening leading into the stone before us.

The majesty of the beast that easily matches the size of the Dragon Queen of Wyrms back home strikes me—only she isn't a Wyrm dragon.

This beauty is a Western, like Dart.

Four muscle-carved legs, two glorious gold and burnt orange wings, and a strong tail that ends in a treacherous-looking ball-spike.

With each step closer, her champagne scales shimmer and catch the magical light, making her look like a dazzling opal glistening in the light of a raging fire…only with two-foot-long teeth and that scary ball-spike on the end of her tail.

"Who have you brought for a visit, darling?" she asks, her voice a melodic purr I recognize.

I shake myself inwardly. How could I recognize her? I've never set eyes on her before.

Merlin stares up at her, entranced. There's no mistaking the devastation in his gaze or the raw wonder. "These are dear friends, my love. From far away and long, lonely centuries into the future."

He shifts his footing, raising a trembling hand to brush the side of her jaw. "Oh, my sweet and glorious Cazzie. There's so much I have to tell you."

"Why does your pulse race, Emrys?"

"I'll explain everything in a moment, but first," he gestures to us, "Dartamont, Fiona, and Sloan, this is Cazzienth Empress of the West, and this is the lair of the free dragons. They are family and will take good care of you until we return. Saxa, please show my friends to my chamber, little one."

"You're leaving?" I ask.

He offers us an apologetic smile. "It has been almost twelve hundred years since I've seen my Cazzie. I need a moment alone with her. We'll return as soon as I figure out what happened."

Before we have time to respond, a great surge of power erupts, and Merlin transforms into a massive chestnut brown dragon. With a few running steps, he launches off the ledge of the plateau, and Cazzie joins him in practiced synchronicity.

Dark next to light, they soar into the cavernous space, climbing in a wide arc before disappearing into the deep shadows of the distance.

"Wow. Did ye know he could do that?" Sloan asks, eyes wide.

My mind is fritzing out at the sight. "Nope. That was incredible."

Sloan nods. "Animal Transfiguration is common for druids but other than yer saber-toothed cat, I've never known anyone to shift into any form beyond normal earthly animals...and certainly nothing as big and powerful as a dragon."

"Do you think he can breathe fire?"

The two of us stall out on that one.

Amazeballs.

Saxa emerges as Cazzie and Merlin fly off. She is a sunshine yellow dragon with dark gold wings and a blunt snout of the same color. She's bigger than Dart but not as big as Cazzie or the Queen of Wyrms back home.

Before we get acquainted with her, a massive, purple dragon comes out of the cave opening as well. He scrambles behind Saxa, advancing with a strength and speed that makes the plateau shake beneath my sneakers.

When he overtakes Saxa and charges straight at us, Dart seems undaunted.

I pee a little.

Still, my protector gene kicks in, and I take a step closer to Dart in case he's underestimating the threat.

Be at peace, he says into my mind. *They are merely curious. They sense I am different...I come from a lineage they are not familiar with, and that sparks their interest.*

So. Many. Questions.

How does he know what they're thinking and feeling? What are free dragons? How do they sense the lineage of others? Is there a way to get in and out of Merlin's cave without riding a dragon through the sea?

"We come in peace," I say, so everyone's on the same page and there won't be any ill-informed munching on the strangers.

The purple dragon lowers his snout and takes a long, deep breath. "You smell wrong. What creek do you bathe in?"

I'm not sure if he's talking to Dart or me but I decide to answer anyway. "We're from a place far away. Bathing in creeks isn't a thing there. We have plumbing, and I hosed Dart down after our last bad-guy chomping battle, so I suppose we smell like Toronto municipal water."

He tilts his head to the side and chuffs. "Come, hatchling. Saxa will tend to your rider. There is much to learn from one another."

"Uh...maybe we should stick together." I reach to press a hand on Dart's wing, not liking the idea of being in a strange dragon cavern and separated from him.

The male dragon snorts smoke and rounds on me. "You face no danger from us, rider. Merlin told us to care for you and we shall. Even if we opted to disregard his request, what do you think you could do to fend off our will?"

I hear the amusement in his voice and straighten. "Please don't joke about hurting Dart and don't discount me as a threat. If you hurt my boy, I *will* come for you."

The purple dragon stretches his neck so the beast's snout is less than a foot from my chest. It would be the work of a moment to chomp me, but I hold my stance.

He draws a deep breath and eases back a bit.

Is he assessing my scent to test if I'm serious?

I am. I may be small but—

A huge gust of moist air hits me and knocks me back. I topple backward, landing hard on my ass before getting somersaulted against the rock wall.

Ew… gross.

Mucousy dragon snot covers me.

Dazed and dazzled, I sit up and hold out my hands. Long strings of glistening goo dangle off my fingertips. "That was rude."

The rumble of male laughter makes me even angrier. "Let this be your first lesson, dragon rider. I smell how young you are, so I shall offer you patience. There is a great difference between bravery and arrogance. If you fail to understand what you're up against, you shall likely end up dead and put your mount in danger."

I can't believe how gross I feel. Dragon snot is like being covered in rubber cement.

I'm one giant gooey glue glob.

I huff. "I wasn't arrogant."

"You were, and you failed to prove your threat."

"I wasn't ready." I fumble to get back to my feet. "That wasn't a true show of my skills."

"Of course not." He turns toward the edge of the plateau. "Come, hatchling. I won't invite you again."

Dart looks at me, and I can tell he's torn.

"Let him go, *a ghra.* It'll be good fer Dart to learn about dragon ancestry while we find ye somewhere to clean up. He is smart, and ye must start trustin' him to take care of himself."

I sigh, hearing the wisdom in Sloan's words. "Okay, fine. Go with the mucous monster but be alert and be careful. He may be a dragon, but he's still a stranger."

Dart moves in to swipe my cheek with his tongue like always

and stops before licking me. *You are disgusting at the moment...but I love you.*

He runs toward the edge of the plateau and dives off, super-sizing in mid-air and pumping his wings to catch up to the arrogant purple male.

"I love you too, buddy."

CHAPTER TWELVE

S axa couldn't be more apologetic for my current state of phlegm-covered grunge. "There is a bathing pool in Merlin's private chambers should you wish to clean up."

"Yes. I wish to. Very much."

Saxa glances down at me and smiles. "While it was amusing to see you challenge Utiss, he speaks the truth. If you think yourself a greater threat than you pose in reality, it endangers both you and your hatchling dragon."

"Got it. Lesson one delivered and received."

We arrive outside a dark opening, and she tilts her head as if finding me a curiosity. "There was another reason Utiss sullied you, though humankind often misses his subtlety."

Subtlety? I am head-to-toe dragon boog.

"It seems I did miss it, yes. From where I'm standing, it feels like snotting on me was meant to put me in my place for being protective of my dragon."

"No. Not at all."

"All right, so what was it also about?"

"You *do* smell odd and will be noticed as outsiders by the

captive dragons. Bathing in our waters will dilute the strangeness of you while you are here. Utiss was simply encouraging you to heed his warning and ensure your safety."

Sloan chuckles. "We shall certainly heed yer warning and bathe in yer waters, but I doubt anything will dilute the strangeness of Fiona."

"Har-har." I crinkle my nose at Sloan, him standing there all dry and stupidly handsome as ever. "Thank you, Saxa. We'll wash up and wait in here until Merlin gets back."

"That would be the wisest course, yes."

Saxa leaves us and heads back the way we came.

Sloan calls on faery fire and lights the way so he and I can step into and assess Merlin's private chamber.

The interior is simple enough.

There is a sleeping pallet on the floor covered in fur pelts, and a hearth dug into the stone floor next to it. For furniture, he has a couple of wooden chairs next to a round cafe table, an oversized armoire against the sheer stone wall, and five bookshelves brimming with texts and overflowing onto the floor in stacks of books.

"Well, I know what you'll be doing during our downtime."

Sloan pulls his gaze from the books and grins. "Can ye blame me? It's an opportunity to look through the private collection of books and texts belongin' to Merlin. When does a person get a chance like that?"

"When he's mysteriously sucked back in time during a voyage through an enchanted ring of druid stones?"

"Och, right. Then I best take advantage of it."

While I look around, he lights the three iron candle trees. A golden glow casts dancing shadows across the rough stone walls, reflecting off fragments of crystal or quartz or something equally shiny.

"This must be the bathing pool." I study the rocky crag in the floor. It's a puddle of water and spans about five feet wide and seven feet long. There doesn't seem to be any place that a trickle of water is feeding it so it must be filling from the sea outside the cavern somehow. "How cold do you think it is?"

Sloan pulls his shirt over his head and starts on the button of his pants. "I'm sure it's nothing we druids can't warm up to enjoy. Here, let me help ye."

He comes over and pauses, searching for a place to touch me or tug on my clothes or something. "Och, he got ye good."

"There's no helping it. I'm covered. I'll go in like this." I think about taking off my shoes to keep from sloshing in soakers the rest of the day but decide against it when I take stock of the craggy opening. "As is, then."

Not knowing exactly what to expect, I take a little jump and pencil dive feet first into the seawater. It's cold but not brutally so. The moment I bob back up so my head breaches the surface, I cast *Internal Warmth,* and all is well. "Come on in, hotness, the water's fine."

Standing on the bottom, the water splashes and ebbs up against my chest. Thankfully, dragon snot dissolves fairly well in seawater.

Sloan finishes stripping down and joins me.

I think I got the raw end on the need for the dip, but with Sloan naked and dipping with me, I got the better end of things on that front. "Hello, nakey man o' mine. Come here a minute."

Sloan chuckles, gripping my hips and holding me at a safe distance. "Ye've seen me naked enough to restrain yerself. Don't forget, we're in the private quarters of a friend of ours and expect him back at any time."

"Then I better hurry and take advantage of you while I can." I slide my hand under the water and waggle my brow. Sloan grips my wrist and shakes his head. He's over six feet tall and has ape arms, so there's not much I can do to coerce him.

When he doesn't relent, I give up and sigh. "Are you seriously not going to let me take advantage of you?"

"Seriously." He raises his hand and pushes to submerge me again. "Another dunk. You've still got dragon snot in your hair."

I let him dunk me if it means getting Utiss mucous out of my hair. Under the water, I rake my fingers through from my scalp to the end of my lengths, shaking it out, trying to dislodge all further grossness.

When I come up this time, I watch Sloan and wait. "Did I get it all?"

He grins. "Ye got it all the first time. I was just messin' with ye."

"Rude." I thrust my hands across the surface and send a spray of water that catches him in the face.

"Och, game on, Cumhaill."

I yelp as he lunges at me, and the two of us devolve into a frenzy of slip and slide grabs and wild splashing and dunking and laughing. It takes a solid five minutes before we're both choking on water and breathless.

"Do ye concede, female?" He holds me in a headlock.

"Never," I choke, seawater stinging my nose.

"Then I must take pity on ye and be the bigger man here." He lets me up.

"News flash, Mackenzie, you're the *only* man here."

Movement in the shadowed corner inside the door brings a stranger into our midst. "Technically not the *only* man."

Sloan straightens and raises his hands out of the water, readying to defend. "Who's there? Come out where we can see ye."

The man steps forward and a shiver runs the length of my spine. He's not an overly tall or burly man, but he gives off an eerie aura.

He's no friend of ours.

I don't know how I'm so sure, but I am. My shield tingles

awake to confirm it. "Why are you here? These are Merlin's private quarters."

"I realize that," he says. "I also realize that he's not due back from East Anglia for another week. So, imagine my surprise when three dragon guards returned from a breach of Tintagel air and reported Merlin's early return. And then, even more surprising is the revelation that he brought his niece to court."

"Why is it any business of yours?"

"Because I've known the man since I was a squire in the stables and Merlin has no family in the world beyond this lair. The only living beings he cares about and has ever cared about are dragons."

Bestial Strength. I bend my knees and push up and out of the water. Like a dolphin at a waterpark show, I somersault in the air and land on the stone floor of the cave between our peeping tom skeptic and my naked boyfriend.

The intruder holds up his hands as if readying for an attack, but if it doesn't have to come to that, I'd rather it didn't. I already pissed off Pelleas and Sigberht. I don't need anyone else as a foe.

"Thanks for stopping by, but you don't know my family or me. By the sound of it, you don't know my uncle very well either."

Bending to the pallet of furs on the floor, I scoop Sloan's clothes and toss them behind me.

The man's gaze narrows on me. My wet clothes have suctioned to my body, giving him too much insight into what is going on beneath the fabric.

He rakes me with a lascivious grin. "I make it my business to know the powerful players in this life—that includes Merlin—but something tells me I should pay attention to you as well. Pelleas says you are a druid sorceress. Maybe we should share a meal and you can tell me more about yourself."

Ew, no. "I'm only here for a visit and then heading home as soon as our business is concluded. I'm afraid I won't have time to start up new acquaintances."

The air in the cave is cool and I'm not the only one who notices my nipples poking out from beneath the fabric of my shirt.

I cross my arms over my chest. "Enough about me. Who are you? Does my uncle know you skulk around in the shadows down here when he's not around?"

The man's gaze narrows. "Merlin, you mean? The man who is definitely *not* your uncle."

"What makes you so sure?"

"How could you be his niece? His sister died centuries ago."

Oh, well, there's that.

He studies me and my shield tingles against my back. "Do you even know her name?"

Sloan finishes getting dressed behind me and joins the conversation. "Born in 541, under the given name Myrddin Wyllt, Merlin had a twin sister Gwendydd whom he loved dearly. Fiona is a descendant of her, and therefore, his niece, though granted many generations removed."

The man frowns. "A servant boy with a silky serpent's tongue."

I frown. "Sloan is not my servant. He's my…"

"Husband," Sloan snaps. "I was hired on as her tutor last year, and we wed soon after. I'd very much appreciate ye not lookin' at my wife like she's a horse to be mounted."

I nod and hold up my ring finger to show him my lovely Claddagh band. "That's right. Yes, he has a silky voice and lovely diction. Can't you tell how educated he is?"

Sloan rolls his eyes. "Ye have no business harassin' Lady Fiona, sir. I think it's best ye take yer leave."

The man scowls. "If Merlin had blood kin all this time, why wouldn't he mention anyone over a drink or a game of bones? In all the years I've known the man, he never once mentioned a niece or anyone else."

Sloan shrugs. "I'm not surprised he doesn't speak of Gwendydd or her heirs freely. Upon her passing, the man grew dark in his daily dealings, eventually retreating to live as a prophet and recluse in the forests of Tweeddale. He did everything he could to cut himself off from his family and any memory of his twin."

"But we reconnected," I say, "and he has spent the better part of the past year fighting his way back to becoming part of my family. We have a great deal in common, he and I. He's taught me so much."

The man arches a brow and smiles. "Yes. A fellow druid, I hear."

"I am."

"How long have you been practicing?"

"Almost a year. Merlin has been a mentor from the beginning days. I'm quite a natural if I do say so."

His eyes glint, and he grips the sword at his hip. Pulling the hilt, he slowly unsheathes his weapon. "And if I chose to test your proficiency and challenge you?"

I activate my armor and call Birga to my palm. Spinning my staff in my hands, I give the man a little show of what's in store. "You'd be wise to sheath that sword and take your leave, sir. If you give me your name, I'll tell my uncle you visited."

"You might well tell the man you arrived with, but I am certain it isn't Merlin. I would make a bet on it."

"You would lose that bet, Wolfric." Merlin strides in from the corridor, his gait stronger and more confident than I've ever seen. Shoulders back, he joins us, his hand resting on the hilt of a sword he wasn't wearing when he left.

Wolfric studies the man before him and frowns. "How is it you return from East Anglia before the herald or any other men arrive?"

"I flew upon Fiona's dragon. If you are here, I assume it's because Pelleas has been spewing off in the tavern. Surely he and Sigberht mentioned our arrival upon a blue winged beast and how my ill-mannered niece almost knocked him off his dragon when he advanced on us."

"They mentioned your arrival but nothing of your niece facing off against them."

"Then you have the answers you sought. Good day, Wolfric."

The man's grin widens, his teeth showing. "I don't believe for a second you are Merlin or that she is your niece."

Merlin drops his chin. "I tire of this. Stop pestering us with your nonsense and get out of my cave. Can you not see the girl is soaked to the bone and shivering?"

He throws his hand toward a stone hearth near the pallet, and a fire ignites. "Shuck off your riding clothes and warm yourself. Sloan, you'll find tunics and trousers in my cupboard for Fi to wear while her clothes dry. I'll escort our unwanted guest out and return your privacy."

I nod. "Thank you, Uncle. I appreciate that."

After Merlin leaves with Wolfric, I tug and pull at the wet clothes suctioned to my skin. When I finally get everything off, Sloan wraps one of the furs from the sleeping pallet around me and pulls me into his lap in front of the fire. "There now, luv. Call *Inner Warmth* and let's try to make it so yer lips aren't so blue."

"Are you saying blue's not my color?"

"Blue lips are definitely not yer color."

I hear the undercurrent of annoyance in his comment and realize he's referring to last week when Galina Romanov—daughter of one of the most powerful crime families in the eastern bloc—kissed me with her blue vampire blood-lust lipstick. Xavier was helpless to resist attacking me. "What doesn't kill you makes you stronger, right?"

He brushes the edge of the fur pelt down my neck and scowls at the scars where Xavier's fangs punctured and tore my flesh. "If ye hadn't had yer armor engaged, he would've killed ye for certain."

I shiver, but not because I'm still cold.

"But I did, and he didn't, and I'd rather not dwell on that if you don't mind a blatant change of subject."

"Fine by me. What shall we talk about?"

"I was thinking about what time we're in. If Dora is almost fifteen hundred years old and hadn't seen her dragon since she lived as Merlin almost twelve hundred years ago, that means she was three hundred the last time she saw Cazzie. Since Merlin was born in 540 CE, that places us sometime in the mid to late 800s, doesn't it?"

"That sounds about right."

I free an arm from the warmth of furs and flip my shirt over so the back will dry too. "What is the world like in ninth-century England?"

He thinks about that for a moment and tucks my arm back inside my fur blankey and snuggles me in. "For the most part, it's a time of invasions and raids. The Saxons are invading what will be Wales. The Vikings are raiding their way down the coast led by Ivar the Boneless."

"Ragnar's son? Oh, he's creepy."

He leans around my shoulder, his brow arched. "You know the history of the Danish Vikings?"

"I watched all seven seasons of *Vikings* and am waiting for the fifth season of the *Last Kingdom*. Yeah, I know things. Destiny is all," I say in my best Dane voice.

"Ye say that like it means something."

"It does. That's Uhtred son of Uhtred's tag line. He has this really cute accent and always says that at the most poignant moments. Destiny is all."

Sloan's chest bounces against my back as he chuckles. "Ye realize those are television programs, right?"

"Based on true events."

He kisses my cheek and slides out from underneath me. "I'll give ye that much."

As he heads across the cave to check out what's in Merlin's armoire, I lean forward toward the flames and finger comb through my hair. "I'm hungry. Any chance this is a time when men ate those big drumsticks and drank tankards of mead?"

Sloan chuckles, opening the double doors to the large, wooden wardrobe. "I don't think there was ever a true era of drumsticks and mead, luv, but yes, I'm sure there's a good chance ye might find it on the menu."

"Excellent." I test my bra and underwear to see if they are dry, and thankfully, they are. Shucking off the furs, I get myself covered up.

"Yikes, my gitch is on fire."

Sloan looks over, alarm plain on his face.

I snort and wave that away. "Sorry, not literally, but they're hot against my girly bits."

"Well, don't singe yer girly bits. Neither of us will like that."

"True story." I finish pulling on my underthings and reclaim the fur pelt to tighten around my shoulders as I walk over to join him. The floor is rough and jabs at the tender flesh on the under-side of my bare feet.

When I round the door to the armoire, I assess what Merlin has for me to wear. "The man is as tall as an ancient oak."

Sloan nods. "I don't think any of the trousers will stay up on ye. I'm thinking ye wear one of his simple tunics as a dress until yer clothes are dry."

I finger through the selections hanging and go with a simple brown one. "I don't see much of a choice…unless I stay wrapped in this fur for the next few hours."

Sloan winks. "As much as havin' ye naked and wrapped in fur appeals to me, I don't think it's prudent given the company in the dragon lair at the moment. Besides, ye can't go to the tavern fer a drumstick and mead wearin' only a pelt of fur."

"Good point. Tunic it is."

CHAPTER THIRTEEN

Once I'm satisfied that I'm dressed appropriately and can pass as a woman in the ninth century, I force myself to put my soggy sneakers back on, and Sloan and I strike off, looking for Merlin.

Thankfully, it's not that difficult to locate him because he's shouting mad and we're able to follow his angry rant through the cavernous maze of passageways that make up the dragon lair.

We find him pacing back and forth in front of his beautiful champagne-colored dragon, and as he shouts and gesticulates, her head slowly pivots to watch him.

She doesn't seem the least bit concerned.

If anything, she seems to find it endearing.

"Emrys, my heart, if you wish to save face in front of your friends and not have them regard you as a madman, I suggest you end your tirade."

Merlin glances at us as we enter and rolls his eyes. "My apologies. That bastard, Wolfric, never should've been down here. Everyone knows this is *my* space. No one is welcome without my express permission. I am sorry he bothered you."

"No bother," I say. "As long as you're not bothered I seriously considered running him through with Birga."

"Next time, go with the impulse. It will teach the next member of the guard that there are consequences for intruding into my life. Despite what they might think, I do not fall under the purview of their governing. I answer to the king directly as I did the king before him, and even then, I'm a free agent."

Wow. This is Merlin fired up. "All righty then. Spear first ask questions later. Got it."

Cazzie makes a sound much like a clucking of a tongue and grins at us. "Emrys tells me you've come a long way. I am pleased to have you as my guests."

I sober and bow my head. "We are pleased to be here and to meet you, Empress. May I say, you are truly the most resplendent dragon I have ever seen."

She chuckles. "Oh, sweet child. Of course, you may say so. No female of sound mind would object to such flattery. Now, let us arrange a meal for you and Emrys will explain why he believes you are here."

My stomach growls in response, and I set a hand over my belly. "Eating sounds wonderful."

"Saxa mentioned that Utiss and Bryvanay took your hatchling out on a hunt. Shall we go out to the plateau and see what prey they bring?"

"Sounds good." Swiss Chalet take-out sounds better, but when in ancient Tintagel...

Cazzie pushes up from lounging in her mossy nest and straightens onto all fours. She's easily forty feet tall and muscled like a tank, but somehow the first adjective that comes to mind is feminine.

She steps across the stone floor, and the glimmer of gold and silver treasures she was screening in the background strikes me.

She catches my gaze and tilts her head toward the pile of loot. "I ask that you not touch my treasures, child. Each item has a significant meaning to me, and I'm afraid I won't take kindly to you taking liberties."

"We wouldn't dream of it, milady." Sloan lowers his chin.

"You don't need to worry," I say. "The Dragon Queen of Wyrms guards a similar stash, and I've seen what happened to people who took liberties, as you say."

Images come to mind of the crunched and crushed dead bodies I waded through the first time I found myself in the dragon lair.

"Is your queen's collection more impressive than mine? Surely not."

I hear the edge in her voice and shake my head. "Oh, no, Empress. She merely guards the treasure for her Man o' Green companion. I don't know if any of it belongs to her. Your collection is inspiring."

She glances back at it and smiles. "Yes. It truly is."

Merlin winks at me and smiles. "Come, Cazzie. Let's go see what's for supper."

The four of us roam the dark, stone passageways and Merlin fills us in on what he's figured out so far. "This is the autumn of 865, and my self of this time traveled to Wessex upon hearing the news of the death of King Aethelberht. A few weeks ago, I would've attended the coronation of his son Aethelred, and soon after, we got news of the Great Heathen Army bearing down on East Anglia."

"And ye went to lend aid?" Sloan asks.

"I did. It was a horrid, bloody battle, as most are, but the Vikings fought with crazed violence rarely seen. Most Viking raids of the time were about pillage and plunder. This was about conquering the land."

"Ivor the Boneless." I make a face. "He was awful. His mother should've listened to the seer's warning and never allowed Ragnor into her bed that month."

"Television program." Sloan frowns at me before turning back to Merlin. "How do ye think we ended up here and why?"

"I suppose I'm to blame for that," Cazzie says. "Not the me of now, but the me of your time."

I hold up a finger. "The you of our time? What does that mean?"

Merlin offers me an apologetic smile. "I haven't been forthcoming with the personal details of my life, and I apologize because now it has affected you. When I return from East Anglia next week, I will find—or at least I did find—Cazzie and the others dead. I never knew what happened. I simply found the four of them down here in the dark."

I swallow, letting that sink in. "So, is that why we're here? Are we supposed to stop the slaughter?"

Merlin shrugs. "I haven't figured out what we're supposed to do yet, but I promise you, I won't lose Cazzie this time."

Sloan draws a deep breath and exhales. "Altering the timeline has consequences, sham. Ye know that."

"I know. We have time to think about that. For now, I'm happy to be back here to make this right."

I hold up my hand. "You said Cazzie died, so how could she bring us back here?"

Merlin grins. "When I found her and the others lifeless in our home, I did the only thing I could think of to keep from losing everything. I used the union bond between us to extract Cazzie's spirit to join us as one."

"Kind of like me holding Brendan's spark," I say.

He tilts his head from side to side. "Similar, yes, but your brother remained dead, and the spark you embody is an essence meant for him. I have literally had Cazzie living within me."

"Like a symbiotic host," Sloan says.

"Exactly," Merlin says. "For almost twelve hundred years, we lived as one."

My mind trips on that.

I can only imagine how it would change me to have Brendan

actively sharing my body and mind. I would be ten times crazier, more daring, hilarious—

"Oh, my." My mind spins out as I truly take in Merlin for the first time since we got back. "Cazzie is your inner goddess... the glam... the sparkle... she's your Empress-ness."

Merlin nods. "To a large extent that's true, but I think after all these centuries, part of me loves those things too."

"Who are we kidding? You rock it on stage in spandex and sequins."

"Yes, I do." He nods, lost in thought for a moment before his smile falls. "As disturbing as it feels to be alone in my body, I won't allow history to repeat itself."

"So, how do we stop it? Did she tell you what happened? Could you tell from the scene?"

"No. The four of them were whole and looked healthy and peaceful...but they were dead."

"That suggests maybe magic or poison," Sloan says.

"Cazzie said the last thing she remembered was going to sleep one night, and she never woke up."

"That, at the very least, isn't so horrible," I say.

"Except for her being dead."

I wave away his scowl. "You know what I mean."

"Yes, he does," Cazzie says. "And yes, I would much rather that than violent bloodshed or painful torture. It is, however, unfortunate that I was unable to tell him anything more that might help us this time."

"But you think it was Cazzie's intention within you that brought us back here to fix things," I ask.

"I do."

Sloan crosses his arms and leans back. "She's not with ye now?"

He shakes his head. "The moment we passed through the circle of stones in the forest, she was gone. It was horribly disturbing at first, but when I laid eyes on Cazzie alive and well, I started to piece it together."

I follow his gaze as it lands on Cazzie. It's lovely that he gets this chance to reunite with her again. "Okay, well, at least now we know the how and why and when. All we need to figure out now is the what. What do we need to do so it doesn't happen the same way again?"

Sloan frowns. "What do we do to ensure that when we change things, the timeline doesn't get skewed so badly it changes everything?"

I shrug. "Right. Easy peasy."

The four of us make our way back to the plateau and look out across the darkness of the cavern. Now that we've been down here a few hours and my eyes have adjusted, it's not as dark as I thought it was at first.

"Here they come," Cazzie says, her gaze fixed on the darkness off to our left.

I squint to see, but all I've got is a black void and shadow. It takes a long while before I see the movement of what I assume are dragons in flight.

"It looks like lamb or venison for dinner for the three of you," she says, swishing her tail.

Dart arrives a few moments later with the massive purple dragon and a slightly smaller black one. All three of them carry a dead animal in their mouths. Utiss and Bryvanay each have deer and Dart has a dead sheep.

My blue boy looks as proud and happy as I've ever seen him. When he sizes down, he leans forward and flops his kill at my feet. *We went hunting across the countryside, and I caught your dinner.*

I feel a bit like I did when the neighbor's cat used to sit at the sliding glass door and leave me dead moles and mice. Only the dragon catch of the day is a lot bigger.

"Thank you—each of you. This is so thoughtful."

Merlin assesses the kills and seems pleased. "Come. We'll take the sheep up to the kitchen, and I'll send one of the staff down to butcher the deer."

"The kitchen staff?" I repeat. "You have kitchen staff in your dragon lair?"

He looks at me and chuckles. "No, girlfriend, but the lair is below Tintagel Castle. We'll go up, get you something appropriate to wear, and make our contributions to dinner."

"Awesome." I scrub Dart's horn and lean closer to pat his scaly jaw. "Are you good down here with the dragons, buddy?"

He nods. *Yes. Saxa said she will teach me to blow smoke rings.*

"Nice. Well, you two have fun, and we'll check in later. Be good and call for me if you need me."

Merlin grabs the sheep's front legs in one hand and the back legs in the other and swings it up and over his head to rest on his shoulders. When he straightens, he looks brawny and masculine, and I'm having trouble recognizing the Dora in him.

Where is his flashy, flaunty feminine side now?

Was it only Cazzie's presence that gave him glitz?

I guess time will tell.

"Be safe." He casts Cazzie a poignant glance. "We'll be back by dark. If you need us or if anything unsettling should happen before then, call for us and Sloan can portal us back in a flash."

Cazzie tilts her head to the side. "Go show your friends the castle, darling. From what you said, we have days before the plot to harm us unfolds. We shall figure out who's behind it long before then."

He nods. "Without a doubt."

There's a moment of quiet when their gazes lock, and they seem to have a private conversation. It's lovely to see how much the two of them love one another. It's a connection beyond the bond of dragon and rider.

They are *in* love.

"I'm glad we're here for you," I say as we follow Merlin through the lair to an iron gate that blocks a set of ascending stairs. "We'll figure out what went wrong the first time and make things right."

Merlin passes a hand over the gate lock and Sloan swings the door open so we can access the stairs. "About Cazzie and me," Merlin says. "I know what you two must be thinking. Perhaps I should explain."

Sloan shakes his head. "We think the two of ye share a wonderful love, and we're happy to help right a wrong that left ye at odds fer much too long. That's all. Yer a dear friend, and we know ye suffered things over a long life. If Cazzie is the one to soothe those wounds and bring ye joy, blessed be."

Merlin stops climbing at the next landing and twists to look at me. "Is that how you feel, Fi?"

"Of course. She's spectacular and sassy and sweet. You love who you love. End. Of. What's important is figuring out who wants to kill her and how to stop it."

"The other option is to leave the timeline and simply take her home," Sloan says.

Merlin shakes his head. "I thought of that, but losing her and having her essence within me influences who I am and how I interact with the world for the centuries to come. How many lives did I touch? How many kings and state leaders did I advise? How many things would I do differently if I hadn't had her within me? That's too big a change to the timeline. No matter how much I want her to come with us, I can't allow that."

"Wow, that's a tough call."

Merlin hikes the sheep higher on his shoulders and lifts his chin. "We'll think of something. Let's not worry too much about it yet."

I hear the tightness in his voice, and my heart aches for him. He may not *want* to worry about it yet, but it's obvious he is.

"We'll figure it out."

Wandering through the Castle of Carlisle during my time with Fionn stands out as one of the most magical moments of my life. It was a short stay, but how can you be back in Arthurian times and not have your mind blown?

Today is even more special.

It's the same mind-blowing experience of architecture, culture, and customs, but this time I get to share it with Sloan.

"Are you super stoked?" I link my arm with his and fall into step...which is tough because he has such long legs that his strides are way longer than mine. "Do you know anything about Tintagel Castle, hotness?"

"Of course. It's the birthplace of Arthur and where a young Morgana was brought and raised as Uther's ward. It's considered to be one of the most iconic castles of the Arthurian era."

"Huh...I didn't know that." I'm not sure what the two of them hear in my voice, but they both stop climbing and look at me.

"Are you all right, girlfriend?" Merlin asks.

I consider that and try to answer him honestly. "I hadn't connected this place to Morgana. Knowing this is where she lived for a large part of her life burped up some bad memories."

Merlin was there when I stopped Morgana's escape from her banishment, and both he and Sloan were there while I fought the possession of Morgana's dark grimoire. They know how hard it was on me, so nothing more needs to be said about that.

Merlin offers me a sympathetic smile. "Morgan le Fey wasn't always the maniacal dark sorceress you encountered through her spellbook. There were many years when she stood as a strong supporter of Uther, Arthur, and the kingdom's people. She was a beloved part of the royal hierarchy in the early days."

"You knew her well, way back when?"

Merlin nods. "I did. Morgana and I had a colorful history before she chose the power of dark magic and was banished. There was a time when I thought we might end up married and ruling together. Things didn't work out that way."

No. I guess not. When you lose your hold and go full dark, things tend to get tainted.

Merlin looks off as if seeing this castle in another era filled with memories. "Tintagel was one of her favorite places and the place she settled when she returned after many years studying abroad. I don't think any of us understood how powerful a sorceress she had become...or perhaps we were simply too blind to see it."

Sloan shrugs. "When someone returns after a long separation, they're bound to be changed. It's easy to understand how ye missed it."

Merlin bounces on the balls of his feet, hiking the sheep up higher on his shoulders. "She seemed to be the same passionate leader she had always been. She came of age to claim her family money while she was away. Then, upon her return, she got straight to work funding the repairs to overhaul the castle to bring it back to its former glory. Then, when the work finished and the castle was like new once more, she invited knights and squires to attend her here in the first of her grand tournaments."

We crest the last of the stairs, and he points at an oil painting hanging at the end of the hall. It depicts Lady Morgana standing in an oxblood leather coat with a fine chain mail tunic and a gold crown topping her long chestnut hair.

She's perched in the royal box of an auditorium addressing two-dozen knights in armor standing before her on horseback.

"She was a beautiful woman," Sloan says.

Merlin's mouth quirks up in an uneven smile. "She was.

Unfortunately, power can make even the most beautiful people ugly in the end."

The stairs to the dragon lair ended in the back room of a small chapel, and we make our way past the ten wooden pews outside to a courtyard. People are bustling around, men leading horses into the stables, little girls feeding the chickens running loose, and fishermen bringing in their catches.

Sloan takes it all in, and the sheer wonder on his face makes me smile.

"What are you most excited to see, hotness?"

"Och, everything: the architecture, the culture, the clothing, the castle workings, the battlements...all of it."

"First, we eat," Merlin says. "Then I'll give you the tour so you know your way around, and the two of you can explore."

We follow him through a set of double doors, past a couple of simple tables, and into the kitchen. From the pinched frowns being thrown our way from four or five workers, I take it people other than the castle staff don't usually access the kitchen, but when they see we're with Merlin, they go back to their business.

Merlin heads straight back to a long, wooden table and unburdens himself of the sheep. When he straightens, he flags over a guy about my age with a blond, bowl-cut hairdo.

"Cenric, we bring you a sheep to be butchered, and the dragons brought in two deer as well. Have Eastmund and Hama butcher them on the plateau and leave the limbs and entrails for the dragons."

"Yes, sire." Cenric bows his head.

"Also, we are ravenous from our travels. What did Ms. Marigold prepare for the end-of-day repast?"

"Barley browis with applesauce."

"Lovely. Is there any left for those of us who missed the dinner bell?"

"What's the rule, moppet?" A rotund woman with a missing tooth waddles in a side door with a fistful of carrots dangling from their greens. "If ya miss the meal, ya do without until the next sitting. I'm not runnin' an inn."

Merlin offers the woman a flirtatious smile. "Marigold, my dearest lady. I would never take your time and hospitality as a given. I only hoped that my niece and her husband could get a taste of your fine cooking after a long journey."

She sets the carrots down and whacks his arm with a wooden spoon. "If ya think the flirtin' will get ya fed, think again, Merlin. I'm immune to your sorcery."

He laughs, and the sound is a burst of easy joy.

My stomach takes that moment to growl, and I press my hand over my belly. "Sorry. It's been quite a day."

For the first time, the roly-poly woman looks me up and down. "By the saint's grace, deary. What are ya wearin'?"

I look down at the tunic I put on from Merlin's armoire. "One of the dragons and I had words, and my travel clothes didn't fare well. I'm afraid it left me with no choice but to wear my uncle's tunic."

"Uncle, ya say?"

"Oh, pardon me," Merlin says. "Miss Marigold, this is my great-niece, Fiona, and her husband, Mr. Sloan Mackenzie."

"It's a pleasure to meet ye, milady," Sloan says, dropping his chin.

She looks Sloan over as if weighing in on him. "I'll have ya know, I've never allowed a man of your kind into my kitchen before, Mr. Mackenzie. But since yer kin to Merlin, I'll make an exception."

I stiffen. "His kind?"

Sloan holds up his hand to stop me from losing my shit and calmly smiles at her. "Did ye know six percent of the Knights of Arthur's Court were men of color?"

She frowns. "Color? I meant ya bein' a Gael and all. The color of your skin is of no consequence. Why would I care about that?"

I manage to hide my smile behind my hand as I rub my mouth. "Well, he's quite a civilized Gael, I swear."

Sloan arches a brow at me, and I chuckle.

She notices the platinum band on my ring finger and then finds the matching band on Sloan's. "Domesticated him, have ya?"

"I'm trying. He's a handful though."

Merlin laughs. "Please. *You* are the handful."

I grin up at Ms. Marigold. "That is true."

Ms. Marigold chuckles. "It's good to keep the men on their toes. So, it's not a man ya came for then. Are ya here for the tournament?"

"Oh, right, one of the dragon guards mentioned it earlier. He said a lot of strangers have been arriving."

She nods. "Lady Morgana's Champion competition is scheduled to begin tomorrow to celebrate the life of one king and the future of another. Tintagel Castle has hosted such events for centuries. I'm sure your uncle has told you all about it."

"In fact," Merlin says, "I have not. I confess with everything that's been going on, I forgot. A champions tournament is rather low on the list of topics of concern at the moment."

She clucks her tongue. "Forgot? Dear me, your journey took more out of ya than I thought."

"In his defense," I say, "our arrival here was a rather unexpected detour from our original plans."

She casts Merlin a pinch-faced look. "That sounds about right. He needs to settle down, your uncle, find himself a fine woman, and not be jaunting off across the countryside. The man is a rapscallion to the bone."

I think about Dionysus and how much he would have enjoyed her use of the word. "As unexpected as our arrival has been, we're here now and looking forward to spending a few days learning about the workings of things here at Tintagel."

"A tournament sounds quite exciting," Sloan says. "I expect the travelers and strangers hail from all over the countryside. Will they stay within the castle walls?"

"Most make camp on the mainland. There is a field of tents set up for the men so they can remain close to their dragons. Of course, some champions stay in the guest housing." Something about that brings her back to scowling at me. "That tunic is quite dreadful."

I shrug. "It was the best we could do in the lair at a moment's notice."

"It was Utiss who crossed ya, I'm guessing."

I chuckle. "I don't think he likes me much."

"That old beast doesn't like much of anything." She frowns down at me. "When will the wagon with your chests of belongings arrive?"

I look at Merlin for help with that and thankfully, he snaps out of his reverie. "We came upon her dragon, with only the clothes she wore. I'm afraid Utiss fouled them quite spectacularly, and they are currently hanging to dry, freshly laundered in the lair."

Marigold grunts and gives him a look. "Men. They don't think beyond their bellies and their pricks."

Merlin laughs. "How have I become the whipping boy of this conversation? I brought you fresh lamb and venison."

She clucks her tongue again and looks around the busy room. "Sunni, nip down to the laundry and see if Miss Maxene has something decent milady can wear."

The blonde waif bows and rushes off.

My stomach growls again, and Ms. Marigold reaches around my shoulder and turns me toward a side door. "Come, Lady Fiona. Let's get you fed and dressed. It won't do to have ya lookin' like something the dragon dragged in."

I chuckle. "No. I suppose not."

CHAPTER FOURTEEN

After our stomachs are full, Sunni takes me to a private room and helps me into a long, mint green dress. It covers my feet, drags on the floor, and the cuffs of the sleeves hang nearly to the floor as well. It takes me a moment to figure out how to secure the gold belt. Then she helps me with the gold and burgundy cloak that finishes off my layering.

"Ye look lovely, *a ghra,*" Sloan says when I return. "The picture of a true English lady."

I laugh. "Focus the lens of your camera, Mackenzie. You can stick me in a dress, but there's no need to insult me by mistaking me for a lady."

When the two of us got dressed back in Merlin's cave, Sloan kept his olive green khakis from home and topped them with a navy and black tunic of Merlin's. Belted, it hangs to his mid-thighs and makes him look every bit the part of a Middle Ages man of means.

"Was that true, what you said to Marigold about there being black knights?" I ask him.

Sloan nods. "Six percent...which, in truth was one out of the forty-nine men, but it sounds more impressive."

Merlin nods. "Yes, Sir Morien was black. An interesting man. He was reserved and kept to himself for the most part but fought valiantly. It's smart that the two of you pose as a married couple. That should keep the wolves from our door. These tournaments become breeding grounds for finding a matrimonial match."

I slide my fingers into the crease of Sloan's elbow and smile. "I'm happily married to my tutor, thanks."

Merlin grins. "Between the languages Sloan speaks and the fighting methods he knows and his breadth of knowledge on pretty much any topic, even if someone challenges you on a black man being the tutor of an English lady, Sloan can sell the lie."

"True story."

When we have our story straight, the three of us stroll the corridors of the castle. Merlin points out things he thinks might interest us and Sloan absorbs it with a smile of true wonderment. The castle is laid out in a square with buildings set together along the exterior stone wall and an open courtyard in the middle.

We begin the tour by taking a right as we exit the kitchen and Merlin points out the armed guard standing on the step of the next building over. "The weapons keep here is quite impressive. With the tournament upon us, there will certainly be a guard on that door until the champion is named and people begin to return home. Next to that, the guest housing."

We pause at the bottom of the steps outside the guest rooms, and he frowns. "I told Ms. Marigold the two of you were staying down in the lair with me, but she wouldn't hear of it. She sent Sunnifa to make arrangements for you to stay in the castle proper."

I make a face. "I'm fine on a pallet of furs near the dragons."

He nods. "I knew you would be, but after thinking about it, I accepted on your behalf for two reasons. First, it's better not to start a scandal about being a lady and living down with the dragons, especially after run-ins with Pelleas, Sigberght, and Wolfric. Second, if you're up here and mingling with the people of the castle, you might pick up on who's plotting to harm the dragons."

I understand what he's saying, but it doesn't make me any keener. "I don't like the idea of being so far from Dart in a strange place."

He nods. "Remember what I said the other day...he is not your baby boy. He is a mythical creature with the knowledge and wisdom of the ages. I will be down there with him and won't let anything happen."

Sloan watches me consider that and shrugs. "It's not a bad plan, *a ghra*. If we figure out who has designs on harmin' the dragons, we not only save them, we are free to go home."

"If someone wants to kill the dragons, *my* dragon is down there without me."

"Only during the sleeping hours," Merlin says. "Nothing says you can't spend your days in the lair with your beloved uncle."

I hear what he's saying, and despite not being a fan of leaving Dart down there without me, I concede. "Fine, but not only am I holding you responsible for Dart's safety, but also for what Utiss and the other dragons teach him. I have a feeling Utiss will fill his head with bad habits and a bad attitude."

Merlin frowns. "Utiss is old and set in his ways, but he is also brave and loyal and a leader to his kind. Anything he teaches Dartamont, whether you agree or not, will be in the best interest of Dartamont's development."

I wholeheartedly disagree. "Is this a pep talk because if it is, it sucks. I don't feel any better."

Merlin shrugs. "Not a pep talk. We'll call it straight talk. Now, shall we continue with the tour or do you want to go in and claim your rooms?"

Sloan's brow tightens at the mention of ending the tour early, but the poor guy says nothing, leaving it to me to decide.

"Definitely the tour." I wink at my guy. "We'll claim our rooms later once we've seen everything there is to see."

Merlin sweeps his hand through the air, and we strike off again. "Next, we have the eastern hall…"

After we finish the tour, Merlin goes back down to the lair, and Sloan and I wander. We end up on the raised platform looking out over the sea. Perched up here, we have an unobstructed view of the span of open water, the rocky cliffs below, and the rolling green landscape beyond the jut of land the castle sits upon.

The wind catches the skirt of my dress and sends it streaming behind me in loud flaps of fabric. I pull a strand of hair from my face and let the wind take that too. "How beautiful is this?"

"Breathtaking." Sloan smiles when I catch him looking at me, not the view.

I roll my eyes and point at the white water crashing against the cliffs far below. "The birthplace of King Arthur. That's beyond cool."

Sloan nods. "It is. The castle is weathering well considering it's almost five hundred years old."

"You'd know better than me about weathering castles. I'm a Canadian. We have no sense of history or buildings with architectural character. You're the champion of damp and decay."

"Do ye think ye'll ever let me live that down?"

"Don't count on it. The Sloan Mackenzie I had to put up with during those first days and weeks was an arrogant snood."

"And Fiona Cumhaill of those first days and weeks was a stubborn, clueless annoyance."

"Says you."

He chuckles and wraps his arm around my shoulder, pulling me against his chest. "Aye, says me."

"It's funny now, but boy, did you rile me up then."

His smile softens. "Ye knocked my world on its ear from the start, *a ghra*. I couldn't fathom how anyone so guileless and ill-prepared fer druid life could storm into every situation with her fists up and ready to fight. I thought ye were a lunatic."

"Nope. Just a child of Niall Cumhaill."

We stand out on the viewing deck for a while longer and catch sight of four dragons exiting the sea cave below. Dart and Saxa and Merlin in dragon form and Cazzie have taken to the air, their silhouettes dark against the brilliance of the coming sunset.

"How could anyone plot to destroy dragons?" I ask.

Sloan shakes his head. "I have no idea. It will be my greatest pleasure to foil the plot of whoever thinks to do them harm."

"Mine too. We have to figure out how to save them and yet keep Merlin's timeline on course."

"I am working on a few ideas. Let me think on it for a bit longer."

I squeeze his hand. "You do you, hotness. I have faith in your mental mastery."

We turn to leave the barbican platform and my shield tingles to life.

Sloan senses my snap to alertness and stiffens beside me. "What is it?"

"My shield is waking up. Nothing to panic over, but there's something."

He lifts his gaze, and from the top of the stairs of the viewing platform, scans the activity of the castle grounds below. Merlin said there are about a hundred people who live and work within the walls of Tintagel. Another hundred or so, like fishermen, hunters, and their families, live outside the castle walls on the other side of the small causeway that leads back to the mainland.

With the tournament starting tomorrow, there are another hundred visitors at least.

"Do you see anything that sparks your instincts?" I ask him.

"No, but it's yer instincts that play a bigger part in sussing out trouble."

"Or manifesting it."

He chuffs. "A fine distinction where yer involved."

"True story."

Instead of descending the stairs to the inner court as intended, we continue on the high side of things and make our way to the platform Merlin pointed out as the constable's outer chamber.

From there, we duck through the inner chamber and come out on the roof of the chapel.

I scan the scene below.

Nothing alarms me or triggers my shield.

"Got it," Sloan says, turning his back to the courtyard to smile at me. "In the shadows of the drawbridge gate. I think we've drawn the attention of our Peepin' Tom again. It seems he's gathered a few friends."

I release my hold on my fae vision and stare across the castle grounds to find Wolfric and a couple of other men staring at us from the shadows. "Their auras are all kinds of tainted and hostile."

"I'm not surprised. It's likely the men ye showed up when we first arrived or perhaps they heard the tale and are plannin' what they should do with the willful female who dared stand up to them."

I raise my hand and wave, jumping down to the courtyard stone. "In that case, we should go introduce ourselves."

"Och, I don't suppose that's a good idea."

"Why not? It's not like we're here to make lifelong friends or anything. Maybe stirring things up is the way to find the bad seeds in the mix."

"Or maybe it's simply stirrin' things up."

Water squishes in unpleasant rushes between my bare toes as I walk, and I regret my choice to wear my shoes into the bathing pool.

Live and learn.

"May I at least ask that ye temper yer first impulse to show these men yer their equal? In this time, that won't be well received."

"You can always ask, hotness."

"All right, but will ye oblige me?"

"No promises."

Sloan makes a grumbling noise in the back of his throat. It's a sound Da and Granda often make too when I'm talking to them.

As we approach the passageway that leads toward the drawbridge, I assess the crowd. Five men...all of them wearing the red and gold tunic of the Dragon Guard of Tintagel. All of them glaring at me like I'm about to pee in their porridge.

"Hello, gentlemen. I noticed you watching us. Did you have a question? Curious about the new arrivals? Did you maybe want to ask me about my uncle or my dragon? Is there anything I can help you with?"

Sloan rolls his eyes and steps in behind my hip. "Ye must excuse Fiona's forwardness, gentlemen. Raised by her father and five brothers, she never had a governess to teach her the finer points of being an English lady."

I give him that one. "That is true."

"Merlin claims he's your uncle?" The speaker is that russet-haired Ewan McGregor guy from the mid-air confrontation when we first arrived.

Merlin called him Sigberht, Earl of Dukeshire.

"My uncle many times removed, yes. With a man as long-lived as he, there are more than a few generations between us."

Wolfric nods as if this is what he expected me to say. "Pelleas says ya have quick reflexes and the gift of sorcery like Merlin. That's how ya vaulted out of the bath like a boulder out of a catapult sling, ya? And how ya stopped Alden's disarming spell mid-air."

He tilts his head to a slightly younger, scruffy man with chestnut eyes, hair, and beard.

I offer Alden a smile. "I don't practice sorcery, no, and I'm certainly not as gifted as Merlin. I am a druid, like him, though. My gifts come from a connection to nature, not sorcery or other sources of magic."

"But you have a dragon and a form of magic."

"Yes. I do."

"And ya think yourself a match for us in a fair fight." Sigberght scratches the russet scruff of his beard. "Ya said as much to Wolfric and to me."

I pause before answering. *Danger, road out ahead.*

What am I missing? How did this get turned around on me? I was supposed to be knocking them off balance, not the other way around.

"I hold my own against most men, yes. My confidence wasn't directed at Wolfric specifically. He and I got standoffish because he was looming in the shadows watching a married couple bathe and got defensive when I took offense."

They don't seem to care about that.

"What's this about?" Sloan asks, his voice clipped.

"It's about Lady Morgana's Champions competition. Never has a female's plaque been raised on the board, but if you think yourself able, we invite you to be the first. I shall nominate you to join us."

Oh, I see. "No, thank you, boys. I'm not taking the bait. I don't need to prove myself, and honestly, I'm not sure how long we're staying."

Pelleas grins and smacks the arm of the guy beside him. "I told ya the little bitch would scurry back into her hovel with her tail between her legs."

"I'm not scurrying anywhere. I simply have no interest in embarrassing a group of men who underestimate me as an opponent simply because I have breasts."

They recoil at the mention of my breasts and grimaces darken their ugly mugs.

Sloan gently squeezes my elbow and tilts his head back the

way we came. "Perhaps that's enough visiting fer one day. We should get back to the lair and check in with Merlin."

Sigberght frowns and steps to block our retreat. "Surely, if you truly possess the skills of a dragon guard, we would be remiss if we didn't take the opportunity to meet you on the field of challenge and learn from your strengths."

I chuckle. "Which is not-so-subtle guy speak for you wanting to kick my ass and teach me who's boss."

I have to admit the more they push, the more my Irish ire prickles, and I consider it. But no. It's not what I'm here for, and our priority is finding the person who kills the dragons.

Right.

I reset my conviction and step back. "I truly appreciate the offer, boys, and you can believe I'm afraid if you wish, but that's not it. There are simply other matters more pressing, and we have family business to attend to."

"We haven't even shown ya what this year's prize is," Pelleas says.

"It won't make any difference, I'm afraid. You have my answer. It's a no for me."

My shield flares the moment Sigberght reaches under his cloak. I'm ready for an offensive, except he doesn't attack. He pulls out a silver dagger and holds it out for me to inspect. "She's beautiful, isn't she? Perhaps ownership of a token as exquisite as one of Lady Morgana's treasures might entice you to change your mind."

The satin-finished blade draws my hand toward it, and my skin tingles with the power it possesses.

There's no missing that it's an enchanted object, and if it once belonged to Morgana, I'm now one hundy percent interested in who might win it.

I inspect the ornate engravings on the blade and the raised lettering on the steel cross-guard. "Is this Elvish?"

Sloan bends forward to get a better view. "Aye, a dialect of the Avalonian elves if I'm not mistaken."

"What does this say?"

Sloan tilts his head and reads it aloud. *"Laytah, im vaegannon cathol arod i hen, a thand dan i thang."*

I snort. "No, I meant what does it say in English, you giant nerd."

"Oh, sorry. Laytah, a well-made blade for the noble daughter, a shield against the throng."

"A blade for the noble daughter, eh?"

Morgana must've been given this before her dark days. I brush my fingers over the intricate vine pattern engraved on the steel and magic surges up my fingers.

The dark blue gemstone on the hilt blinks to life like an eyeball opening when awakened. A gold seam flashes down the center of the stone. Then the golden glow warms the stone's color on both sides from pink to burgundy.

That's not super creepy at all.

"What kind of stone is this, hotness?"

"It's called a dragon's breath opal." He leans around my arm for a closer look. "Very rare. In fact, in our circles, there are only synthetic replicas of the once magical stone."

With the gold line cutting the oval in half, it looks like the dragon's eye is peering out of the dagger's hilt to assess its surroundings.

"You are an über eerie girl, Laytah."

My cells ignite and I'd swear the blade has a consciousness like Birga does. I'm still considering that when the air fills with an unearthly song.

It's haunting yet beautiful and holds an entrancing cadence and silky-sounding words. When it ends, I pull my fingers back. "Did I do that?"

"I believe ye did, *a ghra.*"

"I did *not* mean to."

Sloan arches a brow. "When do you ever mean for the things you do to happen?"

"Almost never."

The men have closed in, their curiosity piqued.

"How *did* ya do that?" Pelleas snaps.

"No idea. It just happened. Did anyone understand the words of her song?"

Wolfric nods. "It was a ballad about the bravery and skill of Lady Morgana."

Sloan frowns. I'm not sure if he disagrees or is simply trying to translate the words himself. "Well, I think with the lovely Laytah as the prize, Fiona will accept yer offer to join the competition."

I whip my head around. "I will?"

Wasn't he the one advising me to fall back and give the Dragon Guard of Tintagel a wide berth?

"Of course, ye will. If her creator forged this lovely dagger to serve a noble daughter, who better to wear her? I think it was meant to be."

I see his point but also hear there is more not being said. Well, whatever it is, Sloan would never hang me out to dry. There must be a darned good reason he's opting me in.

"All right. Sign me up. When do the games begin?"

By the looks on their faces, I'm getting a rush of mixed reviews. They don't seem so keen and cocky about me joining them as they did five minutes ago.

Sir Earl of Dickshire takes the dagger back and tucks it back under his cloak. "The Banquet of Champions begins in a few hours in the Great Hall. The first event is the dragon trial in the morning."

"Excellent." I step back and give them a little wave. "We'll go claim our rooms and freshen up. See you in a few hours then. May the best woman win."

CHAPTER FIFTEEN

"Okay, 'fess up, Mackenzie," I say when the two of us are in our guest room. "Laytah's song wasn't an ode to Morgana at all, was it?"

He shakes his head. "No. Laytah is most definitely an enchanted object, and she was singing about being the drinker of blood and the taker of life."

"Lovely. And here I thought we could be friends."

Sloan shrugs. "It's not that different from Birga's thirst for blood, though I'm surprised an elven piece is so bloodthirsty."

"Could she have been influenced by her time with Morgana? Maybe she started out being a tool of goodly defense and was tainted?"

"Och, that's more than possible. I'd bet that's exactly what happened, but the effect may or may not be reversible. A weapon like that with a consciousness wanting to spill blood would be a terrible influence on a mortal man."

"What are you saying? You think she could enthrall the dragon douche squad into killing people indiscriminately?"

He lowers his chin. "With her current outlook, I'd say she could inspire the Ted Bundy of the ninth century."

"Why now?"

"From what I gathered from the welcoming committee, I'd say she's been in a keepsake chest and was chosen as the prize fer this tournament. She likely was recently unpacked and brought back into the world."

"Then I went and woke her up."

Sloan nods. "That's the part that makes me think you need to be the one to win her. Elven craftsmanship is extremely refined. If her creator intended her to be the weapon of a noble lady, perhaps she sensed you, and that's what woke her. If that's the case, perhaps yer the perfect person to handle her and restore her."

"We either fix her and stop her from creating a serial killer or we lock her away in STOA so she can't hurt innocent people."

"That's my thinking."

"But I have to win her first."

Sloan nods. "Win her or steal her, yes."

"Steal her? How double-crossy of you. Don't you think I can win her on merit?"

"Of course I do, but that depends on how much time we spend here and how long the tournament lasts."

"I suppose if it's between leaving her here for a ninth-century massacre or stealing her away and time jumping back to Toronto, it's a no-brainer. Although it could cause a ripple effect."

"My thoughts exactly. When we see Merlin and Cazzie return to the castle, we'll go down and find out what this tournament is all about."

I laugh. "Maybe we should've found that out before you voluntold me to be part of it. I think my reckless spontaneity is finally wearing off on you."

"Wearing me down, more likely."

"Potato-tomato."

He presses his hand to the small of my back and guides me toward the door. "I say we spend the next few hours exploring and learn more about Morgana's heirlooms and other cursed or enchanted objects that might be lying around here waiting to awake."

I hold out both sides of my dress and curtsy. "As you wish, milord."

He grins and sends me a lascivious gaze. "Maybe tonight we'll play lord and lady, and you can say those words to me again."

"Mhmm… as you wish, milord."

The two of us spend the next couple of hours exploring the architectural nooks and art-filled crannies of Tintagel. At every opportunity, we discreetly touch things to test if they possess any enchantments. We're also busy pulling out our phones to take pictures on the sly.

It's easier to be shutterbugs here than at Carlisle Castle when Fionn pulled me back in time because here, one of us can act as a lookout.

"Having fun?" I ask when we've covered every inch of the public spaces within the castle, and the last of the sunlight has surrendered for the day.

"More than I can express. I think exploring ancient castles for cursed objects with you is my most perfect date night ever."

"So sweet. Who needs long walks on the beach and chocolate-dipped strawberries and Gran's homemade blackberry pear wine?"

"Och, that sounds wonderful too. Still, I wouldn't trade the past few hours for anything."

I slide my arm around his back and lean my head into his shoulder. "I was thinking about a few of the pieces we saw around the castle. If it comes to us stealing Laytah, maybe we should take them back with us for STOA. They'd be in way better condition than most of your artifacts."

"Ye want to steal from the past so we can have better quality antiques in the future?"

"Hey, don't look at me like that. You were the one who opened Pandora's box."

"I suggested removing a powerful dagger from the general population for the health and safety of innocents, not stocking my wares."

"Why not do both? Does that violate some kind of historian code or something?"

He arches a brow. "Or something."

Whatevs. I thought it was an inspired idea. Given the opportunity to stick a few artifacts into the folds of my skirt, I absolutely will.

I'm still thinking about that as we make our way back to the chapel and the gated stairway that leads down to Merlin's dragon cave. Even though we didn't see the dragons return, I feel Dart through our growing connection and know he's back.

"Hellooo, the dragon lair," I say, mostly because I don't want to walk in on one of my friends having dragon sex with his empress love.

Awkward.

"In here, kids." The deep timbre of Merlin's voice resonates from down the passageway, and we track him into a section of the lair we haven't been in before. "Did you two have fun exploring this afternoon?"

We step into what I can only guess is a dragon common room, and I smile at the scene. Saxa and Dart are tugging on opposite ends of a deer, Utiss is curled up, snoring in the shadows of the corner, and Bryvanay is sitting with Cazzie and Merlin, the three of them lounging around a pit fire.

When we join them, Merlin sits up from where he was lying on his side on a thick area rug and makes space for us.

I hike up the skirt of my dress, lower myself to the floor cross-legged, and flop the fabric down around my knees to cover things up. "Do you mind if I let Bruin out for a while? He likes to stretch his legs and might want to explore a bit himself."

Merlin shakes his head. "Go ahead and release him. I mentioned your bear to the dragons earlier and told them not to be surprised if he makes an appearance."

"I'm looking forward to meeting him," Saxa says. "Dartamont says he's an ancient mythical like us."

I grin. "In a way, I suppose he is. Yes."

I release my hold on my spirit bear and Bruin materializes on the stone floor between Sloan and Dart.

"Hello, everyone."

"He says hello." I relay his greetings. When the dragons smile at me, I wonder if they understood him without the translation. "Can you hear him?"

"Oh, yes," Cazzie says. "Dragons have a natural affinity for over three hundred languages."

"A natural affinity?"

She nods, and her champagne scales shimmer in the light of the fire. "Yes. There is an archive of information that passes through the genetic code of our species. There are certain things that all dragons naturally know without being taught or told."

"That's cool. I wish that were true for humans. Can you imagine if we naturally understood chemistry or algorithmic math or any number of the other horrid courses of study we're subjected to growing up?"

Sloan chuckles. "I think it has more to do with the survival of the species and less about skipping classes at school."

"Same diff."

Merlin chuckles. "So, tell me about your time here at Tintagel. Did you claim a room and look around? Is there anything I need to know or anyone I need to address or apologize to?"

I catch the look he sends Sloan and sigh. "Seriously? You don't think I can spend one afternoon on my own without causing trouble?"

Merlin chuckles. "Is that a rhetorical question?"

I'm not exactly sure why he'd need to address anyone on our behalf, but in any case, he doesn't.

I wave away his concern and decide to forgive him his skepticism. "We had a great afternoon. We explored and touched a lot of antiques...which, of course, aren't antique yet. We met a few of the locals...oh, and I entered Morgana's Tournament of Champions."

Merlin's jaw tenses. "Why would you do that? I thought I was clear about you interacting with the men of this time being a bad idea."

I hold up my hands. "Don't shoot the messenger. In this one instance, you can't tie the poor decision to me. That is Sloan's honor today."

Merlin flashes me a look that blatantly says he doesn't believe me.

Rude. "Seriously. We were getting heckled, and I totes ignored it and passed on snapping up the bait. It was my stalwart lover here who turned the tables."

Merlin has the good nature to look apologetic. "I assume there's a story behind why you thought competing is a good idea?"

I chuff. "So, if he does something stupid and reckless, there has to be a reason?"

Merlin grins. "Now you're getting it."

Sloan chuckles, and I let him fill in the blanks. After everyone has been updated on Laytah and our bonding moment and the dagger's thirst to take life and drink blood, a surly scowl darkens Merlin's expression.

"I remember the dagger you're describing. It was a commissioned piece for Morgana from Uther for her thirteenth birthday."

"Lucky number thirteen." I raise a weak fist into the air. "Now it's lost its way and wants to guide people into murderous bloodshed."

"For the moment," Sloan says.

Merlin purses his lips. "An elven master craftsman forged it. Sloan's right. The taint might be reduced if not removed."

"Ye might want to see if ye can do that before they award it," Sloan says. "That way, if Fi doesn't win it or if we're drawn away before it finds its champion, it won't be thirstin' to pollute its new handler."

"Your lack of faith wounds me, hotness. Of course, I'm going to win it."

Merlin straightens his legs along the floor and leans back on his elbows. "A sound idea. I'll work on that tonight at the banquet. It's customary to display the prize at the head table. I should be able to get a few moments with it in my possession without raising a fuss and drawing anyone's unwanted notice."

"Speaking of drawing notice," I say. "How is it that the citizens of Tintagel openly have dragons and talk about sorcery and magic? They are, for the most part, humans, aren't they? Why are they so aware of the magical world? Is that a ninth-century thing?"

Merlin shakes his head. "No, it's a Tintagel thing. This is the birthplace of Arthur. This is where the tales of the boy and the stone come from, Excalibur and the Lady of the Lake. It has been a place of sorcery, prophecy, dragons, and magic for centuries. That's why I live here and why Cazzie and the dragons live here. The rest of Wales and Breton might be going into the Middle Ages stomping out magic for Christianity's sake, but dragons are living proof that it exists."

"That's part of the reason they hold Morgana's tournament," Cazzie says. "It's a challenge of the magical men of the kingdom to see who's most powerful."

"Oh, so it's a magical tournament?" I ask.

Merlin nods. "A dangerous one, too. Don't for a moment think the men involved are battling to win a trinket of Morgana's favor. This is a no-holds-barred pissing match for empowered men with dragons to prove who's the fiercest of the land."

"Awesome. So, it's a medieval joust but with magic and dragons?"

"No, Fi. It's a battle to the last man standing—"

"—or woman," Cazzie says.

"—or woman," Merlin amends, "that tests the champions' magical prowess, daring, powers of deduction, and, of course, ability to cope with and adapt to danger."

"Okay, so *Goblet of Fire* with a *Highlander* slant. I can manage that." I straighten and lay the accent on thick. "I'm Fiona mac Cumhaill of the Clan mac Cumhaill. There can be only one."

Sloan rolls his eyes.

Merlin leans closer. "These men fight dirty, Fi. They aren't naïve followers of the legends of a benevolent and beautiful Morgan le Fey. These men are ruthless seekers of conquest and power. Don't think Laytah's selection was random bad luck. I guarantee you they feel the dagger's dark power and hope to add to their cache of strengths."

"Not gonna happen," I say. "There's no way I'm letting that dagger fall into corrupt hands. Sloan said it's the kind of weapon that could incite another Ted Bundy killing spree."

"He's not wrong," Merlin says.

"Who's Ted Bundy?" Cazzie asks.

"A serial killer who murdered women in our time."

"Gruesome. Did he eat them?"

"No, darling. More to the point, this could be much worse because men bound to dragons have the longevity to kill over many centuries."

Those words hit like a sucker punch to the belly. Acid rises in my gorge, and I swallow down the burn.

I hadn't thought of that.

If I make enemies of these men, they might show up on my doorstep in Toronto and seek revenge. *Hey there, remember me? I'm going to kill your family because you thwarted my evil plans.*

Yeah no, I don't think so.

"If longevity is a byproduct of the union with a dragon, could the arrival of the champions have something to do with the murder of the dragons?"

Merlin blinks at me. "How'd you get there, Fi?"

"The concept of *Highlander* is kinda sticking with me—there can be only one. What if one of the contestants wants fewer dragons in the world and therefore fewer men to challenge his power and longevity? What if one of them wants to wipe out dragons to elevate himself and his dragon?"

Cazzie frowns. "The men who participate in the tournament certainly have the kind of power and knowledge it would take to put four of us down."

Merlin shrugs. "The timing works. There are a dozen local contestants and another dozen that come from all over the countryside. The tournament offers access to Tintagel that strangers normally don't have."

"It's a sound theory," Sloan says.

"It's as good a theory as any at the moment. Tonight, when I get back from the champions' banquet, I'll ward the lair against other dragon guards and specifically the tournament's competitors. Maybe that's the first step in keeping the dragons living here safe."

I exhale, feeling a great deal better for at least coming up with something to do to protect the dragons. It still isn't sitting well that Dart is hanging around here with four dragons who died in the previous timeline.

I can't dwell on that, or I'll go bonkers.

"Okay, team. Onward to the banquet." I hold up my finger pointing to the exit.

Merlin rolls to the side and gets to his feet. "Give me five minutes to change and clean up. I wasn't expecting a night out."

I chuckle. "With me around, you need to expect the unexpected, my friend."

CHAPTER SIXTEEN

By the time we arrive at the Great Hall, three-quarters of the rustic dining lodge is full and the people still funneling in will pack it to capacity. I follow the lines of the three rows of wooden tables banked end to end toward the far wall where another long run of tables sits perpendicular at the front.

By the look of the two velvet-upholstered thrones, one larger than the other, I figure that's where the king and his lady sit when they're here.

Since King Aethelred is newly crowned, I bet he's never even sat there...or at least not as the king.

Merlin said his self of this time went to Wessex to show both his respect for the deceased king and support for the son and heir.

How cool is it that history is in the making, and we're here to witness it?

I take in the rich reds and golds in the floor-to-ceiling fabric panels that decorate the walls, the royal banners hanging from the wooden rafters, and the eighty or more people shouting, chatting, and laughing.

It's warm in here and a bit smoky.

A hole in the roof lets some of the heat escape, but the smoke from the hearth has collected high in the rafters and beams above our heads.

Is the excitement in the room simply because there's a banquet or because Morgana's tournament has brought so many new faces for the competition?

So many new male prospects for marriage according to Merlin and Marigold. I scan the attendees' faces and am completely secure in saying that I've snagged the catch of the castle.

To each their own.

Merlin points at a place near the front, then taps my elbow and gestures to the head table. "Champions sit at the front, girlfriend. Remember to play nice. Don't underestimate these men, Fi. I'm serious."

"Got it. I already had a sickening thought of them living long enough to come after my family in our time and came to the same conclusion."

"I'm glad we're on the same page."

We are.

As we make our way down the rows of people shuffling to step over the wood benches to sit, more than a few of them turn to give me the stink eye.

It seems the women are going for pursed glances and disapproving frowns while the men stare with eyes alight with malice.

Yay me.

I guess making an impression is better than never doing anything daring enough to be noticed, amirite?

When I arrive at the front, I scan down the length of the head table to where the two dozen other contenders are already seated.

Huh, no one saved me a seat.

Imagine that.

Bestial Strength. I grab the sides of a barrel keg stacked beside the wall, lift it down to the floor, and rim-roll it to the end of the table. Little do these fellas know that I've been relocating kegs for close to a decade at Shenanigans.

Like butter, baby.

Liam would be proud.

Climbing onto the top of the keg, I get myself seated at the end of the long, head table and smile at the other contestants. "No problem, gentleman. I'm very capable of seating myself. No need to jump up. I've got it."

I frown down in front of me. I'm going to face the same issue with my place setting as well. That is until my beloved Sloan strides to the front to set a plate, fork, and tankard of ale in front of me.

"Show them who's boss, *a ghra*," he whispers.

"*Go raibh maith agat*," I say, thanking him in Irish.

"*Go ndéana sé maith duit*," he says, wishing me well.

When he goes back to sit with Merlin, I smile at all the hostile and curious faces. "I heard this is a banquet. Am I presumptuous to think there will be food?"

Ms. Marigold has the spectacular timing to step through the open doorway on my right carrying a large platter heaped with a turkey and surrounded by potatoes and root vegetables. Behind her comes the kitchen entourage of Sunnifa and three young men I recognize from the kitchen, each of them carrying a similar platter.

"Right, ya are, Lady Fiona," Ms. Marigold says. "Dinner is served."

The arrival of the food warms the artificial chill of the stifling air and the daggered looks melt away.

Marigold is kind enough to cut the bird and serve me first. Otherwise, I am quite certain I wouldn't have received a morsel at all to eat.

I scan the crowd to see if I'm supposed to wait until everyone is served before eating, but it seems that's not a custom here, so I join the feast and dig in.

Looking at my plate, I giggle. "Hey, Mackenzie!" I hold up the King Henry drumstick and my tankard of ale. "Now we're talking."

Sloan leans back from the long line of people at his table and chuckles. "Yer ridiculous, Cumhaill."

Dinner progresses with hearty conversation buzzing among the three long tables and a fair bit of male bonding across the head table—excluding yours truly, of course.

Meh. Being a girl while growing up with five brothers and all their friends, being left out of the conversation isn't foreign, and I don't let it bug me.

These boys have no idea who I am and no interest in finding out. I pick apart the meat on my plate, fingering large chunks into my mouth. It's not overly warm and quite greasy but fills the empty ache in the pit of my stomach.

That's all that matters.

Munching along happily, I listen to the conversations on my end of the table, which ranges from friendly wagers on the tournament's outcome to speculations about how the young king will rule, to whether or not anyone has a shot escorting Sunni into the keg room after the evening comes to its end.

I smile at Ms. Marigold's kitchen helper.

Sunnifa has soft features, flaxen and gold hair, and pretty hazel eyes. If I were to guess, by her name and her complexion, I'd say she was of Scandinavian descent.

She certainly stands out next to all these ruddy, dark-haired Englishmen.

"Are you finished, milady?" she asks, ready to clear.

"I am, thank you, Sunni." I hand her my plate and wait while she sets it on her tray before handing her my cutlery.

When she finishes with me and moves on, Merlin comes up to the head table to say hello...or at least that's how he makes it seem.

In truth, he's here to test the dagger and see if he can reduce its dark intentions. "Are you enjoying yourself, Fiona?" he asks, standing in front of the table.

"With these fine gentlemen to keep me company, how could I do anything but?"

His smirk makes me smile inside.

"Did you see this year's prize, Uncle?" I point at the dagger mounted in a wooden holder at the center of the table.

Of course, no one is sitting in the king's or queen's throne, so that's where Morgana's dagger lies on display.

Merlin strolls down the length of the table and lifts it off the display to examine it.

"Who do ya think ya are touchin' the trophy of the champions?" a scruffy, dark-haired brute says. He slurs his words, and it's obvious he hit the mead like the champion he thinks himself to be.

Merlin's brows arch so high up his forehead that they disappear under his brown waves. "I think I'm Emrys Merlin, the man who went with King Uther to commission this dagger for young Morgana. Who the fuck do you think you are?"

The dark-haired brute grumbles and sputters and goes back to his tankard.

Merlin meets the steely gazes of the other champions and frowns. "Do any of you take offense to me reminiscing with my niece for a moment?"

When no one says anything, he huffs and comes back down the table to stand with me. "So, you met Laytah earlier, you said."

I take the cue and tell him over again about meeting the dagger.

He's not listening, of course. I sense the familiar signature of his magic and take the long way around my story to give him time to do whatever he needs to exorcise the evil out of the tournament prize.

"Then, when I touched the raised engraving on the blade..." I continue prattling on, highlighting the song she sang and how her entrancing tune made my blood sing. "Sir Wolfric said she was singing an ode to Lady Morgana."

Which we know was a complete fabrication, but I'm not about to go into that in the present company.

"Then, Sloan thought that since the blade was forged for a noble daughter, I should put my hat in the ring to win her."

Merlin holds the dagger up toward the lit chandeliers, and the bleeding edge of the ancient blade catches the light. "Did Wolfric mention that entering into this competition is not something one should do lightly? Once listed on the champion's board, you are obligated to see things through until the event is complete and the winner declared."

"No, but I am wholeheartedly ready to play."

"Play?" the man next to me says. "This isn't a game to be played at, little girl. An attitude like that will get you killed in the first hour."

I feign an apologetic smile. "I meant no offense. I simply find competition fun. I love a challenge. I'm looking forward to the tests and trials to come."

The comment about it being fun and me being ready to play serves two purposes. First, it gives me an advantage tomorrow if they underestimate me or my commitment to winning. Second, it distracts the men sitting close to me from what Merlin is doing.

Now they're glaring at me instead of watching him.

I continue to express my excitement for the morning until Merlin shakes himself from a deep reverie and strides back to the center of the table to mount Laytah on the display rack.

"Are ye ready to retire, *a ghra?*" Sloan asks, joining us at the head table.

I shrug and look at Merlin. "Are there speeches or announcements or anything?"

Merlin shakes his head. "Just men drinking and measuring the size of their cocks."

I press my hands against the table and stand. "All righty then, that lets me off the hook. We're good to go. Good night, gentlemen. I'll see you in the morning."

On the way out, I thank Ms. Marigold for a lovely dinner and Merlin walks us outside into the open air of the inner courtyard.

After the stale hour of the Great Hall, I pull in the fresh, night air in greedy gulps. "Okay, the suspense is killing me. Did you get Laytah evened out? Is she still maniacal or has she been cleansed of her evil intent?"

He frowns. "I didn't have any effect on her at all. The dark taint feeding her is strong. She wants her mistress and has no interest in being cleansed of the impulse. Sloan is right. We can't trust her in the hands of any of these men."

Well, poop.

The three of us let that hang heavy over us as we stroll back to the stone tower housing the guest quarters. There doesn't seem to be anything more to say.

I gotta win Laytah and take her back with us.

"Until the morrow then, niece." Merlin bows his head and lays on the old-timey charm. "Straight to bed, you two. The trumpets of dawn will sound earlier than you think and you'll need to be well-rested."

I chuckle. "Are you cockblocking us, Uncle?"

He rolls his eyes. "Oh, that I possessed that much power. No. I simply want you in top form. I meant what I said. This tournament isn't for the timid, Fi. These men will come for you with ruthless aggression."

"Got it. There can be only one."

When Merlin mentioned the trumpets of dawn sounding, I thought that was a figurative term like waking up with the roosters or early bird catches the worm. Nope. Sloan and I are sawing some serious logs cuddled up on our tiny straw mattress when those brass horns sound.

I jolt out of bed like I've been electrocuted and land halfway across the room atop a furry, brown mountain.

"Och, Red, get off." Bruin grumbles and rolls, toppling me onto my ass on a mat made of bullrushes. "That was *not* the way to begin our day. I thought my days of trumpeting were behind me. Stupid time-travel adventures."

I thump my chest to restart my heart, then untangle my legs and struggle to get up. "You're not wrong, buddy. Is that how they plan to eliminate me from the competition? By giving me a coronary?"

Sloan sits up at the side of the bed and scrubs his hands over the morning two-day stubble on his jaw. "I don't know about a plot to give ye a heart attack, but that was unnecessarily abrupt."

"Abrupt? Yeah, understatement of the century."

Muttering to myself, I haul myself over to the dry sink and pour water from the floral clay pitcher into the matching basin to splash my face.

Last night, when we returned from dinner, the girl downstairs gave us a warm pitcher of water to wash up. It's cold now, which is fine because the shock of the temperature will help me wake up.

"I don't suppose they have Colgate and a traveler toothbrush lying around for guests?"

"Likely not. I did see some mint in the window box downstairs though if ye like."

"Better than nothing."

"I'll pinch us some when we go down."

I forgo the green dress and any illusion that I'm anything like an English lady and pull on my black stretch pants and my Guardian Druid t-shirt Bruin got me for my birthday.

Well, Bruin picked it out online, but Emmet and Ciara ordered it for him. Bruin, thankfully, hasn't ordered anything online since I ended up with a twenty-seven thousand dollar landscaping bill when he tried to help me build a grove.

The t-shirt is much smarter shopping.

It's super cute and has a snarling bear face on it with the saying, *Guardian Druid: The bear of scare has claws of might. We won't go down without a fight.*

Bruin thinks it's amazing and suits us well.

I do too.

After pulling my crazy, red curls free of the neck hole, I check myself in the postage stamp square of a mirror. I probably look too twenty-first century, but if I'm flying dark in this competition and battling chauvinistic and power-driven men, I gotta be me.

"Is this a stage tournament? A weekend thing? Man, I wish I knew what to expect."

Sloan pulls on his pants and the same navy tunic he wore last night. "From what I learned at dinner, it's one long challenge. It's supposed to test yer wits and skills and force ye to fight and think on yer feet."

"One long challenge? Like, how long?"

He grabs the belt he borrowed from Merlin and straps it around his hips. "That depends on how many competitors there are and how long it takes to whittle ye down to one."

"Oh, okay. So, the faster people drop out or get put out, the sooner it'll be over. What are we looking at on the outside?"

"The man sitting next to me last night said the longest event recorded lasted five days."

"Five days! I don't want to be out there battling those ninth-century jerks for five days. I want to go home and snuggle Daisy and read stories to the twins with Jackson and Meggie."

Bruin snorts. "Manx, Doc, and I planned to take Dart into the forest for a wander…and my ladies will be missin' me."

Sloan steps up to stand in front of me and rubs my shoulders. "I'm sorry. Yer both in this predicament because of me and I regret puttin' ye there."

I wave that away. "Not your fault. You were right to be concerned about Laytah being loose in the wild. I agree we need to do this. I guess I figured we'd finish this afternoon, grab dinner, figure out who's got designs on killing the dragons, foil them, and go home."

Sloan blinks at me. "Ye figured us a busy day."

"I did. I guess five days gives you and Merlin more time to work on the dragon murders."

He frowns. "We need to be gone before the herald arrives and notifies everyone that Merlin of this time is returning with the traveling party. Then we need to figure out how to change the timeline without changing the timeline."

There's always something.

"Och, I want ye to take this." Sloan tugs his bone ring off his finger and slips it over the knuckle of my thumb. "If these men are gifted in magic, ye never know what might be glamored. Maybe it can save ye a bump or two in the process."

"S'all good. I heart you, Mackenzie." I push up on my toes and kiss him. "Bruin, let's go kick some dragon guard ass."

My bear grunts and dematerializes to bond with me. *If it means I get to crush some skulls and work off some hostility, I'll forgive the early hour.*

I giggle. "That's the spirit."

CHAPTER SEVENTEEN

Sloan and I make our way downstairs and are welcomed by a crush of men loitering at the bottom of the stairs. Their booming chatter and camaraderie end with deafening silence as they notice our arrival.

"Gentlemen." I ignore the leering and scowls.

I recognize a few of the men from the head table. The rest of them must be their entourage.

Maybe today we'll get introductions.

Or maybe not.

I get the feeling they're fine with the status quo—they all know who I am, and I don't need to know them because I won't be around long enough to matter.

Sloan presses a hand to the small of my back and guides us through the throng. "Friendly bunch," he says as we exit into the courtyard.

"Do you think it's about more than the competition for the dagger?"

Sloan chuckles. "Aye, I think it might be your sparkling personality and feminine presence."

"Well, there's nothing to be done about that. I am who I—"

A rush of nausea hits me, and I stop in my tracks to steady myself.

"Fi? What's wrong?"

Something twists in my belly, but it's an odd sensation...like I'm sick, but I'm not. It takes me a moment to figure it out, but when I do, my heart races in my chest at triple time. "I think Dart's sick. The closer we get to the lair, the stronger the sensation grows."

Sloan takes my hand, and we jog through the courtyard and into the chapel. Another round of gut-wrench hits as Sloan works the spell to unlock the iron gate. Then we're racing down the hundreds of stone steps.

"What's wrong? Where is he?" I ask Saxa as we enter the lair.

The yellow dragon looks ill herself as she turns tail and hurries ahead of us. "He's in the nesting area. Merlin is with him. This way."

Dragons move at an unexpectedly fast pace considering their size. Sloan and I have to run to keep up.

Which does nothing to calm my nerves.

When she turns and leads us into a large cavern, I find Merlin with his hands pressed against Dart's scales and a fierce scowl on his face.

"What is it? What's wrong?" I ask again.

Merlin shakes his head. "Sloan, come in here and help me. He's been poisoned."

"Poisoned?" The word croaks out of my mouth, pitchy and breathless. "Is it the poison that killed them the last time?"

"I don't think so, no."

"Then who? How? Why?"

"It's my fault," Bryvanay says behind us. "The two of us were out late last night. Some of the men from the feast were headed back to their camp on the other side of the bridge. They said there was a great deal of food and bones left from the feast and that we should help ourselves. I wasn't hungry, but Dartamont ate a great deal."

Dart lets out a pathetic wail, and tears brim hot in my eyes. I rush over and scrub his horns. "Oh, my blue boy. It's all right. Sloan and Merlin will make you feel better. You'll see."

"I am sorry for his suffering," Bryvanay says.

I wave that away. "It's not your fault. My Da always says, 'Evil is as evil does.' It could as easily have been you poisoned, or the both of you."

"It's the damnable tournament," Cazzie snaps. "We should've anticipated something like this. Those men get meaner and more dangerous every time this ridiculous event happens."

My mind shorts out on that. "You think the competitors poisoned Dart to knock us out of the trials?"

"Of course they did," Utiss hisses. "What does killing a dragon mean to them? Nothing. They know the first event is a dragon rider trial and took out your mount. It was the quickest and easiest way to eliminate you from the competition."

Sloan looks back at me, his eyes far too glassy. "I'm so sorry, *a ghra*."

The sorrow in Sloan's gaze cuts me to the quick. My lungs lock tight, and I start to shake. "You can't *fix* him?"

Sloan curses and runs to catch me as my knees give out. "Och, my love, no. I meant I'm sorry for puttin' the two of ye in harm's way. I wasn't givin' ye bad news about your boy. I'm sorry I wasn't clearer."

I cling to him, my tears hot on my cheeks. "You mean he's not dying?"

"Not if we can help it," Merlin says, "but I need Irish back here."

I push Sloan away and back toward my baby dragon. "Oh, thank you, Divine Lady. I thought..." my throat clutches closed around the words.

I can't even say it.

The dragons lift their chins and turn their heads toward the plateau in unison. It's such a synchronized movement that it's obvious something triggered it.

"What's going on?"

Saxa turns to meet my gaze, and I can tell by her expression, whatever is happening, it's not good. "The trumpets have sounded for the contestants to assemble."

"Okay. I'll go do that, and we'll see how Dart's feeling when I'm done checking in."

Saxa shakes her head. "No, Fi. You need to assemble for the beginning of the competition. If you're not there with your dragon in the next five minutes, you'll forfeit your spot."

Five minutes?

I assess the guys working on helping my blue boy and wipe the tears remaining on my cheeks. I'm no longer heartbroken— I'm pissed.

"So that's it? They poison Dart as some twisted show of their male dominance, and we're done before we even get started? That's bullshit."

"It is," Utiss grumbles. "And I won't allow it. I will be your dragon, and we will crush these men who dare harm one of our kind."

I blink.

Can I ride a beast as large and powerful as Utiss?

"I'm not sure...I mean, Dart and I only started dragon training a week ago. I don't think I'm good enough to handle you."

"You're smarter than you look," he grunts. "Of course you're not good enough to handle this much dragon. The reality is, all you need to do is hang on. I've lived in Tintagel for centuries. I know every inch of this countryside and can navigate any course they put together. You need only stay atop me and do as I say."

I don't appreciate his tone or implication that I should sit and shut up, but what choice do I have? He's right. It's the only way to get even.

"Fine. Do you have a saddle? I don't think Dart is feeling up to super-sizing so I can remove mine."

Utiss grumbles something in a language I don't understand and turns toward the room's exit. "I am a free dragon. No man will ever saddle me."

"What about a woman?"

He scowls. "You will make do holding the spikes of my collar."

He stomps off, and I'm torn. I can't leave Dart now...but if I'm to make it to the start line, I have to go.

All will be well, Dart says into my mind. *Go with Utiss and make them pay for this. I love you.*

Another round of tears prickle in my sinuses and sting my eyes. *I love you too. Don't you dare die on me. We have a long life of magic and mayhem ahead of us.*

Yes, we do. Don't worry. I'm feeling better already.

Connected as we are with our union growing each day, I feel the lie. Still, I let him have his moment. *Be a good patient, blue boy, and get better quickly.*

I will. Now go.

I run, kiss Sloan on the mouth and Merlin on the cheek, and dash for the exit. "Fix him, boys. You do your part, and I'll do mine."

I catch up to Utiss on the plateau and waste little time climbing his elbow spike to hoist myself up onto his side. My sneakers are finally dry enough not to slosh, and I'm thankful that no water gushes between my toes as I pad my way up his shoulder.

Centering myself at the back of his neck, I rub my hands against my thighs and find a foothold and grip position for my hands. I wish we had more time to work out the mechanics of things, but you get what you get.

"Let's kick their asses, Utiss. They came after my family and will pay for that."

"We are of one mind in that."

I grip tighter as I feel his muscles tense beneath me, and between one racing heartbeat and the next, he launches off the edge of the cliff and plummets toward the surface of the sea below.

Utiss is much more dragon than I'm used to, and I find his instructions to hold on and let him handle things is sound advice. Instead of worrying about what he's up to, I focus on casting a protective bubble around myself before we crack the surface of the sea and I drown.

"Shape Water." I don't think this is how its creators intended to use the spell, but it does the trick in a pinch.

Tucking tight to the leathery plate of Utiss's collar, I check the structural integrity of the bubble I erected around me.

So far so good.

In the initial moments of our descent, it keeps me dry and gives me a pocket of air to breathe as we shoot like a torpedo through the undersea channels.

Having Utiss help me is an unexpected boon.

Not that I wouldn't prefer Dart to be healthy and sharing this with me—because I totally would—but Utiss offers strength and confidence that will give me an edge against the other dragons and their riders.

From what Merlin said, the dragon guard dragons are both afraid of and revere the free dragons.

Especially Utiss.

We emerge from Merlin's dragon cave in a thrust of power and soar into the air. Arcing wide over the water of the sea, Utiss brings us over the crowd of maybe two or three hundred people gathered to witness the beginning of the tournament.

Utiss circles looking at the ground, and drops into an open space barely big enough for a dragon.

Ohmygoodness, he's going to squish—

I close my eyes as people scream and scramble.

Utiss lands, narrowly missing a man with a cane and a club foot. "Dude. You almost squished those people."

He smiles back at me. "I know."

I roll my eyes. "Okay, what now?"

"This is the human part. Go see who looks surprised that you are here. Get a sense of who wanted Dart out of the competition. That will give us our first clue in finding the ones who thought it wise to poison a dragon."

While I'm very thankful Utiss has taken a personal interest in Dart, having him so invested in the retaliation of his attack is alarming—and slightly dangerous.

As Utiss predicted, when I push through the crowd, I see the contestants. They are facing the audience in a long, curved line, broken in the middle by a red podium with the Tintagel banner hanging down the front of it.

I hustle over and join the line of contestants.

Most of the men glance over at me, looking pissy that I bothered to show up. That doesn't bother me nearly as much as the three that look surprised and curiously hostile that I'm here at all.

No need to make note of who they are.

They are exactly who I suspected they would be.

Wolfric. That weaselly jerk has the gall to gesture at me and whisper something to Pelleas and good ole Sigberght, Earl of Dickwad.

I'm disappointed in Earl Dickwad.

I can see Wolfric being a sniveling sneak, but I thought the earl and I were fellow russet-haired warriors who understood one another and wanted to crush the other upon the field of battle.

Guess not.

"Lady Morgana's Champions competition," the announcer

says, "is part of Tintagel's history. It is a test of strength, intelligence, and the ability of man to control a beast as willful and ornery as a dragon."

I dislike this man immediately.

Dragons don't need people to control them. Yes, they might be willful, but hello...they're dragons.

I think if you're a mythical creature with ancient knowledge and magic you get to be a little willful. I don't think ornery is a good description at all—well, except maybe for Utiss—but that's more a personality trait than a species trait.

Sure, dragons might need to be taught something or shown another way of doing things to fit in better with human society. For example, instead of razing the countryside and gobbling up a flock of sheep, maybe use an intricate network of roadkill, farm animal die off, and illegal poaching confiscations to fill their tummies.

Thinking of filling their tummies reminds me of poor Dart. Of course, he would eat the food offered him. Adolescent dragons have insatiable appetites. It takes a lot of calories to keep those bodies growing.

The announcer finishes rambling about the glorious history of the competition and the future of a new king. Then he gets to the part about the trophy.

"This year's token for the champion is Lady Morgana's thigh dagger." He holds up Laytah, and instead of looking at her, I watch the other contestants.

Several men seem to have no interest in the piece, some look on with hopeful appreciation, and half a dozen have the same creepy wide-eyed possessed look of Gollum drooling over the one true ring.

Wolfric, Pelleas, and Earl of Douchedom fall into that category.

"Now, the moment you have anticipated," the announcer says, pointing off in the distance into the morning sun. "Directly north of here, on a small island in the channel, we have hidden ten maps with the first clue to the competition. With twenty-one competitors, that will thin out the competition by half."

By half.

Wow, okay, maybe we will get it done by this afternoon after all. Since no one is going anywhere, I figure there's more that needs to be said. But nope… everyone's staring at me.

"What? Did I miss something?"

The announcer offers me a patient smile. "Is there something you wish to tell us, Lady Fiona?"

I glance around, searching for a clue. "I don't think so. Why? What do you think I should say?"

"I was told you were pulling out of the competition this morning."

I shake my head. "No. I'm ready when you are."

His wrinkled brow crinkles more. "We were informed that your dragon isn't participating. You do realize you need a dragon to be part of this competition, don't you?"

Aw, so that's what this is about.

"Yeah no. Dart was poisoned last night by some competitors too spineless to face a girl on the gaming field. Unfortunately, he is very much under the weather."

"Poisoned is quite an accusation, young lady," the announcer says. "I am sorry to hear your mount is under the weather. You are wise to withdraw so you can tend to him."

"Oh, I'm not withdrawing. I'm no quitter, and neither is Dart. Merlin and Sloan will have him back on his feet soon. In the meantime, I'll be riding Utiss, the free dragon of Merlin's Cave."

"Utiss?" one of the men barks. "Impossible. He has never allowed a rider."

I shrug. "I don't know what to tell you, fellas. The big guy is mighty pissed someone poisoned Dartamont, and he wants to ensure those responsible pay. Who am I to deny the dragon his revenge?"

I watch Wolfric, Earl Dickwad, and Pelleas as I speak and am happy to see them pale at the thought of Utiss coming after them.

"Is that all?" I smile at the announcer. "Can we let the games begin?"

The old guy sputters a bit, but what more is there to say? He nods at a young man standing beside a small fire. "Let it be so."

The archer takes the arrow in his right hand, nocks it, holds it in the flames until the blunt tip ignites, and fires it at the wicker rendition of Morgan le Fey standing sentinel on the cliff's edge.

When she goes up in flames, the men bolt off toward the open lands, and I run back to Utiss.

The massive purple dragon sees me coming and dips to the side for me to make a quick mount. I get into position. "There's a small island directly north in the channel. They've hidden ten maps somewhere there. We need to get a map to continue."

"Got it. Hold on."

I do as he says and still, the force of his strength is tough to bear. Utiss is a beast, and within a few powerful pumps of his wings, we catch up to the early leaders and lead the pack.

Twenty-one dragons in the air is an incredible sight.

I've been so impressed by Dart and his growth and his power that I never realized how much more he'll become when he's fully grown.

I see now why it's good for him to spend time with the older dragons. They can teach him things his siblings can't. His mother could—if she was that kind of a mother and didn't have twenty-two other adolescent dragons to take care of.

Being with me, it's good that he gets a broad education about all things dragon. I live in a dangerous world, and I want him to be all he can be.

I seriously need to put a pair of swimming goggles in my pants pocket. Or, duh…maybe figure out a spell to save my eyes from streaming.

Look at me thinking like a druid.

I chuckle. Sloan would be so proud.

Utiss knows where he's going and that leaves me free to think about what we might face.

Where will the first clues be hidden? If this is part of the "test your intelligence" part of the competition, I assume they won't be on a table in the open or have banners marking the location like on *The Amazing Race*, Tintagel edition.

It would be so cool if they did.

We tilt erratically to the side, and I lose my footing. My feet swing free in the air, and I grip his collar with as much force as I can manage.

I hang on as if my life depends on it—because it does. If I lose my grip, I fall and die.

CHAPTER EIGHTEEN

A spear zings past my hip, and I grunt, swinging my legs and trying to find purchase once again. I manage to plant my sneakers on one of the overlapping plates of Utiss's shoulder scale and regroup. Who the fuckety-fuck targeted me and tried to skewer me off a dragon?

Utiss tilts his wing and catches a gust of wind, pulling us up and back. The shift in position changes my center of gravity, and I get my feet solidly beneath me.

My hands ache, and I have trouble letting go of my hold, but I force my fingers free so I can turn and see who is attacking.

"Bruin. I've got a green dragon with an asshole firing spears at me. Can you spirit over there and knock him off his dragon?"

Can I hurt him?

"Since he just tried to kill me, sure. Go ahead."

Bruin releases from me in a rush. *Yer the best, Red.*

"Tough as Bark." My armor engages a moment before a flaming arrow hits me right in the fleshy part of my boob.

Ah! The point hits and I bat it away, but not before it singes my new birthday t-shirt. "You asshole. This was a gift. Bruin, get the guy with the stupid red hat too. He wrecked my bear druid shirt."

Bruin roars off to my right, and I smile as he materializes on the green dragon. The look on the jerk's face is priceless.

What? You didn't expect a bear to appear on your dragon's back? Sucks to be you.

Bruin rushes forward and tackles the spear-thrower into the air.

The guy lets out a baleful scream, and a few of the other dragons have to peel back not to get taken out by the scramble of a flying grizzly.

A moment later, he spirits out and reappears behind the guy who thought it would be a good idea to shoot flaming arrows at me.

"I love that shirt," Bruin snarls, reaching up and swiping him with a massive hit.

Claws out. Blood spray. One less contestant.

"Behind you, Bear." I point at a man on a red dragon with a short snout. The dragon rider is conjuring up a magic offense and has his sights on my bear.

Bruin roars, pushes off his position, and spirits away as the ball of magic hits the dragon he was on. The dragon shrieks, rears around, and sends a long stream of blue flame into the field of contestants.

I don't know if he doesn't realize who attacked him or is too pissed to care, but things go to hell from there.

Or not really.

Utiss and I are ahead of the turmoil with half a dozen other riders. We take the opportunity of the dragon fight to gain distance between the rest of the pack and us.

"I enjoy your bear," Utiss says, amusement thick in his graveled voice. "He is my kind of male."

I chuckle.

Look at us bonding.

Bruin catches up with us and materializes beside me. "This is so much fun. Is there anyone else I can attack fer ye?"

The sheer delight in his question makes me smile. "I guess you've never done airborne dragon attacks before. A new experience for you."

His grin is wide, his long, white canines slightly bloody. "After all these centuries, it's exciting to have new experiences."

"You may wish to focus on finding your clue," Utiss says. "We're approaching the island now."

Bruin settles in beside me and lays flat to distribute his weight. I scan the island below and try to figure out where we're going. It's a long, oval island densely covered in forest and no apparent buildings or monuments. "Looks like a ground search. Do you know anything about the terrain below?"

Utiss angles his head, drops his shoulders, and we descend fifty feet or so. "It is covered in trees and vegetation. There is a rocky section around the crest of the top point and an inland pool of water near the center."

None of that sparks any ideas.

"Do you know where they hid the first clues in the past?"

"In any number of places: deep in stone caves, under fallen trees, one year they were strung up in an empty wasp nest right next to an active one. It took men two days to find that one."

"Are they ever hidden with magic? Could I find them that way?"

"Not usually. Simply placed somewhere hard to find and hard to get to."

It's pretty obvious that this part of the challenge is meant for the riders and not the dragons because other than a rocky beach on the top edge of the island, there's nowhere suitable for Utiss to land.

"Bruin, this island is uninhabited, so if men came over in the last day or so, you might be able to pick up their scent, right?"

"Aye, if they haven't masked it somehow."

Right. But they weren't anticipating a spirit bear joining the challenge, so I'm fairly sure they wouldn't have masked anything.

"Okay, the mighty bear takes the first third of the island. Utiss, if you drop close to the canopy, I'll drop into the trees and search the middle section. We'll make our way back to the dragons at the opposite shore. Does that make sense?"

Utiss drops close to the treetops and slows down. "As much as anything else."

Cool. That works for me.

If the ancient dragon doesn't think it's a bogus idea, I'll take that as a win. When we get to the leading edge of the island, Bruin spirits away. I jog off the center of Utiss's spine and ease down the slope of his ribcage.

"It won't get any lower or slower for you, Fiona."

"All right. I'm going." The last time I flew off the side of a dragon, a bolt of magic shot me off and I had no say in the matter.

Jumping off by choice seems crazy.

Another dragon swoops in close, and the rider looks at me like I've sprung a couple of extra heads.

Oh, it's my armor.

"Yeah, it's pretty freaky the first time you see it, but it's well worth wearing it. You never know when you're going to jump off a perfectly good dragon and fall to your death."

"Quit stalling." Utiss tips so suddenly that I lose my balance and fall.

"Diminish Descent." I watch the leafy top of the canopy as I fall, directing my feet to guide my descent into an opening between trees instead of crashing into branches. Wind whistles in my ears as I get that amusement park rush of butterflies as I fall.

For the most part, my plan works well, except for the blast of orange energy I don't see coming. My shield goes off a moment before the magic hits me in the back and sends me face-first into the trunk of a very hard tree.

The impact rattles my bones, but with my armor up, I sustain no lasting damage.

I wish I had the chance to see who took a cowardly pot-shot at me from behind, but I'm too busy peeling my face off the bark as I slide bunglingly toward the forest floor. I should've called *Feline Finesse*.

Hindsight.

When my feet finally hit the ground, I scan my surroundings and try to think of another way to search for the clues and where the event organizers might've hidden them.

Bruin's working on the scent of things…

"Commune with Animals." I pause, dropping to one knee to press my palms against the grass and focus on my connection with nature. It's been days since I've been in my grove, and even though this isn't a fae source of power, the natural state coupled with the abundance of woodland creatures is a balm to my soul.

Closing my eyes, I open my senses and take time to learn about the animals here. The small, scurrying animals are scared and sitting motionless while they sift through their fight or flight options.

I come in peace, little ones. Have you been disturbed by others lately? Maybe men tromping through your forest in the past few days?

When nothing comes back to me, I think about how easy Gran makes all things nature and wildlife look.

The shadows of a couple of dragons flying overhead snap me from my mental musings and reinforce the urgency of keeping the foot on the gas.

I reach out with my fae energy and try to find a bigger animal, one that wouldn't be so timid when faced with the incursion of strange humans tromping through its home range.

There aren't many animals of any size.

The biggest animal I can sense is a red fox watching me from beneath a bush. As curious as the little guy is, he's also wary.

Which is understandable.

Reaching out, I brush him with a gentle suggestion of friendship and ask if he's seen or smelled any strangers recently.

The images he sends me in reply are more impressions than words. But yes, the fox saw men come through here yesterday.

Where did they go, little one?

He considers taking me but catches the scent of the dragons and other humans on the wind and hunches back under the protective cover of his hiding spot.

That's okay. You hide. Can you picture it for me?

I see the images. A rocky outcropping. A craggy tree on a rocky slope. A hole in the stone.

Thank you, little one. Stay safe.

I leave him and scan the forest around me.

Snap.

The twig breaking directly behind me makes me vault forward to gain some distance. *"Feline Finesse."*

I dive forward into a front handspring. Landing ten feet away, when my feet connect with the pithy ground, I spin to face whoever was sneaking up on me.

Pelleas has his sword drawn and was about to stab me in the back.

Rude.

Flexing my right hand, I call Birga to my palm and grin. "Back-stabbing is both cowardly and ungentlemanly, but what's unforgivable is you poisoning my dragon because you're too much of a weasel-faced pussy to face me without cheating."

That sparks a fire in him.

He lunges forward, and it's on.

Poisoning Dart and sneaking up on me from behind gives me the impression he lacks in talent and confidence and is compensating. When we go hard at it, I realize how flawed my theory is.

He's a damned good fighter and keeps me on my back foot more than Sloan would like.

"Bestial Strength." I hope to level out the playing field.

I raise Birga with both hands and brace as he comes down with bone-shattering force. If *Bestial Strength* and my armor hadn't been active, a strike like that would pile-drive me into the ground.

As it is, I grunt and absorb the hit. Pelleas launches himself over a root, and I thrust my hand toward the ground. *"Entangle."*

The roots whip up in response to my call and grab hold of his ankle. I take his momentary distraction as a chance to catch my breath and check my surroundings—

My shield ignites with a fiery burn a heartbeat before I'm knocked forward by the point-blank strike of an electrical blast.

Sensation rips down my spine.

That would've crippled me if my armor hadn't been active. No time to dwell.

I backpedal to reposition myself for a fight on two fronts. Spinning Birga in my hands, I hold position while the two of them move in. Birga is excited for the battle, anticipating the blood she will spill and consume.

I eye up my second opponent.

I don't know him, but I remember his square jaw and crooked nose from the banquet. He's got his palms out and is conjuring up another round of magical energy.

It's orange...like the blast of energy that hit me and knocked me face-first into that tree.

Coincidence? Maybe.

As the next ball of orange energy comes at me, I choke up on Birga and knock it out of the park. "Batter, batter, batter, swiiiing batter."

His eyes widen as his spell shatters and sails back at him.

Bruin materializes and dives into the mix. The astonishment on their faces is too funny. "Have your fun, Killer Clawbearer.

Maybe don't kill the one with the orange magic. The one with the sword, however, helped poison Dart, so have at it."

Bruin roars, and I leave him to it while I cast a privacy spell to seal in the noise of our battle.

While he has his fun, I try to figure out where the rock outcropping is. If the fox's vision is correct, there's a hidden cavern beneath it where the clues are.

The baleful screams of men echo around me, and part of me regrets the violence. I would've been happy to have a healthy, competitive race to the finish line.

They initiated the bloodshed.

I think about what Utiss said about the island's topography and wonder if the crevasse is closer to the far end of the island.

That's where he said the rocky landscape is.

But no.

In the fox's vision, all around the mouth of the cavern were densely growing trees.

Bruin trods over to me and grins. "What now?"

"I got it from a local source that men were here over the past couple of days, and they dropped into a rock outcropping surrounded by forest. He showed me a craggy tree on a rocky slope. I think if we find it, I can lead us into the hole in the rock where the clues are."

"On it," Bruin says. "There was nothing like that on the part of the island I already searched. It was marshy and flat. I'll take a look around for a craggy tree and rocks. Shout if anyone else wants to play."

"Will do." When he breezes off, I scan the forest. The distant clash of metal-on-metal makes me feel a little better. Maybe it's not all about killing the girl who dared to enter the contest.

Deciding to avoid getting tangled in another fight if I don't have to, I scan the canopy above and climb.

With *Feline Finesse* still in play, I move through the branches as easily as walking on the forest floor.

A blast of fire sizzles through the air below me, and I crouch behind a screen of leaves. A man wails and writhes on the ground thirty feet below with Wolfric and Earl of Dickdom kneeling over him.

So, it's not only me they want to crush.

Something catches the Earl's attention, and he turns. He must have a gift of sight or location or something because he looks straight past the branches and leaves and meets my gaze.

Gone is the veil of feigned diplomacy he showed me yesterday. His eyes glint with malevolence as he reaches back and catapults a ball of flame at me.

I'm about to retreat when something even stranger happens. His presence wavers in front of me as the bone ring on my thumb bursts to life.

The ring cuts through the man's glamor.

He isn't even the redhead, Sigberht. He has dark, shaggy hair and a scar across his left cheek. When I look at him, my shield goes wild, and I'm not even sure who I'm seeing.

Who is he? Why did he glamor himself as a local?

My mind spins with a million questions until he reaches forward and I'm under attack.

I react fast to the fireball, but not fast enough.

The flames singe my shirt and heat my ribs. *Tough as Bark* saves the day. Out of my crouch and running, I navigate the canopy as quickly as I can.

Over a branch.

Under a nest.

Through the thicket of leaves.

Bruin, if you can hear this. I've got the other two men who poisoned Dart on my ass, and they're not playing nice.

I'm not sure if he'll hear me over our mental connection or not. It depends on how far apart we are.

Another flaming projectile blasts through the foliage and I

have to tuck and roll to the side to avoid getting hit. I fall for a bit, getting poked by sticks and whipped by branches.

It doesn't faze me.

It does knock me to the low branches to face the incoming assault of two very hostile men.

"Wall of Thorns." I call the scrub on the forest floor to close in around them. *"Confusion."* I drop a few more feet to get a better vantage point. *"Insect Plague."*

As the air erupts with the buzz and hiss of insects, I drop to the ground below and take off running. I try not to be a vindictive person, but when their screams rise behind me, I gotta say, it gives me the warm fuzzies.

Is that wrong?

I'm still running full-tilt when Bruin breezes around me and I slow down. "What did you find out, buddy?"

He materializes into his beautiful hulking form next to me. "Follow me. I found your hole in the rock."

CHAPTER NINETEEN

Forgetting the battles and hostilities of being attacked by Pelleas, Wolfric, and the Earl-not-Earl guy, I follow Bruin and switch gears back to the challenge of finding the first clue in Morgana's tournament.

Thankfully, the island isn't big, and with me dropping in the middle section, by the time we climb the rise of rock, I figure we're pretty close to being back to the rocky end of the island where the dragons are.

Bruin stops at the top of the rock and hunches down to look in the hole. "Was this what you saw?"

I lean forward and examine a three-foot-square opening into the ground below. "I think so. I guess there's only one way to find out."

Before I step off the edge and drop in, Bruin raises his paw. "Me first, Red. Even with your armor on, you're not invincible. We learned that the hard way."

"If you want first dibs for access into the hole, I'm not about to argue. Maybe you can clear out all the cobwebs and grossness while you're at it."

Bruin laughs. "I'll do my best."

When he disappears, I give him a few minutes to investigate, then I follow. I can make out rocks and dirt thirty or so feet below, so I sit on the edge and let myself drop.

Diminish Descent does the rest.

Straightening at the bottom, I wrinkle my nose and try not to inhale. "Gross. It smells like rotting assholes down here."

Bruin laughs. "All the feminine charms of my girl coming out fer the world to see."

"Faery Fire." I hold up the ball of blue light against the darkness. "Hey, I'm authentic. Some people think that's better than charming."

"Och, make no mistake, Red. I'm one of them. I take ye as ye come and am happy to have ye."

"And I appreciate that. So now, let's get this clue and get outta Dodge. I want to kick this contest in the hoo-haw and be done with it."

There's only one direction to follow underground, so we get going. "Merlin said this tournament is a challenge of skill, strength, and intellect. I think we've proven ourselves the scrappy underdogs so far, but by the time we finish, I want it known that we rock socks and they are misogynistic asses."

Bruin chuckles. "Don't let them get to ye, Red. The people who matter know yer the bomb."

"I know, but maybe it'll help the women of this time if the powerful men of the area learn a healthy respect for the abilities of a lady. We're more than cooks and baby-makers."

Bruin chuckles. "A mere ten generations ago, when the goddess ruled the land, women were free to make choices, own land, and take oaths. When the church overtook England, that's when women's rights began to vanish. I don't suppose ye'll change anything by showin' them yer a strong and capable female."

I sigh. "All right then, I'll kick their asses for my satisfaction."

"That's likely best."

I raise my arm and cast light against the far wall of the tunnel. It's a dead end. "It can't be. There has to be something here."

I release my fae vision and search the area again. "I've got nothing. You?"

Bruin's got his nose up and is sniffing the air. "Maybe something."

Good. Maybe something is good.

"All right," he says, pressing his black nose close to a spot on the dirt floor. "There's a density of scent here that suggests they were touching something."

"I am awed by your awesomeness once again."

Bruin smiles and drags his massive paw over the floor of the tunnel. "I do try."

I brush my hand over the dirt, opening my senses up to anything that might jump out and get me. Nothing comes back to bite me in the ass. My shield remains inactive as I uncover a piece of wood hidden by loose dirt.

"Can it be this straightforward? Find the box and open it?"

Bruin grunts. "I don't know. Are any of yer warning bells ringin'?"

"No. Nothing."

"Och, then maybe the trick is that there is no trick."

"Mind bendy."

"Only for the people who were screwed over enough times to expect a double-cross of some sort."

Agreed.

I dig in the dirt, and as I brush my hands over the soil, I project a spell to help me find what I need.

In a challenge of men, I stand alone,
and ask that the unseen be shown.
With good intentions, I seek the prize,
to keep it from those evil guys.

. . .

I laugh at how that came out, but hey, it works, and intention is everything. I find the edge of a piece of wood beneath the soil and trace my fingers all the way around until I've outlined all four sides. "Let's have a look. You ready?"

Bruin snorts. "I was born ready."

"Yeah, you were. Ready. One. Two. Three."

I flip back the wood and grin at all the scrolls rolled in the box. After a quick count, I clutch my fist in triumph. "All ten are here. We're first."

"Hells yeah, we are."

I pull one out, unroll it and take a moment to study the clue. Once I've got it, I stick it into my bra.

On a hunch, I take out a second scroll, unroll it to ensure they're all the same, and giggle as I cast a spell on it.

Take from me, and you shall pay,
Your path is wrong and far away.
Trickster map it's up to you,
Take him off to Timbuktu.

I giggle and place it in my pocket, then replace the lid of the wooden box. Once it's recovered with dirt, I press my hands on the soil.

"*Earth to stone.*"

As the ground hardens to rock around the box, I straighten and brush off my hands. "All right. Back to Utiss, then to the next destination."

The two of us make quick work of getting back to the opening of the rock formation, and I kneel with my palms on the dirt.

"*Heaving Earth.*"

The ground shakes and shimmies beneath me and raises me until I can reach the lip of stone above and climb out. "Thank you, earth."

I send the soil back to the bottom of the passage below and frown at the stone opening.

"Shape Stone."

It's a moment's work to seal the opening shut so all traces of the entrance point to the underground hidey-hole are gone. Normally, I wouldn't be such a dick in a competition, but apparently, that's what Lady Morgana's tournament is all about.

Little surprise.

I'm about to climb down when my Spidey-senses go haywire, and a heaving horde of bugs, spiders, and snakes slither and scramble for me.

"Gross." I search for an escape as the ring of creepie-crawlers tightens around my feet.

"I don't think they're real." Bruin swats at the ground and clears long swipes of rock with each swing of his mighty paw. "I can't smell any animal scent from them."

"Magic bugs?" I get control of my kneejerk reaction and look at things with a bit more objectivity. "All right. Now that I'm focused, I sense the signature. It's some kind of illusion. Forget them and let's get back to Utiss."

"Sounds good to me."

Taking to the trees once more, I climb up into the canopy and encourage Bruin to take his spirit mode and scout ahead for the best route.

I hurry along, invisible to the other contestants until below me, four other competitors wander around looking in the hollows of trees and turning rocks.

Sorry boys. You're cold.

If any one of them had been kind to me or even not hostile, I might consider giving them a hint, but they weren't, so I won't.

Merlin told me not to lose focus on the prize, and I haven't. Laytah is mine to lose at this point, and I won't lose her. Lives depend on that.

Eventually, the trees thin and I drop to the forest floor. I've lost the protection of the canopy, but if I'm right, Utiss and the dragons can't be far now.

Throughout our journey, the ground has morphed from pithy soil to tangled scrub to pebbled rocks. Despite my best efforts, it's difficult to mask the sound of my steps on this ground.

I could cast *Stalk Silently* or *Fleet of Foot* and dash for it, but I've expelled a lot of energy for one day and am worried I might deplete myself entirely for the battles to come.

Rounding a large boulder, I scan for—

A hard uppercut to my jaw snaps my head back, and I stumble to keep my feet under me.

I grip the trunk of a tree to keep from falling and take stock. Damn, the inside of my head is in complete disarray. It's as if my brain has been ransacked.

Mr. Punch first and ask questions later, crunches the stones behind me and I push off the tree and spin. I manage a strong palm thrust to my attacker's throat in time to avoid the dagger in his left hand.

"Wolfric. Imagine meeting you here. Decided not to search for the clue but scavenge for scraps, did you?"

His cold smile tells me I nailed that. "Better to use your brain than exhaust your strength."

He's a bloody mess, and I don't even feel bad for the guy. You come after me and mine, and you're going to bleed.

He comes at me hard, and the fight continues with a flurry of fists. His run-in with Bruin earlier has left him sloppy and a little lame on his left side.

I manage to disarm him with a solid twist of his wrist. When he loses his dagger, he seems to realize this isn't going to go well for him.

I sense the surge of his magic building but have no idea what kind of skills he has. I push off his shoulder to gain some distance and call Birga.

"*Siphon.*" His command comes off as a whispered hiss but even breathless, it works. I feel my magic draining and can only assume it's boosting his.

Not good.

Still, I'm a good fighter even without magic. I get Birga's tip up and keep him at a safe distance, swinging and defending so he can't get inside my defenses.

Only he's not trying to.

He's stalling.

Either he's waiting for the Earl Dickwad imposter to catch up with us, or he knows druid strength and stamina stem from our fae power, and he's wearing me down to swoop in.

I hate to admit it, but neither of those options bode well for me. "Bruin. Now would be a good time for you to get your furry ass back here."

A rock the size of a grapefruit hits the side of my head and knocks me spinning.

Did Wolfric throw that?

I don't think so.

Can he command nature?

I don't know.

My balance is off from the strike to my head, and I barely get Birga up to block before a massive branch cracks down on me. Wolfric can command nature because no one is swinging that branch.

I recoil, off-balance, my strength all but gone.

"Killer Clawbearer, I need you."

I deflect the next strike and stumble backward. As I fall, Wolfric tackles me to the rocky ground. My hips hit the rocks a second before my hands brace his weight on top of me.

Scrambling beneath him, I fight to get him off me as he reaches into my pocket.

He pulls out my bogus scroll and rolls off me, grinning like he's the shit.

"Give that back, you bastard," I snap. "You didn't find it, and you didn't earn it."

He holds his hand out to the side, and the branch snaps into his grip. "I disagree. I think putting up with you for two days has been trial enough. I earned this clue and then some."

He reaches back to take his swing and Bruin materializes beside me and knocks him flying backward. With a murderous roar, Bruin sends the birds flying and the butterflies in my chest fluttering like crazy.

Wolfric scrambles to his feet and turns to run.

"Let him go, Bear," I say as Wolfric runs away like the coward he is. "He's so not worth it."

When it looks like Bruin's rage is drowning out his reason, and he might give chase, I grab his furry ankle. "No, seriously, bear, let him go. He stole my trickster map. We got the last laugh."

Bruin roars once more to let it out, then his muscles tense and twitch as he shakes it off.

The urge to fight runs strong in him.

Rolling to my knees, I push myself up, and we close the distance to the rocky shoreline where the dragons are waiting.

"It took you long enough," Utiss snaps.

I grunt, gripping his elbow and struggling to pull myself up onto his collar. I'd depleted my magic before Wolfric siphoned off what was left.

If lives didn't depend on what happens, I'd curl up next to my bear and have a nap. "Nice to see you too, Utiss. I think we're doing spectacularly. We're the front-runners."

"Except you're not."

I chuckle and wave that away. "I fed Wolfric a bogus clue. He's going on a wild goose chase."

"Earl Sigberht left ten minutes before him."

"Hubba-wha…no way. Bruin and I were first to the clues and hid them well. There's no way that Sigberht imposter got a clue and beat me here. I call bullshit."

"I call cheat," says Bruin. "That's why Wolfric was waiting for you. He gave his buddy a head start."

I frown. "Two against one. Smart."

CHAPTER TWENTY

Wrought by the elf of mythical acclaim
A prince made king with heralded fame
Freedom from the great prison of stone,
Tests the mettle to the marrow of bone
A little sister, a noble daughter
A shimmering blade, who sings of slaughter
Where the essence of gods and giants merge
Destiny, fate, and magic converge

I finish reading the clue aloud and wait to hear what they think. Utiss is huffy with me because he wants a destination, but I can't give him what I don't have.

Man, I wish Nikon was here.

The Greek is a marvel with riddles.

I read it out again, this time slower and thinking about possible other meanings for each word.

"Okay, so the first four lines are about Excalibur, right? *Wrought by the elf of mythical acclaim, A prince made king with heralded fame, Freedom from the great prison of stone, Tests the mettle to the marrow of bone.* That's Arthur pulling Excalibur from the stone."

"Yes and no." Utiss pumps his wings and tilts right toward the setting sun. "It's about Arthur pulling the sword from the stone, but that wasn't Excalibur. The Lady of the Lake gave Arthur Excalibur when his sword broke in battle, and she gifted him a new one."

"What? Why did I think that was Excalibur?"

"I would answer that, but Cazzie told me to be kind."

I grunt at him. "Fine, so I've blended two myths. A young Arthur pulls a sword from the stone to prove he's the rightful king."

"Caliburnus," Utiss says. "Commonly referred to as Caliburn."

"Fine. Arthur pulls Caliburn from the stone and becomes king." I flick my hair out of my eyes and turn my head so the wind pulls it away from my face.

"A little sister, a noble daughter." I read, one hand gripped on Utiss's collar and one holding the scroll. "Merlin said Laytah was a commissioned piece that Uther had a master craftsman forge. If it was the same Avalonian elf of mythical acclaim, that would make Laytah Caliburn's little sister, right? And she was forged for a noble daughter."

"Makes sense to me," Bruin says.

I think so too. *"A shimmering blade, who sings of slaughter.* That is Laytah. But wait...do the officials know that? I thought when Wolfric made up that bull crap about her singing Morgana's praises, that it was because her true intention was a secret."

"A secret from you, maybe," Bruin says. "It could be they simply wanted to keep the new girl in the dark."

Utiss grunts. "What does that matter? Where do you want me to take us? Once we return to the mainland, I need a destination."

"Where was the sword pulled from the stone?"

"Legend has it, the stone with the sword trapped in it,

appeared in a churchyard in Montesiepi Chapel, in Chiusdino, Italy," Utiss says.

"Do you think that's where they'd hide Laytah? Would they reenact the whole stone thing and put the dagger in the stone?"

"It would be a much smaller stone," Utiss says. "Almost ridiculous to picture."

It is silly to picture.

Bruin looks up at me and shrugs his muscled shoulders. "Chiusdino is far, Red. If we're wrong, it'll lose us a day of travel each way. That might give Earl of Dicks the time he needs to win the tournament."

I don't want to do that.

"What about tracking him specifically? He has magic. Can we track his signature or scry for him? Or maybe the binding magic from his dragon's shackle?"

"Possibly," Utiss says. "I can sense magic in the air, although I have no way of knowing what it is. It could simply be a faery taking a midday flight."

I sigh. Why can't this be easier?

Oh, right, because it's a tournament of skills, survival, and smarts. "Where is that magical energy headed? Is it out of the way, or can we follow it for a bit while we think?"

"For the moment, it doesn't take us off course."

"Good. That gives me a few more minutes to figure this out." I close my eyes and push down the aching hunger in my belly and my need to pee. Connecting with the rhythm of Utiss in motion, I empty my mind and invite cognitive brilliance to shine its light on me.

Sadly, brilliance evades me.

Where the essence of gods and giants merge, Destiny, fate, and magic converge.

"What is the origin location of dragons?" I ask. "Merlin said the blood of gods and giants fell and merged with fae prana to create you. Where was that?"

"Across the lands from Breton to Gaul to Naples to Hibernia to Moravia to Bohemia."

Poop. That's not helpful at all.

"What do you think that last bit is about—dragons obviously —but in what context? *Where the essence of gods and giants merge, Destiny, fate, and magic converge.*"

"The Dragon Guard of Tintagel possesses the largest army of dragons anywhere. Twelve dragons held captive and within their power. It is a point of pride for them."

"Where do they house the dragons when they're off duty?" I ask. "Is there a stable or a lair for them when they aren't being shackled into servitude?"

"There is. It's in an underground cave found on the mainland side of the drawbridge. Why do you ask?"

"Partly because I know I'm missing something and partly because it's pissing me off that these men think they have dominion over dragons. How does that even happen? How did they get the upper hand on them and chain them as beasts of burden?"

"The same way most men in their position seize the upper hand—by being cowards. They raided a lair, killed the mother, and confiscated the fertilized eggs."

"That's deplorable."

"They would never be able to control a freeborn dragon but those who have never known the joy of being at one with the sky and serving no master have little fight in them."

"I'm sure the magic shackles have a lot to do with it too. No one wants to be a slave."

"You are idealistic, Lady Fiona. They are dragons. I would rather die than bow to lesser men, yet they make no effort to liberate themselves."

"But they know no better...and they won't until someone educates them on the joys of being at one with the sky and serving no master."

The low, graveled rumble of his amusement undulates under my feet. "I underestimated you. You are still arrogant, but you are nobility-driven. That somewhat makes up for you being a loud voice in a tiny package."

"Um...thank you?"

Bruin chuckles and lifts his shiny, black nose. "I hate to break up yer bonding moment, but could we get back to the current dilemma? Where are we headin' for the next part of our quest?"

I sigh. "I honestly don't have a clue. If you boys have any suggestions, I'm listening."

"Actually," Utiss says, dropping his shoulder and veering to the left and down. "I do have an idea."

Bruin and I wait to see where Utiss is taking us, and it becomes clear once I see the castle perched out in the sea. "Back to Tintagel?"

"Almost. When you spoke of the bound dragons, it got me thinking. The tournament officials would have needed transport to the island where they hid the clues. Logically, that would have involved dragons. If they used the dragons to set the first clue, perhaps they know more. If they can tell us the final destination, maybe we can skip the other tasks altogether and go straight for the dagger."

"Point to you, dragon. More than just a scary beast, you have ancient wisdom too."

"You are an odd female."

"You're not the first to tell me that."

With a new destination in mind, I'm jazzed. Yes, the dragons might be bound to the men of Tintagel but are they loyal to them? Where I come from, loyalty is earned, not demanded.

I think Utiss hit on something.

"If we can find out where Sigberht, Earl of Dickdom went, we might be able to stop his cheaty ass from getting that dagger."

Bruin chuffs. "If yer right and he didn't need the clue, why did he come to the island as part of the competition?"

"To not come would expose himself as a fraud. Oh, and speaking of him being a fraud…when I was fighting him in the forest, Sloan's ring stripped an enchantment off him, and I saw beneath his glamor. He's not Sigberht, Earl of Dickville at all. He's another man entirely."

"What other man?" Utiss asks.

"I don't know. I'd never seen him before. He's a dark-haired brute with two different colored eyes and a scar on his cheek."

"One green and one brown?"

"Yes."

"What kind of scar?" Utiss asks.

"A red line from his cheek to his ear."

Utiss mumbles something in tongues and pumps his wings harder, taking us straight toward the castle.

"Does that mean something to you?"

"It does. It would also explain who kills us in the next few days."

I don't follow, but my curiosity is piqued. "Who do you think glamored himself to be Sigberht?"

"From your description, Yvain, Lady Morgana's son, attacked you."

"Yvain? I've never heard of him."

"Morgana was pressured into marrying King Uriens of Gore, and she bore him a son. He grew up serving Camelot as one of the Knights of the Round Table, but his character darkened after his mother fell from grace. He made no secret that one day he would find a way to free her from her prison and reunite them."

"So you think he found a way and is making his move to unleash Morgana on the world once again?"

"I do."

Okay, that's bad.

Just having Morgana's grimoire near me was almost more dark power than we could manage. If Yvain found a way to bring the woman back, we have to stop him.

"The dagger," I say. "Laytah has something to do with his plan, doesn't she?"

"I would guess so, yes."

"What does that have to do with the dragons? You said you think you know who killed the dragons."

Utiss is giving it his all now.

Each rhythmic *thwoomp-thwoomp-thwoomp* of his massive wings propels us closer to the lair. "In the end, Morgana blamed Merlin for the turn her life took. She studied magic as his apprentice, and when she twisted it to her gain, he stopped. She never forgave him and swore one day she would return and take everything he values from him."

"So, you think in the previous timeline, Morgana escaped her prison and killed Cazzie and the rest of you?"

"I do."

"Then where did she go for the next eleven hundred years?"

"I can't say."

"And Yvain needs the dagger to perform some kind of ritual to release her?"

"That would be my guess."

"Then I definitely need to win her."

Utiss grunts. "You miss the point. There is no way Yvain would leave the ownership of the dagger to chance. I bet he knows where the dagger is and knew he could claim it at any time. He's likely gone to fetch it and will arrive at the castle as the conquering hero."

"I knew he was cheating. Do you think he's in league with the tournament officials? Did he convince them to give him an advantage?"

"Not willingly," Utiss says. "The tournament holds too much

honor and tradition to betray it. The three men on the committee are arrogant dolts, but I respect their integrity, and they revere the event. Yvain, however, is a powerful sorcerer. He could make them his puppets with a twist of his wand."

Well, crappers.

Utiss goes quiet for a bit, the only sound being the wind blowing in our ears. "We need to get back to the castle and warn Merlin. We need to figure out how Yvain plans to bring back his mother and what we can do to stop him."

I grip the ridge of the dragon's collar and we dive toward the surface of the sea.

The moment Utiss lands, I release my hold, jog down the hill of his shoulder and slide down to land on the plateau. My bond with Dart is growing stronger every day, and I think worrying about him for the past hours has ramped that up even more.

I sense him and am relieved to feel his pain and discomfort have subsided.

When I round the corner into the dragon community room, I find him resting by the hearth. My poor boy. It's not right that he got caught up in the mayhem that swirls around me.

If he had died...

"He'll be fine." Merlin rises from where he's reading a book on a pallet on the floor.

"Eavesdropping on my thoughts?"

He winks. "You're not so difficult to read that I can't make an educated guess."

He's not the first to say so. I tilt my head toward where my dragon boy is resting peacefully. "I worry. After losing Brendan, I think I'm hyper-concerned that everyone around me remains safe."

"That's completely understandable. Loving people is hard on the heart and tough on the nerves."

True story.

"Why don't you go check on him. I'm sure it will make you both feel better."

Don't have to tell me twice.

I go to him, hug his jaw, and press my cheek to his. "How are you, baby boy? Better? You feel better."

Utiss snorts behind me. "Your baby boy is a mythical beast of unlimited strength and incredible power. You realize that, yes?"

I roll my eyes. "Of course, but you weren't there when he hatched out of his little egg and looked up at me so innocent and cute. He'll always be my baby boy."

Dart chuckles beside me and licks my cheek. "It's fine. Fi looks at life through her heart, Utiss. I am honored to be her baby boy."

I scrub the front horn of his three and kiss it. "So, not poisoned and dying anymore?"

"It wasn't as much fun as it looked, so I stopped."

"Excellent. Scratch that off the list of things to try."

Sloan chuckles behind me and wraps his arm across my shoulders in a hug. When he presses a kiss to my temple, I lean into it and accept his strength as the gift it is. "Poisoned and dying is off all our lists, please. It is highly overrated."

"What happened with the tournament?" Merlin asks. "I wasn't expecting you back until much later."

"We have a rather alarming theory and need to tell you about it."

Utiss and I spend the next ten minutes filling them in on how Sloan's ring broke the glamor on Sigberght and how we think he is Yvain here to free Morgana from her exile.

Merlin frowns. "If you're right, it would explain what happened to Cazzie and the dragons. Morgana hated me for my part in stopping her and swore if she got free, I would never be truly happy."

"Killing the dragon companion of someone sharing a fated bond would certainly achieve that," Sloan says.

"I would've been destroyed if I didn't have Cazzie's essence within me."

"The Merlin and Cazzie combo was fabulous." I wink at Cazzie. "All your feminine glitz and glam bled through and allowed Merlin to live another life completely."

Cazzie flutters her eyelashes. "Then I suppose being dead isn't such a hardship. If we are bound evermore, I think I'd like that."

Merlin pulls his long, dark hair away from his face. "No. This time around we have an idea who's coming for you, and it'll be different. I'm not losing you again and certainly not to Morgana and her whelp."

"So, what's our plan?" I ask. "How do we find Yvain and stop him from releasing her?"

The dragons all turn their heads simultaneously toward the doorway.

"What do you hear?" I recognize the scenario.

"The castle bells are ringing," Cazzie says. "It seems Tintagel is under attack."

CHAPTER TWENTY-ONE

S loan *poofs* Merlin and me up to our room in the castle. We rush down the stairs and out to the courtyard. The bells have stopped ringing, but the effect they've had on the people of the castle is still wildly underway.

"Where are they all racin' off to?" Sloan asks.

I press back against the wall to keep from getting trampled. Two hundred people are stampeding toward the drawbridge gate, and it's creating quite a bottleneck.

Merlin points at the flow of traffic and pulls us into the sea of bodies. "Whoever sounded the alarm will wait to draw a crowd, then will explain the panic. Follow the people, and we'll find out what's going on."

The three of us join the frenzied exodus from the castle and things get really cozy, really quickly.

I'm crushed against a man—a fisherman by the smell of him—and offer him an apologetic smile. "Excuse me. Why were the bells ringing?"

The man dips his chin in greeting, and when he sees Merlin, he pulls his hat off and clasps it in his folded hands. "Rumors of ships sailing down the coast has folks worried. People is afeared it be the savages. One of the guard reports they'll overtake us by morning."

My gaze lifts to the night sky but unlike in the city, nightfall in the ninth century is pitch black. I look sideways and frown at Sloan. "You mentioned Ivor the Boneless and the Danes attacking down the east coast, and I know the Norse Vikings were active now too... but here? Did they make it through the English Channel and up and around to Tintagel?"

"Not that I know of, but the Picts and the Gaels might be considered a threat. He said down the coast, so that would be coming from Ireland or Scotland."

"Celts? We're about to be attacked by the Celts?"

Merlin shakes his head. "No. By now the Scots are set and settled, and the Vikings who invaded Ireland have come to terms and no longer pillage. They're all about trade and colonization."

"Well good. I didn't want to be invaded by my ancestral people."

Sloan snorts. "I don't suppose it makes much difference when spears and swords are cutting the air and blood is being shed."

"I suppose not...still, I'm glad."

Once we get through the crush of the drawbridge and the castle gate, we allow the bustling crowd to sweep us across the narrow strip of land that connects Tintagel to the land beyond.

There is a growing buzz in the air, and I can't help but be moved by how truly frightened the locals are.

Growing up in Canada, I don't think there's ever been a day when I've feared for my safety—well, before being branded with the mark of the Fianna.

That's partly because of the period I live in, but mostly because I was fortunate enough to be born in Canada. Even in the twenty-first century, there are too many places where people fear invasion or soldiers or bombs on the daily.

"There." Sloan points up at the sky in front of us as a dragon takes off into the night.

I strain to see, but it's too dark to recognize who it might've been. I do, however, recognize the three contest officials standing on their podium up ahead.

My elbow gets bumped as the crowd packs tighter. Everyone seems eager to get close enough to hear what's about to be said.

"Are the savages coming?" someone shouts.

The man who started us off this morning nods. "It has been reported three massive ships are approaching from the north. Two with forty oars and one with sixty by our count."

The woman beside me gasps into her hand.

"What does that mean?" I ask.

"Those are large ships, milady. They will carry a great many heathen savages...perhaps a hundred and fifty or two hundred in all."

That explains the widespread worry.

"What's to do?" someone asks.

"We leave the castle at once. Everyone gather your essentials. The wagons will leave as soon as they are full so hurry or you'll find yourself left behind."

No one likes the sound of that.

One of the other officials raises a hand to quiet the noise. "I'll have men at the stables to help load and get the caravan on its way. Bring only what you can carry or can't bear to lose."

"What about the castle?" someone shouts.

"The Dragon Guard will stay to fight and secure what is ours. But the castle means nothing if our lives are lost. Go now. Prepare to leave."

As the crowd thins out, Merlin pushes forward until we reach the three men at the podium. "Three ships coming from the north?" he says. "Who reported the sighting?"

"It was Sir Sigberght, sire. He saw them during his return flight from the first leg of the competition."

I frown. "I returned from the same place and saw no ships."

The three men scowl at me. "Are you calling Sir Sigberght a liar?"

"Maybe."

Merlin shakes his head. "Never mind. My niece is simply exhausted from a trying day. Carry on, gentlemen. It's much too busy a time to dally."

I bite my tongue until we're out of earshot. "Nothing like making me look like a ditzy fool. There were no ships in the water. Even if I didn't see them, Utiss would have."

"Oh, I know." Merlin waves away my pique. "If Yvain plans to release Morgana and wants the castle cleared, there is a reason. He may not have meant to, but he's given us a clue to his plans."

I look between him and Sloan. The two of them seem to be noodling on that, but I've got nothing. "I suppose, even if it's a lie, the people are safer not being here. If things break out into a battle, I'd rather not have innocent casualties."

"Another good point."

The three of us turn and start back toward the castle.

Sloan presses a gentle hand to the small of my back and guides me between the two of them. The crowd is frantic and wild. "So, if Yvain wants the castle evacuated, there's likely somethin' or somewhere he needs to access to perform his ritual."

Merlin nods. "My thoughts exactly."

"Okay, but when you returned from your journey the first time in this timeline, do you remember hearing anything about the contest being interrupted by an attack of savages?"

He shakes his head. "No. Though, to be honest, I was out of my mind with rage and grief at finding Cazzie and the others dead."

"Then what changed?" I ask.

Sloan frowns. "Perhaps we've already altered the natural course by simply appearing here as we did."

That makes sense. "Because last time, no one saw through his glamor and realized what Yvain was up to? Or maybe having Merlin return a week earlier than expected fouled up his plans."

Merlin grumbles, "Well, if Yvain thinks he's simply going to set Morgana free to kill everyone I love and darken the future, he's got a rude awakening coming his way."

"Hells yeah, he does. We've got enough trouble on the horizon with the Culling and Mingin and Melanippe. We don't need Morgana in her persona of the Morrigan in the mix."

Merlin shakes his head. "So, we stop him from freeing Morgana and keep the dragons from being killed. Two birds, one stone."

"What's our stone?" I ask.

Merlin shrugs. "That's for us to figure out. Come, we need to return to the lair and fill Cazzie and the others in on what we've learned."

The three of us make our way back to the chapel, and Sloan *poofs* us down into Merlin's lair. "I'll go update the dragons and check on Dart. You need to change, Fi. You have holes burned in the fabric of your shirt and are costume malfunctioning."

"I'm pissed about that." I glance down at my ruined druid shirt and scowl.

"Do ye want me to take ye up to our guest room in the castle?" Sloan asks.

"No. I think the tunic I wore before will be fine. Where'd you put it?"

Merlin hitches his thumb over his shoulder. "In my chamber over the chair."

"All right. I'll make myself presentable and find you guys in five. Sloan, can you check on Dart and make sure there are no aftereffects from the poison?"

Merlin chuckles. "Is this you saying you doubt my abilities, girlfriend?"

"No. It's me saying I worry about those I love and want to make sure he's fighting fit before the shit hits."

The two of them stride off, and I make my way back to Merlin's private chamber.

There's a fire in the packed-dirt hearth, and a tall candle tree lit in two of the far corners of the hollowed-out cave. They produce enough light to find the tunic draped over the chair and get changed.

When I hold up the tunic, it becomes very apparent that if a battle breaks out, this isn't the best choice. On a whim, I grab Merlin's knife off the bookshelf, cut his tunic two feet shorter, and pull it on over my pants.

Grabbing a piece of twine, I tie that around my waist, and voilà, I'm ready to star on *What Not to Wear: Medieval Edition.*

I'm about to leave the chamber when my shield tingles to life. I stop to assess my surroundings, searching for what might have set things off.

Nothing.

Bruin? Will you please look around and tell me if anything or anyone seems out of place? My shield is niggling at me. It's not so much danger as a heads-up.

On it.

There's a flutter in my chest a moment before the pressure behind my ribs builds and releases. I fiddle with my shoes to waste time, retying my laces to give him a chance to snoop around.

There's a mangy-looking rat in the corner by the bookshelf nearest the hearth. Only it doesn't act or smell like a rat.

What does it smell like?

Magic.

Awesomesauce. Find Merlin and Sloan to tell them. I don't want to leave and give it a chance to slip away.

On it. Hold tight.

While he's gone, I look around the room to figure out how to waste more time while watching—and at the same time not watching—the rodent tucked over by the furs. Stepping over to the café table, I pick up the book Merlin was reading.

It's written in a language I don't recognize, but if the way the stanzas are penned on the page is any indication, I'd say it's a book of poetry.

Aw…how sweet.

Our magician is a romantic.

A flash of fur in my peripheral vision has me spinning to keep the fiendish furball in sight. The time for playing coy is over. I run forward, throwing my hands at the retreating rodent. *"Dispel Magic."*

My spell hits and knocks him against the stone as he transforms back into a man.

"Wolfric. What a surprise."

He leaps to his feet faster than I anticipate and mutters something. I stiffen like a board and curse.

It's a binding spell, and it hit me square in the chest.

I'm immobilized.

He rushes toward me, grabbing the knife I used for my fashion alterations from the table.

Tough as Bark.

Thankfully, even while fighting against the immobilization spell, I'm able to call my armor.

Wolfric sees the etched roots and branches appearing on my skin and falters in his advance. "What are you?"

Rude. My armor is a little unsettling and not the most feminine thing to look at, but that was harsh.

It also seems to be a rhetorical question because he resumes his attack and reaches me as I break his binding. As he thrusts the blade toward me, I grip his wrist and force his momentum to the side.

The sudden shift in trajectory throws him off course, and I follow up with a stern shove. He stumbles to catch his footing but manages not to fall. Staggering for the door, he makes it to the opening entrance of the chamber and runs headlong into the man himself.

"Merlin," he sputters.

Merlin grabs the man and knocks him back on his ass. Wolfric *thunks* on the stone floor, his head and arms snapping back from the force of the fall.

Sloan throws his arm out, and the knife Wolfric holds is ripped from his grip.

"Back again so soon?" Merlin snaps. "I thought I told you the last time we caught you trespassing down here that to do so again would be the end of you. What the hell is going on? What do you want?"

"Both times he watched us change our clothes. I'm going with Middle Ages pervert."

Wolfric sneers at me but doesn't reply.

Merlin points at a small trunk on the bottom shelf of one of the bookshelves. "Sloan, open my apothecary trunk. There is a clear bottle of green leaves with a silver worm in it. Bring it to me."

Sloan does as he's asked and returns a moment later with the small bottle. He holds it up, and the shiny, silver worm slithers around more like a pinkie-sized snake.

"Open the vial and give me the worm."

Ew, gross.

All kinds of creepy horror movie images flood my mind. "Please don't put the worm up his nose to infiltrate his brain or anything disgusting."

Merlin makes a face and blinks at me. "No. I'm keeping the worm safe. It's the leaves we want. One of you take a leaf and stick it in his mouth, but be careful not to put your fingers in your mouth."

"Why?" I'm suddenly worried about Sloan. "What do your worm leaves do?"

He smiles into the palm of his hand. "This is a silver ring leech. He has hypnotic excrement that can penetrate even the most difficult mind."

Hypnotic excrement?

I giggle. When they look at me sideways, I shrug. "Sorry, psychotropic poop is funny."

Sloan shoves a leaf into Wolfric's mouth and holds his lips shut so he can't spit it out. He resists for a moment, thrashing and forcing Sloan to scramble to keep his hand clamped across his lips, but when he relaxes, glassy-eyed, and his arms hang loose at his sides, it's obvious the worm excrement is taking effect.

"Wash your hands, hotness." I point at the bathing pool. "We don't want you hopped up on worm crap."

He rolls his eyes. "I take back the part about ye being every bit an English lady."

"Good. Now you're getting it."

Merlin ignores us, his focus squarely on Wolfric. "I've known you for almost forty years. Why now have you taken to invading my privacy and becoming a thorn in my side? What's this about?"

He opens his mouth to speak but then a rush of magic snaps in the air. His lips clamp shut, and he lets out a pitiful groan.

Merlin frowns and raises his hands.

"What is it?" I take a step closer and raise my palms to test the power in the air. "Is Wolfric a sorcerer?"

"No. He has a few parlor tricks at best."

"I pulled him out of a rat transformation, and he cast a decent binding spell on me before you got back here. Earlier, he hit me with siphon and drained my mojo dry."

Merlin looks perplexed. "The Wolfric I've known his entire life is arrogant and entitled but doesn't possess the power of taking animal form. I wouldn't think him capable of casting a fishing line let alone casting a siphon spell."

"So, what changed? What is going on?"

Wolfric groans. His hazy gaze and twitching lips tell me he wants to tell us something but each time he starts to make a sound, that rush of magical energy bursts in the air around us and he groans and falls silent again.

"Who is silencing you?" Merlin asks. "Is it Yvain...the man posing as Sigberght?"

His pained grimace indicates no answer is coming.

Merlin presses his palm on the man's forehead and moves his lips, uttering a spell. When he finishes, he steps back and tries again. "Who is controlling you, Wolfric? Who gave you the ability to transform? I know you want to tell me," he says, his voice laced heavily with persuasion. "You need to get it off your conscience."

Wolfric frowns as the subtle energy of Merlin's suggestion is hit with a third rush of power.

It's become a battle of the stronger spell: the one Wolfric is bound by to keep his silence versus the one Merlin cast to compel him to speak.

"C'mon, Wolfman." I lay in some persuasion of my own on the off chance it might help tip the scales. "Let's hear it. Who sent you down here to spy on us and why?"

The snap of magic in the air signals that Merlin's spell has won out. Wolfric opens his mouth, and this time, he begins to speak. "A stranger...with a scar...he searches for—"

Between one word and the next, something within the chamber seems to detonate.

Wolfric screams and then—

Kasplat!

CHAPTER TWENTY-TWO

I spin at the last minute and duck behind the table, but it's Merlin who has the quick thinking to erect an invisible field to contain the damage of a man exploding into a gazillion bloody bits of body.

When I pop my head over the surface of the table, my stomach takes a twisty-turny churn.

Grimacing at the pile of man, I try not to gag. "Oh, that is wrong on so many levels."

Merlin steps back and lowers his hands. When he releases his protective field, the Wolfric bits plop to a wet heap on the cave's stone floor. "I never liked the man, but he didn't deserve to be made a pawn in a game of cat and mouse."

I want to say cat and rat, but it's too soon.

The poor guy hasn't even stopped pooling.

I draw a deep breath and force myself to stop looking at him. "So, the dark-haired man with the scar is Yvain. What is he searching for? Wolfric's last words were, 'He searches for...' What?"

Merlin shakes his head. "I've spent the past millennium mourning the deaths of Cazzie and the others, thinking they died because of what they are. Then we presumed it was Morgana getting even with me and destroying what I love. Maybe it's about something I possess, or they think I possess at the time and us being here fouled up their plan."

I look at the heap of goo and clothing.

Calling Birga to my palm, I poke at the clothes, hooking his coin purse and belt out from the muck.

As gross as it is, maybe it can tell us something. Flicking it clear of the mess, I look for something useful. "I don't suppose you've got any Lysol wipes?"

"All out. Sorry."

"What should we do with him?" Sloan is eyeing the man-muck like it's a science project he's evaluating.

My boyfriend has issues.

Sometimes learning more is *not* a good thing.

Merlin shrugs, taking my lead and picking up the coin purse to have a look. "We'll leave Wolfric to the dragons. They can disappear a body faster and more efficiently than any of us."

I've seen Dart munch down centaur guards in the fae realm, but this seems…blech. I gag. With the sight and smell in effect, it's too much. Closing my eyes, I throw up a little in the back of my mouth.

Must change the subject.

"Assuming there's something here that Yvain needs or thinks he needs to complete the release of Morgana, it stands to reason if we find it and make it unavailable, we're one step closer to stopping him and his evil plan."

"Agreed," Sloan says. "Twice, we found Wolfric lurkin' in the shadows in this room. It stands to reason that whatever his master searches for, he thinks it's here."

"What do ye think it is?" Bruin asks, taking form beside me. He lifts his nose toward the dead guy and makes a face. "That's rather gross."

I nod. "Rather. Yes."

Merlin straightens and starts looking around. "I have no idea. I don't remember what I had in the lair at this point or who might've been after it."

Cazzie joins us and looks at the blood and bone mess on the floor. "A friend of yours, darling?"

Merlin shakes his head. "It was the same man I escorted out of here the other day when we arrived. We think he was searching for something."

"Something important that someone sent him to find down here," I add.

Her eyes widen. "One of my treasures?"

Merlin shakes his head. "While your treasures are invaluable, we think it's something *I* possess."

Cazzie huffs. "I know you value your trinkets, Emrys, but if the thieves knew anything of value, it would be *my* collection they covet."

Merlin nods. "Without a doubt, my love. Let us be thankful the men involved are oblivious to the items of true value in this cave. Your treasures are safe."

"Do you think that's why they killed us on the last timeline?" she asks matter-of-factly. "Do you think they trespassed with the intent to steal from you, and I caught them? I would defend your belongings almost as passionately as I would defend mine."

"Almost," he repeats with a smile.

She flutters her golden eyelashes. "Well, your treasures do tend to be less inspiring than mine."

"Not all treasures need to sparkle or shine to hold value."

She huffs a small cloud of smoke. "Keep telling yourself that, druid."

Merlin chuckles and strides over to the bookshelves. "I used to hide trinkets and small treasures in hollowed-out books."

He pulls out four tomes from three different bookcases. Setting them on the table, he flips their covers open one by one. The first holds a large orange and red gemstone the size of a chicken's egg. The second holds the brooch Dora had Sloan and I recover from the cemetery for her. One of the books is empty. The fourth holds a crystal key.

"See," Cazzie huffs. "Nothing worth dying over."

"All right, so we know what Wolfric is after."

"We do?" Cazzie says.

I nod, pointing at the brooch. "This is Morgana's and is said to be enchanted as the catalyst to bring her back to the living realm. I left it in Merlin's care when we first met because I know he has it in Toronto when we become friends."

Merlin takes the brooch and passes a hand over it, hovering as the power of his magic raises the hair on my arms. The air warms as Morgana's talisman morphs from a lady's brooch to a man's pipe.

When the magic in the air fades, he grabs a leather coin pouch and drops it inside. Then, he steps over to Sloan and ties it on his belt. "It's better with us than left down here, and if Yvain manages to figure out that it's not a pipe, you have the best chance of keeping him from getting it. Whatever happens, Irish, portal off and keep him from getting this."

"Of course."

"Even if you need to leave me behind." I raise my finger and point at him. "Morgana getting free is bigger and badder than me being in danger. Got it?"

Sloan frowns. "I've got it, but—"

"No buts," I say, sobering. "Seriously. I love that you're loyal and protective and a million other things, but for moments like this, we're warriors, not a couple. Lives of the many over the lives of the few."

"Why does it have to be either-or?"

"I'm just saying in the instances that it is, pick the mission's success because Bruin and I are unstoppable and we'll figure something out. We always do."

"Yeah, we do," my bear grunts and lifts his massive paw for a high five.

Sloan doesn't seem happy with that, but he doesn't argue. "So, while Wolfric's searching, Yvain initiates the evacuation of the castle. What's the rush?"

"Good question, Irish," Merlin says. "Maybe he's anxious we're on to him, or it could also have something to do with the next phase of his plan."

"Maybe he realized I saw through his glamor," I say. "Is there a ritual or pagan holiday or some kind of prophecy about today, this week, this moon cycle?"

Merlin and Sloan look at each other and shake their heads.

I scrub a hand through my hair. "We're sure the report of Viking raiders on the way is bogus? I didn't see any ships, but maybe we took a different path back than Yvain?"

Merlin frowns. "There was no raid. When I returned from the king's coronation, the castle was whole and intact. That's why I couldn't understand how the dragons could be dead."

Sloan scans the items on the table again and nods. "Even if our arrival altered a few things," Sloan says. "I don't think the ripple of change would include inciting an invasion of hostile forces from another land. It's safe to assume the evacuation is for the sake of Yvain's plans and has nothing to do with an impending attack."

Merlin nods. "I'll send Utiss to speak to the indentured dragons. Maybe they can tell us where Sir Sigberht traveled in the past few days or weeks and give us an idea when Yvain took him over and what he's been up to since."

"We need to find him," I say.

Sloan grins. "Within a few hours, the caravans will have evacuated the castle. It will be much easier to find him and hopefully stop him without endangering others."

Merlin nods. "In the meantime, we'll go to the castle, grab a bite to eat, and see what we can learn."

I scowl at the Wolfric splatter pile. "I'm not sure I'll eat for a week, but yeah, let's see what we can find out." Sloan *poofs* Merlin and me up to the room in the guest house once again—it's much easier than climbing the hundreds of steps to the chapel—and I make sure we've gathered our belongings and are ready for a final check out. Odds are, with everything going to hell up top, no one will take notice or care if we sleep down in a dragon cave for a few nights.

Assuming we're even here for a few more nights.

Honestly, if Dart's well enough to travel, a quick escape back to Toronto is my first choice anyway.

Before that happens, we need to stop Yvain and make sure the danger to the dragons is over.

Once Sloan *poofs* my borrowed clothes down to the lair, he returns, and the three of us go downstairs.

The castle-wide evacuation is underway, and everyone is racing around gathering last-minute provisions before heading to the stables to join the caravan. We do our best to stay out of the main traffic flow, and by the time we arrive at the east hall, my appetite has returned.

A steady flood of people exits the eating hall as we head inside and sit for a meal. Ms. Marigold has set out small loaves of bread and chunks of cheese for the travelers to take a snack for the road.

"No issues getting a table tonight," Merlin says. "Where would you like to sit?"

Three long banquet tables run down the center of the rectangular room. I point at the one closest to the window and round the end to watch the commotion outside.

Sloan pulls my chair out for me, and when I sit, both of them do as well.

"Are you not leaving?" Marigold asks as she brings us out three mugs and a pitcher of warm apple cider.

"No," Merlin says. "We're confident we'll be fine. If the worst happens and savages attack, we have the dragons to get us away from the danger. We'll spend the next few days in the lair with Cazzie and the others."

"Are you leaving?" I ask Marigold as she pours us each a cup.

"No, deary. My Alfred brought me here to help him work this kitchen when we wed. He took great pride that no stomach went empty in Tintagel, and I won't let him down by being run off by a bunch of savages who may or may not come. I have no plans to leave the castle today or any other."

I smile. "That's lovely. Good for you."

Merlin sips from his mug and sets it down on the pitted surface of the table. "If it's of any comfort at all, we three will defend you to our last breath should the need arise."

Marigold looks me over and doesn't seem to put much stock in me defending her, but bows her head anyway. "May the good Lord watch over us all."

"Your evening victuals," Sunnifa says, setting a tray down with three bowls and three side plates. "Porridge and oat griddlecakes served with Ms. Marigold's homemade applesauce."

Merlin smiles and accepts the plate she offers. "That sounds delicious. Thank you, Sunni."

Marigold ventures off to the kitchen and returns a moment later with a little tin and an extra spoon. "Since there's only a handful of takers tonight, how's about a bit of extra cinnamon to top things off?"

"Much appreciated," Merlin says, pulling his spoon from his mouth. "The applesauce is especially good this batch. I noticed it last night too."

She lowers her chin. "The old tree by the fishermen's dock is having a banner year in spewing forth gloriously sweet ruddy apples. I sent two of the lads down the day before last to pick me a bushel."

"It's delicious," I say. "It reminds me of my gran's homemade applesauce."

Marigold grins. "It's high praise to live up to the cooking of someone's gran. That's a true compliment."

I nod. "In this case, for sure. It definitely is."

The three of us are left to eat in peace while I watch the chaos outside the window. Sloan's right. With that many people leaving, we should be able to find Yvain much easier and with little fear of innocents getting hurt.

"So, what's our plan?" I break an oat griddlecake into pieces to dip it in the applesauce. "Do we wait and see if Yvain comes to the lair to snoop around or do we go on the offensive?"

Merlin chuckles. "I've never known you to sit and wait for the fight to come to you, girlfriend."

Having him call me that makes me smile. "How much Dora is left in you now that Cazzie's essence is her own again? Is my flamboyantly feminine friend gone?"

He reaches across the table and squeezes my hand. "I'm still figuring that out. Being Dora has been fabulous. I love my life in Toronto, my club, my dancers, my drag and trans friends. I don't want to give that up...but I'd be lying if I said Cazzie's empress-ness—as you called it—wasn't a huge contributing factor."

I squeeze his hand and smile. "I guess we'll see how the next few days play out and how you feel when the dust settles. Just know that no matter how you end up or who you identify as, we're behind you all the way."

Merlin winks. "Thanks, cookie."

I giggle at that coming out of Merlin's mouth. He's a brawny, rugged, chestnut-haired warrior man. Him calling me cookie seems wildly odd.

Which is perfect.

I love wildly odd.

"Och, here comes a dragon guard." Sloan flicks his spoon absently toward the window. "He doesn't look at all pleased."

Merlin has his back to the door and lifts his cider to his lips.

Sloan and I strike up a meaningless conversation about the lovely fall weather and how much we're enjoying our time at the castle.

"Merlin. Why are you sitting here at your leisure when the rest of us are busy readying to evacuate?"

Merlin turns. "Because the three of us won't be evacuating. We'll be fine in the lair, Geoffrey. No need to worry about that."

The dragon guard stomps to the end of our table and presses his dirty, calloused hands on the wood surface. "I'm not sure what you're playing at, but when the savages get here, your niece better be long gone. You know what they're like. You've seen firsthand the animals they are."

"My niece is in no danger of being ravished. She's a druid warrior, like me. She has gifts, like me. She is a dragon rider, like me. Even if she wasn't able to defend herself—"

"—Which I am," I add.

"Which she definitely is," Merlin confirms. "Even then, she's not here alone. Mr. Mackenzie and I and the dragons will put up more of a fight than any Viking warriors expect. Don't worry about us."

He grunts, going red in the cheeks. "We don't have time to chase you down and fuss over this. Get your things together and join the caravan or stay and meet your maker. I'll not warn you again."

Merlin nods. "As you wish, Geoffrey. Message received."

"So, you'll leave?"

"No. But you need not warn us again." He waves his fingers in front of the man's face. "As you said, you don't have the time to chase us down and fuss over this."

Merlin reclaims his mug and goes back to sipping his cider. A moment later, Geoffrey shakes himself out of whatever fog of confusion he was under and glares at us.

He looks like he wants to say something more but can't quite remember what that is.

A thundering crash outside has the horses whinnying wildly, and he turns to look out the window.

"You better go check on that."

With a huff and a frown, the dragon guard stomps off to investigate the commotion outside.

"You don't need to see his identification," I say, holding my fingers up to wave my hand in the air between us. "These aren't the droids you're looking for. Go about your business. Move along."

Merlin chuckles. "Did you know George Lucas based the Jedi on the druids? Obi-Wan is an artistic take on yours truly."

My jaw drops. "Shut. Up. You're shitting me."

He holds his expression for only a few seconds before he cracks up. "Yes. I am totally shitting you, but the look on your face was fantastic."

Sloan barks a laugh and holds up his fist to bump with Merlin. "Oh, sham. That was a good one."

I feel robbed. I bought into that with everything I have. "Har-har. You two are so funny."

Sloan sobers and refills his mug. "It was too good not to laugh, *a ghra*. He's right. Ye should've seen yer face. Ye were all in on that one."

"Because it makes so much sense. Are you sure it's not true? When we get home, I'm going to look into it. Maybe George Lucas is a closet druid or has a friend who spilled the beans or something."

Merlin chuckles. "Oh, dear. I've created a stalker."

I grin. "Yeah, you have."

"First, we need to get home," Sloan says. "To do that, we need to find Yvain, stop his plans, and make sure Cazzie and the others don't get killed on this timeline."

I spoon in another bite of applesauce and swallow. "Let's getter done."

CHAPTER TWENTY-THREE

I've never been to a ghost town before. I've seen them in the old westerns Da watches, but as the three of us walk through the empty courtyard of Tintagel Castle, I think this must come close to how those cowboys feel at high noon. In the time it took for us to eat dinner, the chaos of packing wagons and people scrambling to get gone has ended, and now things are dead quiet.

Okay, *dead* quiet sounds eerie and foreboding.

Unnaturally quiet is a better way to describe it.

Why tempt the fates, amirite?

"It's like having a castle all to ourselves."

"Very much so." Sloan scans the building entrances and the empty drawbridge gate.

Sloan grew up in Stonecrest Castle, and the loneliness of that makes me sad. It's no wonder he loves old, crumbling buildings as much as he does.

As a kid, they were his only friends.

I stop as we near the closed drawbridge and do a three-sixty to take things in. "Do you think if we stop and carefully listen, the castle might tell us her secrets?"

"It almost feels like that, doesn't it?" Merlin says.

"It does."

It's cool to be in a time and place when dragons, while not common, are at least accepted by the general public. It's also upsetting to know people will kill them off in the years to come.

Or so they think.

"Where do we begin?" Sloan asks. "How do ye want to go about findin' Yvain?"

Merlin lifts a shoulder. "I suppose if we want to find Morgana's son and he's here doing some kind of ritual, we cast a spell. *Detect Magic.*"

As Merlin's power snaps in the air, the hair on my arms raises on its ends. He put a little extra in that.

I suppose that to stop Morgana's release, giving it your all is likely a good idea.

After he casts the spell, Merlin picks up a pebble and rolls it across the cobblestone of the courtyard. It tumbles and rolls toward the weapon's keep but doesn't stop.

Powered by the magic of Merlin's spell, it takes on a life of its own and keeps going. We pass the door to the armory and watch as the pebble rolls under a closed wooden door.

"Where does that go?" I ask.

Merlin tries the handle and opens the door. The hinges creak as he peers into the dark stairwell. "Down to the lower levels: the apothecary, the dungeons, the treasury, and a few military storage rooms."

"That wasn't on our tour."

"It's reserved for approved castle personnel only. Usually, this door is locked."

"We have a pebble to find, so let's not dally." Merlin lifts his hand and lights our way, touching the wall-mounted torches with faery fire as we go.

The stone steps are crumbly, and I'm searching the area around my feet as we descend, trying not to step on Merlin's magic-finding pebble.

"Where did it go?" I ask when we get to the bottom.

Merlin glances around and shrugs. "It's hard to tell with all his little brothers and sisters lying around."

Sloan chuckles. "Ye do realize that we all sound a little more like her every day."

Merlin grins at me. "That's fine. Fi rocks my socks."

I giggle as he winks.

From the bottom of the stairs, there are three possible choices: left, right, and straight ahead.

"Either the first little dude is dead, or he got away on us." I stare at the floor. "Nothing's moving."

Merlin picks up another stone and casts his spell a second time. He tosses the stone ahead of him like a hop-scotch rock, and it falls still.

"Okay," I say. "I'm going with dead. The magic stone trick doesn't seem to be working down here."

Merlin frowns. *"Find Path."*

Nothing happens.

"All right. We go old-school. Let's spread out and each take a corridor. Holler if you find something interesting. Whatever happens, don't be stupid and try to take Yvain on alone."

I frown. "Rude. Why did both of you look at me when he said that?"

Merlin arches a brow. "Coincidence, I'm sure."

"I'm sure." I point down the corridor I'm closest to and turn on my heel. "Stay safe judgy men of mine."

"Yer the beat of my heart, *a ghra.*"

I wave over my head. "Yeah, yeah."

"Love you, cookie."

I roll my eyes and call faery fire to my palm. "Okay, it's you and me, Bruin. You ready for a bit of recon?"

Always.

I release my bear and point up the corridor. "We're looking

for any sign of Yvain, what he's up to, or anything that strikes you as odd or out of place."

"Good enough. I'll be back."

He whisks off, and I trot down my corridor, peeking into one ransacked storage room on the right and another on the left. It seems the castle evacuation has left a few messes to clean up when people return.

"Milady, I'm surprised to find ya down here," someone says behind me.

I spin and greet the kitchen boy with the blond bowl cut I met yesterday in passing. "Cedric, isn't it?"

"Cenric, actually."

"Sorry. Names aren't my best event."

He looks at me like he's not sure what that means.

"Sorry. I also tend to say things that people don't understand. Don't worry about it."

That seems to set him at ease. "Ms. Marigold sent me to find a barrel of the floor polish they keep down here. She's using the evacuation as an opportunity to move the furniture out of the east hall to do a thorough cleaning."

A strange scuffing sound draws my attention further down the corridor. "Don't let me keep you, Cenric. I'm sure Ms. Marigold is waiting for her floor polish."

Cenric bows and steps back. "I'm sure she is... but are ya lost, milady? Would ya like me to show ya the way back?"

"I'm fine exploring, thanks. You go ahead."

"Very well." He nods and steps into one of the storage rooms I passed.

The strange scuffing sound gets louder as I get closer to the door at the end.

My shield flares.

I focus on the door ahead of me, but the strike comes from behind and sends me spinning.

The spell that hits me locks my muscles tight. I'm rigidly

stiff and tip like a wooden plank to the floor. Magic tingles over my flesh, and I stare up as Cenric leans over me. "I'm sorry, milady. Ya shouldn't be down here. It's a dangerous place for a lady."

Dammit. The kitchen boy blindsided me.

How embarrassing.

I call my armor with thought and fight down the feeling of being at anyone's mercy.

Freedom to Move.

I counter the spell, and its hold breaks as Cenric and now Pelleas move in on me. "I thought ya were a match for any man," the dragon guard says, grinning. "Isn't that what ya boasted?"

I barely get my hands up in time to stop them from grappling me, but I do. I grab Pelleas's face and push him away. *"Frostbite."*

Cenric comes in hard, and I catch his boot across the front of my forehead. My head snaps back and cracks hard against the stone floor.

I must lose consciousness for a few seconds because when I blink back to awareness, they've gagged me and I'm dangling upside down over someone's shoulders.

My mind is a bit like a game of Boggle for a minute, but I manage to lift my head and assess my situation.

Which is shitty, by the way.

I've been captured, gagged, and somehow my armor has been disengaged. Experience tells me only the strongest of foes have the juice to take down my armor.

Neither Pelleas nor Cenric impressed me as being that dangerous.

Bruin? You around, buddy?

With my skull throbbing, I'm not sure if I'm sending that out on our frequency or not.

"You've been a stitch in my side since you arrived, wench, but now you may finally be of use."

I don't need to see the man's mismatched eyes and scarred face to know who has taken me prisoner.

Yvain.

I'm flipped off the man's shoulders and dropped unceremoniously onto the stone floor. My tailbone and elbows hit hard and take the brunt of the fall until I stop against something soft.

I fight not to whimper as it knocks the breath out of me, but my eyes water from the spearing pain.

Fuckety-fuck.

I loll to the side and gasp. The something soft I'm resting against is the lifeless body of Ms. Marigold. What happened? The bright blue eyes of the robust and kind cook of Tintagel are glazed over with death.

Magical burns around her eyes and nostrils tell me part of the story. What I don't understand is why?

What did she do to Yvain or Morgana or anyone for that matter? Nothing.

I shout against the filthy rag stuffed in my mouth, but it does no good. I want to rip the binding from my lips and spear him through, giving Birga the thrill of drinking his dark power.

I can't.

They've done something to my mobility again. I'm not rigid, but I'm having trouble getting my limbs to listen to me.

I stare into the soulless eyes of Yvain, his glamor discarded as he leans over me. He mumbles something in tongues and my ears pop. Then he takes the gag out of my mouth.

Ah, a privacy spell.

"What the hell do you want with me?"

"Only what's mine, Fiona mac Cumhaill," he says. "Only what you stole from me."

"I don't know what you're talking about. I never laid eyes on you until two days ago. What did I take?"

"Haven't you figured it out yet? Who I am? What I'm doing? What I'm after?"

"Yeah. You're Yvain, and you're trying to bring Morgan le Fey back from her banishment. Sorry. I can't help you."

"Oh, but you can. You took me by surprise last time, and I admit, at first I was incredibly bitter about that. Bathalt was a powerful ally, and he assured me he could free my mother."

"Bathalt?" I frown and try to get my hamster running in his wheel. "Bathalt was a lunatic who wanted the immortality of a dark and possessed grimoire. He cared nothing about your mother beyond the power and prestige he anticipated if he could set her free."

"What was wrong with that? We had an accord, he and I. You had no business interfering."

"Except that your mother went full dark. She was banished for a reason. What does freeing her have to do with you killing poor Ms. Marigold? What did you think that would accomplish?"

"Oh, she was the test." He shifts to my other side and reaches past my field of vision. When he straightens, he's holding Morgana's dagger, and it's dripping blood.

"You stabbed Ms. Marigold with Laytah, and it did that to her?"

Drinker of blood. Taker of life.

I look at the old girl, and my heart goes out to her. The magical burns look horrid, and I can't imagine it was an easy death. "That dagger is tainted and dark."

His grin says he already knew that. "It took Morgana great pains to corrupt the elven craftsmanship and transform the dagger into a true weapon to be feared. Then you showed up and tried to take her like you took her spellbook and brooch."

Well, crappers.

Morgana's blood-infused grimoire is currently buried in the cemetery behind my house in the twenty-first century. I'm not worried about him getting his hands on that. The brooch, however…

"Where are they?"

"You think I'd tell you? Not bloody likely."

Pelleas pushes off the wooden table where he was sitting and steps behind a rack of shelving. Grabbing something, he heaves the weight of it with both hands and drags Sloan into view.

Unconscious and bound to a chair, my guy is totally at their mercy.

I curse, struggling to get up. "Let him go."

Cenric pushes me back down. He may be young and not athletic, but he has the advantage of the stronger position while I'm bound, and he's standing over me.

I glare and regroup. "Let him go. He's not a part of this. He's innocent."

Yvain shrugs and examines Laytah with a smile. "Your husband may not have stolen from me like you and Emrys did that night on the balcony, but he is most definitely part of this. I've watched you two together. You are in love and love is a powerful motivator."

"He doesn't have what you want."

"In my experience, lovers share secrets. I'm willing to bet that if he doesn't have my belongings, he at least knows where they are."

Crap. Of course, he does, but he's no more likely to give that information up than I am.

Dart. Can you hear me?

Merlin said we'd be able to communicate over vast distances as our bond grows, but everything is still new.

Dart? Bruin? Hello, anyone?

Nothing comes back to me.

If either of you can hear me, tell Merlin that Yvain, Pelleas, and Cenric have Sloan and me as prisoners. By the smell of things, we're still in the tunnels beneath the castle. They want the brooch and the grimoire.

I assess Sloan's state of unconsciousness.

He doesn't look hurt, so they must've caught him with a spell from behind before he was able to *poof*. I check his hip to see if he's still wearing the leather pouch with the glamored brooch in it.

Nope.

Where...oh, there. The pouch is on the table Pelleas was sitting on, and the pipe seems to still be in it.

Awesomesauce.

Hopefully, that means Cenric or Pelleas peeked in and took it at face value. Yay, Merlin.

"You should've stayed out of my business back at Carlisle. Bathalt was a good man and deserved better than for you to strike him down with a bolt of lightning."

"We'll agree to disagree."

He steps in close, grabs a handful of my hair, and yanks me off the floor. I let out a string of curses and only stop when he flings me into a chair against the wall.

Leaning in close, he sniffs and smiles. "I smell it on you, my mother's magic, her spells. You stole from me and took her life's work as your own."

"Not even close. Try again."

His arm swings, and—*smack*—he backhands me into next Tuesday.

The sting is incredible, and it heats my cheek with a throbbing pulse of its own. I blink as my eyes water and stretch my jaw to try to see straight. Between the stomp to my head and now the beat-down, this dirty old basement is spinning.

Dart? Bruin? Mayday. Mayday.

"You don't want me as an enemy, little girl."

"No. I don't," I say, my voice coming out a little slower and more slurred than I'd like. "It was nothing personal. I couldn't let a douche canoe like Bathalt of Anglia gain immortality for releasing a woman like your mother. It was a no-brainer."

Smack. My head snaps around on my spine. I won't be able to take many more hits like that before I'm pulling a full blackout.

Yvain leans close, and even without his mother's brooch and her grimoire, there's no missing the massive power he holds in reserve.

Like mother, like son.

"I don't know where you came from, Fiona mac Cumhaill, but you will return what is rightfully mine, or I'll return the favor and take everything important to you, starting with Mr. Mackenzie over there."

The warm tang of blood fills my mouth, and I drop my head to the side and spit. Unfortunately, I'm half out of it, and I've now spit blood all down Merlin's borrowed tunic. Yay, me.

"Why come after me and not Merlin? It seems he'd be the one you want, not some girl you don't even consider a threat."

He frowns. "I have other plans to make Merlin suffer for his part in my mother's misfortunes."

"Yeah, killing his dragons, we know."

His look of surprise is a win for me.

"You didn't think we'd figure that out? Well, I'm sorry to tell you, the lair is spelled against you and we warned the dragons. You won't be slaughtering them in any plot of vengeance. Sorry-not-sorry."

Smack.

Yeah. I saw that one coming.

A breeze brushes my hair away from my face, and I smile at the gentle caress. *Hey, Bear. Glad you could join the party. I thought you might miss out on the fun.*

This place was heavily warded. It took Merlin time to break through the spells. Where do you want me?

Is Merlin coming?

Och, about that...

CHAPTER TWENTY-FOUR

Now is not the time for things to start going wrong, but of course, we're talking about my life. Cue the twisting screw. *What do you mean he's not coming?*

We're out of time.

What does that mean?

The herald has arrived. The Merlin of this time is due back from the coronation within the hour. The Merlin of our time rushed back to the lair to ensure Cazzie and the dragons survive. He sent me to help you with his apologies. We need to finish things with Yvain and get out of the castle before he runs into himself.

Well, it's not like I'm lounging here.

I understand, but Merlin is rambling about paradoxes and cata-clysmic events. I stopped listening, but by the sound of things, it's bad.

Do you think I don't know that? As soon as my body is listening to me and I can move, we'll get this show on the road. Go blow in Sloan's ear and see if you can wake him. I need to concentrate.

Okay, cranky pants. Don't kill the messenger.

I chuckle even though nothing about this is funny. I've gotta get control of myself here or else we're toast.

Closing my eyes, I focus on the spell binding me. As scary as it is, Yvain's powers feel oddly familiar. I hate to think about how ingrained Morgana's magic became in my system a few months ago.

The dark magic of her grimoire was both invasive and pervasive.

Still, it gives me a slight edge now as I focus on unraveling the tether of his hold. I blink and work at loosening his spell.

Across the room, Sloan's head twitches, then he freezes. Good.

He's awake, and no one other than me noticed.

Bruin. When you take form, tell Sloan the brooch is in the leather pouch on the table to his right. They haven't realized it's the brooch under a glamor.

If Yvain gets close enough to it, Fi, he'll sense the signature of his mother's power on it.

I thought of that, but so far, so good. Just tell Sloan because if he has any ideas about poofing me out of here, we need that brooch...and the dagger too, if he can swing it.

I'll tell him. Get yer body back in working order.

Working on it.

Minutes feel like hours when you're waiting for the world to go to shit. Yvain is busy reading and tapping the yellowed parchment pages of a thick tome with the bloody tip of Laytah.

I need that dagger...and the brooch...and to get back to my dragon and get out of here.

Yes, I want it all. Is that greedy?

Yvain turns to me, and his grin doesn't bode well. "Let us see if you make a better outlet for the dagger. The castle cook barely lasted a minute before Laytah consumed her essence. I expect you shall prove to be a more fulfilling kill."

"Flatterer." I fight his spell with everything I've got. My efforts are building inside me, the pressure aching in my arms as I fight to move.

With each step he moves closer, Sloan's body tenses. If I've gauged the situation correctly, I'd bet his muscles are bound, and he's working on breaking Yvain's restriction spell too.

"Shall we hold her for ya, sire?" Pelleas asks.

"No need. She's as docile as a lamb under my control. She isn't going anywhere." He winks at me, the gesture pulling at the scar on his face, distorting his expression. "Now, this might hurt a little."

He laughs and shakes his head. "In truth, it will be excruciating. All the more fun for me."

Asshole.

Yvain secures my shoulder with a firm grip and clenches his fingers around Laytah's hilt with his other hand. "Here you go, precious lady. Another noble daughter for you to feast upon."

Magic snaps and zaps me like a bad shock in winter.

Hells yeah, I'm free of the binding.

I lift my knee as hard and fast as I can and shove at his chest, sending him staggering back. He pikes at the waist, and I twist out of the chair.

Sloan's up too and raging mad.

Bruin materializes into the mix and catches Cenric and Pelleas by surprise.

"Get the pipe!" I shout, pointing at the table as Sloan launches toward me.

Of course, his first instinct is to help me, but that brooch is more important. He doesn't bother running. He *poofs* to the table to grab it.

Yvain didn't stay distracted long enough. He and I are in a battle of wills over Laytah.

He's trying to impale me.

I'm trying to disarm him.

"*Earth Bind,*" Sloan says, binding Yvain's feet to the stone before dodging a bolt of magical energy shot by a screaming Pelleas.

Yvain curses at his feet, mutters a counterspell, and pushes forward. The sudden silencing of panicked screams by the door signals that Killer Clawbearer is as efficient as always.

Sloan and Bruin are closing in.

Yvain grapples me. The moment my shield flares hot, I know I won't like what comes next.

My senses ignite as he opens a portal. Then the two of us are standing alone in a cave. He sheaths the dagger at his hip and grips the front of my tunic with both hands. "You *won't* ruin this for me again. I will free my mother."

"Not if I can help it."

He swings back to punch me, and I call my armor forward. The *crack* of his fist connecting with the solid surface of my armor-plated belly is funny as hell, and I laugh at the *crunch* of bone.

"Excruciating? All the more fun for me." Taking advantage of his momentary distraction, I follow his retreat and grab his face with both hands. *"Frostbite."*

As he reels, I grab the hilt at his hip and take Laytah.

He grabs my hand as I pull back and twists my wrist. I lose my hold on Laytah, and my shield burns wild. My armor disengages at the same moment the dagger pierces my tunic.

I try to twist to keep from being stabbed straight into my side, but Yvain is fast and strong.

I cry out as the blade burns into the back of my hip.

Okay, it's my butt, but being ass-skewered by an ancient blade of evil is humiliating.

I grunt and spin, clocking him in the temple with a wicked hard backhand. The blow forces him to release the dagger. Dark magic climbs inside me like a million invading ants. They spread out, and my skin crawls with the sensation of all their little feet pinching me with every step.

Dammit.

The taint of Laytah's evil is invasive, but I won't fall to the same fate as poor Ms. Marigold. I need to get clear of him and get it out.

Resorting to the dark and dirty, I go in for a groin apple grapple and twist those low-hanging fruits like an angry ex-girlfriend.

I don't care how tough a man is. I've never yet met one with the testicular fortitude not to be affected.

He grunts and drops to the ground. "I'll kill you."

I'd love to say something super sassy, but I've got an evil elven dagger sticking out of my ass, and I'm not feeling it.

The snark, I mean.

I definitely feel the dagger.

With a brief window to assess my surroundings, I stagger out to the edge of the cave. Night has fallen, but with the help of moonlight, I see I'm on the top of a rockface with nothing but sheer stone straight down until darkness swallows it.

Awesomesauce.

With no medical clinic handy, I decide to pull the hilt and get this dagger out of my tush.

Wait. There's nothing vital in my ass is there?

If I pull this out, I won't hemorrhage or anything?

I'm pretty sure the answer is no, so I yank her free.

A wave of dizziness hits and I swallow, barfy bile burning up the back of my throat.

Damn, Laytah, I thought we could be friends.

Grabbing the ends of my twine belt, I wrap the hilt and cross-guard a couple of times and knot it tightly.

I'll need my hands if I expect to get out of here.

Yvain is shuffling behind me, cursing. "There's nowhere to go. My cave is twenty miles from the castle and drops straight to the sea four hundred feet down. Even if you make it down, you'll be torn up by the rocks."

That's not encouraging.

I don't care. I can't stay here. Laytah's poison is burning

through my system. My ass is numb, and I'm losing feeling in my left leg.

At the edge of the drop-off, I scowl at the rock and assess the possible finger holds. I've sat with the boys to watch adventure shows where the contestants have to scale sheer rockfaces. This is no different.

Except for the lack of a life-saving harness…and gloves…and climbing shoes…

And the fact that I've never done it.

Cat crap on a cracker.

I don't relish the idea of plummeting to my death and becoming a turkey vulture buffet. What if I become a turkey vulture instead?

Look at me thinking like a druid.

Animal Transfiguration—drop the mic.

But…I've only ever become a sabertooth panther. An eagle or an owl is a different beast. Literally.

I consider the pros and cons of taking a bird form.

Pro: I could launch off the ledge, leave Yvain with nothing, and fly back to the castle.

Con: Even if I manage to change into a bird on my first try—which after Emmet's alpaca-red panda-hippo troubles, I'm not sure I can—I don't know how to fly.

Note to self. Practice taking animal forms when you're not trapped on the top of a cliff.

Dart, if you can hear me, baby boy. I could really use an aerial rescue.

Yvain ambles onto the ledge and flashes me a predator's smile that knots my bowels.

Okay. Debate time is over.

Grabbing hold of a jut in the rock, I swing my foot off the stony ledge and send a prayer up to the goddess.

Today is not a good day to die.

Shape Stone, Feline Finesse, Bestial Strength... I call on any skill I've mastered that might help me. What the hell was I thinking? If I could go back in time three minutes, I would stand my ground, call Birga, and take my chances.

No, I wouldn't.

Yvain has the advantage in his lair. He is powerful, resourceful, and can negate my armor. Besides, taking Laytah away from him is the best offense.

He throws a bolt of energy at me, and I have to drop one of my hands to block. I'm thankful to have heightened strength, but even still, it's unnerving to defend at the same time as climbing.

Yvain must see my anxiety because he laughs. "Even better. I'll entertain myself until you die and gather what's mine at the bottom of the cliff."

Rude.

I scramble sideways to get out of reach. This whole rock-climbing thing isn't as difficult as I thought. Being at one with the stone means wherever I press my fingers, I find a place to hang on.

Sweet.

The pounding of my pulse starts to slow. *S'all good. I've got this.*

A breeze comes up, and I pause. *Bruin? Is that you?*

No. It's not.

The air holds a cloying sweet stench, and another rush of dizziness bombards me. The moment my grip starts to falter, I pinch my eyes closed and focus on holding on.

Fainting is bad.

Horribly, irreversibly bad.

"Warding Wind." I wedge my toes deeper into my footholds, my sneakers doing their best to keep me alive despite this unfamiliar terrain. The swirling wind I call picks up around me, and the air clears.

I press my forehead against the stone and take deep, cleansing breaths until the world settles.

Dart? Can you hear me, buddy? Something flutters against the consciousness of my mind, and I still. "Is that you, Dart? Bruin? Can anyone hear me?"

I search the open air behind me, both below and above. The night is upon us, and even with the moonlight, I can't see anything. Closing my eyes, Dora's teachings from earlier in the week come back to me.

"Open your connection and call him. As your bond matures, you should be able to communicate over vast distances."

I reach for the ribbon of glimmering blue and silver light undulating in my mind's eye. *Dart? Can you hear me? I'm in trouble and could use your help.*

The brush of his consciousness comes only moments before the brush of the breeze signaling his approach. *I hear you, Fi, and I am here to help. Push yourself free of the cliff, and I will fly under you as we practiced.*

Are you sure? We didn't get full marks on that even in training. What if I fall?

If you fall, I will catch you. I will always catch you.

Putting faith in my dragon, I release my fae vision, push off the rockface, and fall backward into the night.

CHAPTER TWENTY-FIVE

Practice makes perfect. Or, if not perfect, at least less terrible than the time before. I use my growing connection to Dart to sense his presence and find that I know where he is, even in the dark of night with nothing but the black void of the sea below me.

The rhythmic *thwoomp-thwoomp-thwoomp* of his massive wings is all the reassurance I need as I get my feet beneath me and ready to land.

The moment the rubber of my sneakers touches his scales, I absorb the landing with my knees and let out a whoop. "Like butter, baby."

Dart's laughter fills my depleted energy stores. *I think we get full points on that one.*

I jog up the line of his spine and grip the center handle of the saddle. "And no one around to see it."

Except for him.

I lift my head and curse as the silhouette of a dragon passes in front of the moon. Yvain. He's like a bad penny. "Do you think you can lose him?"

"I will certainly try. Hold on."

One thing I learned during my hours of flying with Utiss is that the dragon rider doesn't steer a dragon so much as hold on and have faith that the mythical beast knows what he's doing.

Dart has been leveling up by leaps and bounds, and the time he's spent here with the other dragons has given him a confidence and edge he didn't have before.

"Should we go back to the castle?" I ask as we swing wide and take a detour out over the open water.

No need. Merlin's wrapping up there and said he'd meet us at the stone circle when they're ready to leave.

"Leave? What about the dragons? What about Morgana and Yvain?"

You have the dagger and Sloan has the brooch. If we get back to our own time, we've done what we can to stop Yvain.

"And the dragons?" We dive to the side as Yvain comes at us with both his dragon's might and magic. I lurch to the side and throw my hand up to grab hold of the other handle. "Never mind. We'll talk later."

Righting my balance, I stare up at the massive black beast coming at us and scowl at the magic shackle binding its will.

That pisses me off so much.

With my plan forming, I call my connection to fae magic and wait for the next pass of the dragon's attack. As he dips low and extends his talons at me, I throw my spell forward with all the intention I can give it.

"*Open Sesame.*"

I'm not sure if it'll work when I cast it, but then the anklet stops ebbing magical misery and falls away from the beast's foot.

I fist pump the night sky. "Yeah, baby. Fly, be free. You don't have to obey that asshat anymore."

Dart makes a wide arc away from Yvain, and I twist around to watch as the dragon shakes his head. It takes a second, but then the beast roars and whips his tail around with violent force.

Yvain is batted hard into the open air—

"And it's a line-drive into the night sky!" I say in my best base-ball commentator's voice.

Yvain tumbles off into the darkness of night, and I release my fae sight to watch longer. The man isn't as vile and dark as I thought he would be.

He's not a good guy by any stretch.

I guess his obsession to free his mother isn't all rooted in a quest for dark power.

Dart pumps his wings and takes us in the other direction, and I lose track of Yvain.

He went from falling to flying, so I assume—unlike me—he knows how to manifest into a bird. So, not dead but no longer a threat, at least for the moment.

They are ready for us, Dart says on our internal wavelength. *Say goodbye to the ninth century.*

Questions are multiplying like horny rabbits in my mind, but before I can voice any of them, Dart propels us fast and hard toward the forest where we first emerged.

"Wait. What about Cazzie...and Sloan? Have we got everyone? What will the Merlin of this time think? Shouldn't we work through things before racing home?"

Merlin is confident he's handled things, and from what I'm sensing, Sloan agrees.

Okay, if the two of them are confident I won't worry—as much. "All right. Let's do this."

Under the dragon power of my blue boy, we cut the distance between the stone circle of the Tintagel countryside and us. The darkness is full of *whooshing* wings and the air churning from multiple dragons in the same airspace.

The stones seem to glow silver on the ground below, the moon full and at its zenith. I smile at our friends flying around us to give us a sendoff. Saxa's beautiful golden wings shine in the moonlight. Bryvanay arcs, stretching his wings wide. Merlin and Sloan are riding on Utiss and—

"Oh, no, Cazzie!"

The words tear out of my throat as I take in the lifeless form of Empress Cazzienth hanging below Utiss's mighty talons. He has a hold of her by the thick spines of her wings and is pumping hard to carry her.

We failed her.

How did Yvain get to her?

My heart is breaking as Dart makes a final bank in the air and aligns us to the stone circle below.

When he starts beating his wings, I'm at a loss. We can't leave like this. Merlin must be devastated. Why aren't he and Sloan getting on Dart?

Dart dives hard.

I grip the saddle with both hands as we plummet toward the ground. Wait. Everything is happening so fast.

One moment we're flying the night skies over Tintagel Castle, then the rings burst into a glow of gold and orange, and we're pushing through the veil of time and distance.

We emerge in the gray dawn light of an Irish morning with my brothers and Nikon cheering us on.

What is happening?

Dart shoots straight into the sky and circles back to land in the clearing. It takes a moment to release my white-knuckled grip on the saddle handle and run to dismount. I land off-balance and faceplant, but then realize it isn't me only being a klutz.

Blood has soaked my pants, and I can barely feel my legs.

"Very graceful, Fi," Dillan cheers.

I'm the butt of the joke for a few seconds before the circle spits out Utiss with Cazzie, Merlin, and Sloan, then comes Saxa, and finally Bryvanay.

The peanut gallery quickly gets the picture that our maiden voyage through the stones did not go according to Hoyle.

"What the hell, Fi?" Emmet grabs me under my shoulder while Kevin gets under my other side.

"Fuck, Fi," Kevin shouts, holding up a bloody palm. "You're hurt."

"I know."

With them for support, I shuffle to where Utiss lays Cazzie's body. "How did this happen, Merlin?" I say, my throat clogged with tears. "What did we miss?"

"Nothing." Merlin casts me an apologetic smile "Give me one second, cookie, and I'll explain. Don't panic. Everything is fine."

He leans against Cazzie's front leg, wraps his arm under her jaw, and closes his eyes. His magical signature builds until both he and Cazzie are glowing with the most beautiful champagne aura.

Sloan jogs over to me and frowns. "Where are ye hurt this time, *a ghra?*"

"Poisonous dagger to the ass."

"Laytah?" he says, his gaze catching on the enchanted dagger hanging from the twine around my waist.

"Yeah. She's not nice. I think she needs to go in the 'don't touch me' vault and time out for a few centuries."

"Let me get ye to the clinic, and we'll see about yer wound."

I wave that off. "Wait. I need to know what's happening with Cazzie and the dragons. My ass can wait. Merlin's more important."

Sloan frowns but knows he'll never hear the end of it if he doesn't give in. "Fine. Ye can stay long enough to assure yerself all is well. Then I'm takin' ye to the clinic."

"Fine. So, tell me what happened."

"Yeah," Nikon says, frowning. "The rest of us would like an update too. Three minutes ago, you, Sloan, and Dora went through the circle with Dart. Now you and Sloan came through with five dragons, a hole in your ass cheek, and did you say, Merlin?"

I blink at the surprised looks and grin. "Oh, yeah. I guess the magician is out of the bag now. Dora is Merlin, except he had the essence of his murdered empress dragon within him, so he was Merlin plus. When we went through the stones, we went back in time and were supposed to save his dragon. I thought we did... until this happened."

I point at Merlin and Cazzie. The two of them have stopped glowing and as Merlin straightens to stand, Cazzie's eyes open, and she raises her head. "Well, that wasn't so bad."

"You're alive." I hobble forward, and Emmet has to catch me as my feet don't come with me.

"Fi, it's time." Sloan's brow pinches tight, and I know the look. It's his "stop being a stubborn dumbass and listen to me now" look.

I hold up my finger. "So, she didn't die this time after all? The Merlin there hosted your essence, then we brought you here and replaced it so she could live again?"

Merlin nods. "When the Merlin of the ninth century returned to the lair this time, he found Cazzie lifeless, and Utiss explained that I needed to host her essence to keep her alive. Then, we brought her body forward, and I was able to revive her. If we hadn't gone back, I wouldn't have been able to, but technically, her body was only uninhabited for five or ten minutes."

"Brilliant," I say, clapping...well, I try to clap, but my hands don't meet. My motor functions are sloppy and uncoordinated. "Whoa, that can't be good."

"Okay, time to go to the clinic," Dillan snaps.

I wave as my boys gang up on me. "Welcome to the twenty-first-century, dragons. I'd like to stay and celebrate, but I'm losing feeling in my arms."

Sloan harrumphs and wraps his arm around my back and under my ribs. "Yer ridiculous."

"Hey, you're back!" Emmet pats Ciara's leg so she hops off his lap as Sloan and I *poof* into the back yard of my grandparent's home. "How's your back door?"

I roll my eyes. "The dagger didn't go anywhere near my back door. It was squarely in butt cheek territory."

Nikon laughs and offers me his chair around the fire pit. "Do you want to sit?"

"Not for a while, no. Wallace healed me while Sloan sucked the poison out, but my butt is still very sore."

Cue a roar of laughter.

"Sucked the poison out how, Irish?" Calum asks. "Was it like a snake bite scenario?"

"Did you give her mouth-to-ass, Irish?" Dillan asks.

"Now that's love." Nikon laughs. "Although, you have a great ass, Red. I can understand his commitment."

I flick my hand at them all and look at Ciara for some sanity. "What happened with the dragons after we left?"

"Merlin called Patty to let the Queen of Wyrms know there are other dragons in her territory. From what I gather, that's common courtesy. She expressed interest in meetin' the others before they're on their way, so that's what's happenin' now."

"Where's the meeting?"

"Still at Drombeg, I assume. They never mentioned movin' anywhere different."

"Awesome, thanks." I take Sloan's hand in mine. "Back to Drombeg if you don't mind."

"Mind leavin' these assholes, ye mean? Och, no. I don't mind at all."

There's another roar of laughter, and I squeeze Sloan's hand. "Don't worry. You sucking poison out of my ass will only amuse them for a few weeks."

"I used my powers, not my mouth, ye bloomin' idiots. I'd

think ye'd be a little more thankful and less…" he waves, gesturing to them, "whatever the hell this is."

I laugh. "It's fine, hotness. They may be bloomin' idiots, but they're our blooming idiots."

———

Sloan *poofs* us back to Drombeg, and the scene is nothing like I expected. I figured the Queen of Wyrms would be territorial and competitive about having other dragons in her lands, but I've never seen her so engaged.

She and Utiss are flirting, and Cazzie and Saxa are playing with Dart's siblings, and Bryvanay has become a living play center with adolescent Westerns and wyrms climbing all over him.

"It's a dragon free-for-all," I say to Patty.

Patty glances up at me and winks behind his spectacle glasses. "Ye did a good thing here, lass."

"I don't think I get any credit. It was Merlin and Sloan who brought the dragons through."

He nods and lifts the brim of his green cap. "Merlin said Yvain killed them in the original timeline, so they won't be missed, but they can do a great service here."

"Yeah? What does that mean?"

"Bloodlines, Red. Her Benevolence and I have had too many worrisome conversations about what will become of the kids with no other dragons to procreate. Now, with four more dragons alive, that worry is over. Dragons might truly make a comeback."

I'm not sure how that will play out, but thankfully, that's a problem for another day.

"Fiona, darling, come here."

I nod at Cazzie and leave the boys to talk about whatever they talk about when I'm not around.

Likely my latest trainwreck.

Cazzie and the Wyrm Dragon Queen are chatting like old friends, and I'm relieved things are going so well.

When I join them, Cazzie stretches her wing and wraps it around my back. "Fi, I was telling Adalynda how you released Yvain's dragon from servitude by freeing him from his spelled shackles, and we discovered something amazing."

I meet the smile of the red dragon who has intimidated the crap out of me since the first day she threatened to eat me for waking her from her nap.

Adalynda? Huh—I never realized she had a name.

Well, of course, I knew she'd have a name…I guess I never wondered what it was.

The two of them are staring at me. "Oh, sorry. You discovered something? What is that?"

Cazzie flutters her eyelashes and swishes her spiked tail. "Her father, Tyrsinth, was bound to Sigberght Earl of Dukeshire until the ninth century when he was released from the binding spell and gained his freedom."

I blink. "Really? He was your father?"

She lowers her head. "I grew up hearing the tales of how he searched for the red-headed lass who set him free but was never able to thank her."

"Oh, that's lovely. I'm glad to hear he went on to have a family and be happy."

The Queen of Wyrms nods. "He did. I knew I was right not to chomp you, Fiona."

I chuckle and give her two thumbs up. "I'm happy not to be chomped."

Utiss finishes speaking with Merlin, and I head over to take his spot. "And they lived happily ever after."

Merlin holds his arms open, and I accept the offer for a hug. "To have Cazzie back is more than I ever thought possible, Fi. I will never be able to repay you for this."

I absorb the squeeze and hug him back. "You don't need to thank me. Cazzie took us back, and you came up with the plan to save her. I was only along for the ride."

He presses his cheek to the top of my head and sighs. "No. You got me back into druid life. If I hadn't been your go-to dragon guy, I wouldn't have powered up the dragon portal, and we wouldn't have ended up back at Tintagel. This is all you, cookie."

I squeeze my arms around his hips. "You've been outed as Merlin among the fam jam. Sorry about that."

"Don't be. With Empress Cazzienth out in the world again, things were bound to change."

I think about all the things that have changed in our lives over the past nine months, and still, there's so much hanging over our heads. "Will they be coming back to Toronto to make their home?"

His body jostles against me as he laughs. "Do you remember that lecture I gave you last week about the city being a bad idea for dragons? Do you think I'd turn around and invite four more to live with us?"

"If not there, then where?"

"Iceland." Patty joins us. "When we were searching for a new lair site a few months ago, an elf friend of mine suggested a series of volcanic caves in Iceland. They have the same water entry like Tintagel, and with Merlin's druid abilities, I'm sure they can make a home there."

Merlin nods. "We're headed there at nightfall. Patty's friend says the Icelandic people still revere elves, trolls, ghosts, and the like. We believe the dragons will be able to live undisturbed and maybe even grow a bit of a following."

"Iceland is far," I say, reading his expression. "You just got Cazzie back."

He lifts the sleeve of the tunic I'm wearing and taps my dragon band. "Dragon portals make traveling the work of a moment."

I step back and smile at the chaos of new friends.

Having the dragons here means new mentors for Dart and the other dragon young, Merlin's fated bond restored, and powerful new friends in a time when trouble is brewing on the horizon.

"Well then, all's well that ends well. Yay team."

Merlin winks at me and smiles. "Well said, cookie. Yay team."

Thank you for reading – *A Dragon's Dare.* While the story is fresh in your mind, and as a favor to Michael and me, please click HERE and tell other readers what you thought.

A star rating and/or even one sentence can mean so much to readers deciding whether or not to try a book or a new author.

Thank you.

And if you loved it, continue with the Chronicles of an Urban Druid and claim your copy of book eleven:
A God's Mistake

The story continues with *A God's Mistake*, available at Amazon and Kindle Unlimited.

Claim your copy today!

AUTHOR NOTES - AUBURN TEMPEST

AUGUST 24, 2021

I was lying in bed this morning thinking about my story plans for the day and realized it's been eleven months since Gilded Cage launched (Sept 27, 2020) and I'll be finishing the eleventh book, A God's Mistake this weekend.

What a fun ride this series has become.

For those of you who don't know, I leapfrog between two author names. Auburn Tempest for my New Adult/Adult Urban Fantasy and JL Madore for my Paranormal and Urban Fantasy Steamy Romance.

Clan Cumhaill is my pallet cleanse, my giggle-fest, my treat. While I enjoy writing as JL as well, there is something synergistic about Fiona and the gang. They make me smile while I type and I hope that comes through on the page.

Dear wonderful hubby and I have chatted about what makes the Chronicles of the Urban Druid series such a beloved story and I think it's the connection of family and friendship. There is

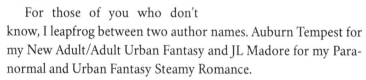

an unshakeable loyalty and respect between characters. While they don't always see things the same way, they respect one another enough to get past those differences of opinion.

Or I might be totally whacked and it's the inappropriate hilarity of the situations they find themselves in that we all love.

Whatever the reason, I'm happy to have discovered them and am pleased you all have joined me for the ride. Last week, I had a reviewer say they can see this series continuing on with so many of the characters still to be explored.

I look forward to exploring them with you.

Blessed be,
Auburn Tempest

AUTHOR NOTES - MICHAEL ANDERLE
AUGUST 24, 2021

Thank you for not only reading this book but this entire series and these author notes as well.

"A God's Mistake this weekend."

I read this in Auburn's author notes and went *WTH?*

I'll get back to that in a minute.

First, I want to congratulate Jenny (Auburn) for eleven freaking books! Not only eleven, but eleven that you the fans still eagerly desire to read and look forward to each time they release. It is not only an accomplishment to have a series this long, but to have a series with as many reviews on the books later in the series as *Chronicles of the Urban Druid* is a huge accomplishment.

It speaks to the love of the characters (in my opinion), thus answering the question, "What keeps the fans coming back for more?" I believe the craziness is the whipped topping, but it isn't the delicious cake.

Unless we are talking angel food cake. I can't understand that dessert because it seems to have been designed from the beginning to be about the topping.

Fiona (Fi to her friends, and we are all friends here, amIright?) is just the right amount of cake and icing.

(Oh, crap, I'm already hungry, and now I'm thinking about cinnamon cake with streusel and white drizzle on top. Dammit!)

So, Fi is this perfect cake, and her brothers, families, and the random gods that appear in her life are the drinks and ice creams that are part of the dessert-fest that is Clan Cumhaill.

I suppose we could make this a drinking metaphor, but I have to admit I don't know S@#% about enough drinks to make the metaphor work. Sorry!

Since I brought up drinking, that is kind of where my head went when I read Jenny's comment about "A God's Mistake this weekend." Seriously, I thought she might have been talking about a bad bender or some other huge mistake that occurred.

I know enough about Jenny to know she stays home. If she could get away with it (she can't, as far as I know), she would. Seriously, I'm not sure how she has such realistic pub scenes in these stories. Perhaps she was a bit of a wild one earlier in her life and now knows enough to keep it sane.

<Snicker. I doubt it.>

It took me about three seconds to clue in that she meant the book title. My bad.

This reminds me that Jenny asked about talking about the story this week. For some reason, I took her question to mean ideas about the cover to give to Kelly O. for the artist to start working. I was wrong then too.

I'd say it was Jenny, but I know myself well enough to admit…

It was me. I just didn't clue in correctly.

Anyway, stay safe and sane out there. I look forward to talking to you in the next book!

Ad Aeternitatem,
Michael Anderle

ABOUT AUBURN TEMPEST

Auburn Tempest is a multi-genre novelist giving life to Urban Fantasy, Paranormal, and Sci-Fi adventures. Under the pen name, JL Madore, she writes in the same genres but in full romance, sexy-steamy novels. Whether Romance or not, she loves to twist Alpha heroes and kick-ass heroines into chaotic, hilarious, fast-paced, magical situations and make them really work for their happy endings.

Auburn Tempest lives in the Greater Toronto Area, Canada with her dear, wonderful hubby of 30 years and a menagerie of family, friends, and animals.

BOOKS BY AUBURN TEMPEST

Auburn Tempest - Urban Fantasy Action/Adventure

Chronicles of an Urban Druid

Book 1 – A Gilded Cage

Book 2 – A Sacred Grove

Book 3 – A Family Oath

Book 4 – A Witch's Revenge

Book 5 – A Broken Vow

Book 6 – A Druid Hexed

Book 7 – An Immortal's Pain

Book 8 – A Shaman's Power

Book 9 – A Fated Bond

Book 10 - A Dragon's Dare

Book 11 - A God's Mistake

Misty's Magick and Mayhem Series – Written by Carolina Mac/Contributed to by Auburn Tempest

Book 1 – School for Reluctant Witches

Book 2 – School for Saucy Sorceresses

Book 3 – School for Unwitting Wiccans

Book 4 – Nine St. Gillian Street

Book 5 – The Ghost of Pirate's Alley

Book 6 – Jinxing Jackson Square

Book 7 – Flame

Book 8 – Frost

Book 9 – Nocturne

If you enjoy my writing and read sexy/steamy romance, my pen name for the books I write in Paranormal and Fantasy Romance is JL Madore. You can find me on Amazon HERE.

CONNECT WITH THE AUTHORS

Connect with Auburn

Amazon, Facebook, Newsletter

Web page – www.jlmadore.com

Email – AuburnTempestWrites@gmail.com

Connect with Michael Anderle and sign up for his email list here:

Website: http://lmbpn.com

Email List: http://lmbpn.com/email/

https://www.facebook.com/LMBPNPublishing

https://twitter.com/MichaelAnderle

https://www.instagram.com/lmbpn_publishing/

https://www.bookbub.com/authors/michael-anderle

CPSIA information can be obtained
at www.ICGtesting.com
Printed in the USA
LVHW101042080123
736715LV00019B/383